SEAL UNDER COVERS

SEAL Brotherhood
Book 3

SHARON HAMILTON

SHARON HAMILTON'S BOOK LIST

SEAL BROTHERHOOD BOOKS

SEAL BROTHERHOOD SERIES
Accidental SEAL Book 1
Fallen SEAL Legacy Book 2
SEAL Under Covers Book 3
SEAL The Deal Book 4
Cruisin' For A SEAL Book 5
SEAL My Destiny Book 6
SEAL of My Heart Book 7
Fredo's Dream Book 8
SEAL My Love Book 9
SEAL Encounter Prequel to Book 1
SEAL Endeavor Prequel to Book 2
Ultimate SEAL Collection Vol. 1 Books 1-4 /2 Prequels
Ultimate SEAL Collection Vol. 2 Books 5-7

SEAL BROTHERHOOD LEGACY SERIES
Watery Grave Book 1
Honor The Fallen Book 2
Grave Injustice Book 3

BAD BOYS OF SEAL TEAM 3 SERIES
SEAL's Promise Book 1
SEAL My Home Book 2
SEAL's Code Book 3
Big Bad Boys Bundle Books 1-3

BAND OF BACHELORS SERIES
Lucas Book 1
Alex Book 2

Jake Book 3

Jake 2 Book 4

Big Band of Bachelors Bundle

BONE FROG BROTHERHOOD SERIES

New Year's SEAL Dream Book 1

SEALed At The Altar Book 2

SEALed Forever Book 3

SEAL's Rescue Book 4

SEALed Protection Book 5

Bone Frog Brotherhood Superbundle

BONE FROG BACHELOR SERIES

Bone Frog Bachelor Book 0.5

Unleashed Book 1

Restored Book 2

SUNSET SEALS SERIES

SEALed at Sunset Book 1

Second Chance SEAL Book 2

Treasure Island SEAL Book 3

Escape to Sunset Book 4

The House at Sunset Beach Book 5

Second Chance Reunion Book 6

Love's Treasure Book 7

Finding Home Book 8 (releasing summer 2022)

Sunset SEALs Duet #1

Sunset SEALs Duet #2

LOVE VIXEN

Bone Frog Love

SHADOW SEALS
Shadow of the Heart

SILVER SEALS SERIES
SEAL Love's Legacy

SLEEPER SEALS SERIES
Bachelor SEAL

STAND ALONE BOOKS & SERIES
SEAL's Goal: The Beautiful Game
Nashville SEAL: Jameson
True Blue SEALS Zak
Paradise: In Search of Love
Love Me Tender, Love You Hard

NOVELLAS
SEAL You In My Dreams Magnolias and Moonshine

PARANORMALS

GOLDEN VAMPIRES OF TUSCANY SERIES
Honeymoon Bite Book 1
Mortal Bite Book 2
Christmas Bite Book 3
Midnight Bite Book 4

THE GUARDIANS
Heavenly Lover Book 1
Underworld Lover Book 2
Underworld Queen Book 3
Redemption Book 4

FALL FROM GRACE SERIES
Gideon: Heavenly Fall

NOVELLAS
SEAL Of Time Trident Legacy

All of Sharon's books are available on Audible, narrated by
the talented J.D. Hart.

ABOUT THE BOOK

Navy SEAL Armando Guzman has just returned from a difficult tour in Afghanistan only to find his sister still making choices that land her in the company of a San Diego drug gang. Vowing he will save her from the bad environment she has placed herself in, he is blindsided by his sister's hotter-than-hot best friend, Gina.

Gina Mancuso is working her first under cover detail, trying to prove herself on a male-dominated police force, even if it means she has to work side by side with the SDPD officer with whom she had a brief, abusive relationship. She is not prepared for the chemical attraction that slams her against the hard body of her subject's Navy SEAL brother, Armando. Their hot affair not only threatens to ruin her mission, but could engulf Armando in a career-ending dispute with local law enforcement.

Armando is unwilling to walk away from his sister, especially as tensions rise between he and Gina's ex-lover. Gina is in a race for time to keep her secret identity from the man she is now sure she loves with all her heart. But will she have to sacrifice their relationship in order to accomplish the mission she was sent to do?

And did you know that now there is a Part 2 to this story? Grave Injustice is the story of Armando and his family 10 years later. After you finish SEAL Under Covers, why don't you try Grave Injustice for the rest of the story? More about this thrilling new story at the very end…

AUTHOR'S NOTE

I always dedicate my SEAL Brotherhood books to the brave men and women who defend our shores and keep us safe. Without their sacrifice, and that of their families—because a warrior's fight always includes his or her family—I wouldn't have the freedom and opportunity to make a living writing these stories. They sometimes pay the ultimate price so we can debate, argue, go have coffee with friends, raise our children and see them have children of their own.

One of my favorite tributes to warriors resides on many memorials, including one I saw honoring the fallen of WWII on an island in the Pacific:

> "When you go home
> Tell them of us, and say
> For your tomorrow,
> We gave our today."

These are my stories created out of my own imagination. Anything that is inaccurately portrayed is either my mistake, or done intentionally to disguise something I might have overheard over a beer or in the corner of one of the hangouts along the Coronado Strand.

I support two main charities. Navy SEAL/UDT Museum operates in Ft. Pierce, Florida. Please learn about this wonderful museum, all run by active and former SEALs and their friends and families, and who rely on public support, not that of the U.S. Government.

www.navysealmuseum.org

IF YOU GOT ANY CLOSER, YOU WOULD HAVE TO ENLIST

I also support Wounded Warriors, who tirelessly bring together the warrior as well as the family members who are just learning to deal with their soldier's condition and have nowhere to turn. It is a long path to becoming well, but I've seen first-hand what this organization does for its warriors and the families who love them. Please give what your heart tells you is right. If you cannot give, volunteer at one of the many service centers all over the United States. Get involved. Do something meaningful for someone who gave so much of themselves, to families who have paid the price for your freedom. You'll find a family there unlike any other on the planet.

www.woundedwarriorproject.org

CHAPTER 1

G INA HAD ROLLED her ankle twice as she hobbled along the wet sidewalk in her red patent leather four-inch heels. She was already flustered since she was running a good twenty minutes behind schedule, but she wouldn't run. The last thing she needed was to fall and end up walking in there with skinned knees or a bloody nose. She really needed to settle her nerves—now—in order to survive the night.

She was determined her first undercover assignment would be a success. She'd made the connection with the girl, Mia, and her gangland friends. The two of them had hung out together a few times, but Gina was about to raise the bar. She was going to get up close and personal with Carlos, the infamous Scorpions of San Diego leader who had taken over for Caesar during his incarceration.

The distinctive, unhealthy bar smells assaulted Gina's senses before she saw the dim lights and the flickering neon sign advertising "Babes." She'd not been to this particular part of town before, and wasn't used to meeting the men who frequented the bar—men who paid to watch topless dancers gyrating on poles way too close to the customers.

At least that's what the guys in the Department had told

her. She could tell they had gotten off on it. Straight as an arrow Gina. By the book Gina. Going under cover on her rookie mission in her red heels. Well, she'd prove them all wrong. She had assets they didn't possess, and she was convinced she was made for such a caper.

It still scared the daylights out of her, though.

Gina hoped Mia was there tonight; otherwise, it would be a quick cab ride home after a text to the team. No sense hanging around a place like this unless there was a reason for it. She was glad she'd left her car at home.

On any other Friday night she'd be in sweats and T-shirt, in her LL Bean slippers or lavender moisture socks, wrapped in the lap blanket her grandmother had crocheted for her in college, reading one of her favorite romance novels. She'd be sipping hot tea, not downing pink umbrella drinks like she was planning to do tonight. She hoped she had it in her to keep her wits tight.

She smoothed her palms down the form-fitting, low-cut, red mohair dress, then put a wad of gum in her mouth and shook her head, which released a few of the curls piled high in a clip. Idea was to give her the "just fucked" look her handler had said she would need.

The irony wasn't lost on Gina. She hadn't been with a man for six months, not since her detective hunk she'd been down and dirty with told her about the wife he'd left back in New York. He wanted to continue as coworkers with benefits—and his version of benefits was pretty intense, since he was into all kinds of experimentation.

"We're separated," he'd said, as if that made it better, as if it didn't count that they'd spent the week prior to this reveal together, naked more than not. The memory of it sent a dull ache to her abdomen.

And before Sam? Well, there was her high school sweetheart, the soccer player who went off to war and never came back. It took some time before she could even think about dating. Then it became just dating for sex, uncomplicated sex. It helped take away the pain.

Her college days were unmemorable, romance-wise, since she'd thrown herself into her studies and made the Dean's list every semester.

Tossing her head back and licking her lips, now tasting of cherry bubble gum, she felt the little glass heart earrings she'd purchased this morning tap against her neck. The feeling was somehow comforting. As if the part she was about to play wouldn't consume her. Those hearts reminded her that she did have a soul, and it was good, unlike the slutty sexual siren persona she was about to play. She was nothing more than bait on a hook. She knew her place in the department. This was her chance to move up.

Her cab disappeared into the night air. She was left without a lifeline as she stepped through the opened doorway of the dark little dive.

A gasp came from several corners of the bar, making her panties bunch and sending shudders down her spine.

Showtime.

Mia was at the bar, just like she'd said she would be. Nestor, the greasy-haired Scorpions enforcer, had his arm around Mia as she was arching her back and raising her shoulders, trying without success to shake him off.

"Hey there, Mia," Gina said as she plucked the black sweatshirt-covered arm off her shoulder.

"Why don't you fuckin' mind your own biz, sweet cheeks?" Nestor stood up, huge muscles making him look like a stubby version of an already stubby Michelin Man.

"Thanks for the compliment," Gina said in her most direct way. She liked that she had a Smith & Wesson 642 Airweight .38 special strapped to her inner thigh, even though it would be a mistake to use it right now. "I'm her date for this evening, if you get my drift."

"I smell some female-on-female sex, and I wanna watch."

"Then go watch your mom in the bathtub. Or, better yet, go jerk off in the men's room and look real deep into those bloodshot eyes of yours." Mia snickered at this.

Gina saw the twitch in his cheek, the slow tilt of his head and narrowing of his eyes. Nestor was going to hit her, so she kneed him in the nuts before he could get himself properly positioned. He immediately bent forward, protecting his groin, nearly falling into her. She pushed him backwards with both hands, easily dropping his intoxicated ass to the floor. He landed on the ground spread-eagled, cracking his head on the concrete floor. Gina flinched.

Did anyone notice? She hadn't wanted to hurt the creep. Gina was relieved when he shook his head and was pulled away by a couple of his buddies.

"Gina, you gotta be careful. Those guys are part of Caesar's, gang," said Mia.

"Like I care? Notice how many of them were going to rush over to protect your virtue?" Gina said as she watched the crowd in the corner carefully. A tall, caramel-skinned man glared at her from under the bill of a red baseball cap as he shoved Nestor into a chair in front of the little stage next to him. He didn't hide that he was perusing Gina's every curve, daring her to show the smallest bit of fear.

Carlos.

Gina sucked in her gut and tried to calm her nerves. He

was every bit as scary as they'd told her in the briefing. She stared right back at him and tried not to blink.

"Let's get out of here," Mia muttered, picking up her enormous red purse.

"You planning on staying overnight?" Gina said as she turned a shoulder to Carlos and pointed to the bag. "Come on, let's have one drink and let these guys drool a bit. It will do them some good."

Hope to God backup gets here soon.

Mia was nearly off the stool. "No, Gina, I mean it. They're bad news. Meeting here was a dumb idea."

While it was good Mia was starting to show some common sense, it would mess up the mission.

"Which makes me wonder," Gina studied Mia's heavily lined, gold-sparkled eyes. She could see her new friend wasn't nearly as tough as she wanted the world to believe. "Of all the dives in San Diego to hang out in, why here, if you're trying to avoid the Scorpions?"

Mia repositioned herself on the barstool, turning forward and focusing on the lighted bottles over the bar as she sighed. "That's a good question. I guess I thought I'd be safer here. And I have you to protect me, Gina."

This tugged at Gina's heart. It was true, Gina was a cop, and so she was able to protect the innocent from the lowlifes of society. Mia was able to somehow figure that out without knowing it consciously. But she was also still putting her faith in men, the wrong men, even though she'd been knocked around by several of them. Caesar's gang had even kidnapped her, thinking they could force Mia's brother, the SEAL, to sell them specialized military equipment and firepower. Only reason Mia was alive was because of her hunky brother and the rest of his SEAL Team 3, who saved the day and helped break up a ring that included some dirty law enforcements and regular Navy guys. All of them were serving time now.

The present operation was considered a cleanup detail, an attempt to eviscerate the rest of the gang, and perhaps catch the guys who were trying to take Caesar's place. "You come in here on Valentine's Day, and you're like candy on a string. Begging for trouble," she shot back to Mia.

The Department is using her, too. Gina wondered if she'd ever get used to it.

"None of them are supposed to touch me. Caesar's orders."

"Except you told me you never visit him. So are you still his property?" Gina saw Mia flinch.

"I'm not his fuckin' property."

Gina took her seat next to the beautiful Latina. "Women are always some guy's property, honey. I'm sure your mother has told you so. That's the way of it, I'm afraid." Gina didn't want to look at Mia for fear she'd see it was a lie. Part of her wanted to cheer over the streak of common sense her friend was beginning to develop, though.

They ordered strawberry margaritas. Gina left a generous tip for the bartender, who gave her a friendly wink. "Pleasure doin' business with you," he said. He turned to serve another customer, then stopped himself and came back. "Say, you gals aren't here to try out, are you?"

"No." Gina said before Mia could answer.

The bartender leaned on the counter and gave Mia a wolfish grin, his head barely clearing the pink and red paper hearts that hung from the ceiling in a ridiculous display of gaiety. "And what about you, little lady? I'd like to see you up on the stage, showing your stuff. You could make close to a grand a night, did you know that?"

Mia sat up straight. "A grand?"

"I never lie," the bartender said in a low, sultry voice. Gina could tell he'd been a handsome man at one time, but years behind a bar, and years of indulging in god-knows-what, had left his face ruddy and tired, and his gut flabby. His aloha shirt was buttoned one button too low to accommodate his thick neck, but it exposed a hairy chest with several gold chains buried in the fur.

Gina glanced at Mia and could see her friend was actually considering it.

"You're joking. You're not thinking of taking your clothes off in front of this crowd?"

"What kind of protection do I have?" Mia turned and asked the bartender.

The bartender pulled something from under the counter with both hands. He held it just high enough that the girls could see it but not so the other customers could. It was a Mossberg Persuader. Gina hoped the man had some training, or he'd be as likely to kill the dancer as protect her from an overbearing customer.

"You rated on that piece?" Gina asked before she could stop herself.

The bartender scowled. "You got a smart mouth, missy. You got friends in law enforcement or something?"

Gina went rigid. Blowing her cover on the first job in the big leagues was not what she wanted to do. "Hell, no. I thought maybe you were some kind of sick cowboy. I hate guns and what they do to people." It was true enough for her to follow her comment with a stare she hoped he'd feel all the way to his toes.

The bartender's hairy arms, covered with tats of naked

women, fumbled behind the counter out of sight, replacing the shotgun. He scanned the gang in the corner, as well as some of the customers at the bar.

He was back on Mia. "If I were in your shoes, little one, I'd be wiggling that cute little ass all over the stage and taking home that grand three or four nights a week. Could do a lot for you and the kid. I doubt Caesar will be very good with child support. None of the rest of that lot would be, actually." He nodded to the corner.

Gina followed his direction and saw the boys taking seats as the music was turned up. All except the tall one with the baseball cap. His arms were crossed as he leaned next to the stage, not bothering to pretend that he wasn't checking them out, making a clear threat out of his continued slow, insulting perusal. Gina felt her pulse quicken and her hands start to sweat. She was sure the top of her chest was red and blotchy. Her stomach lurched.

The lights dimmed and thankfully, Gina could no longer see the guy's face, but she still could feel his eyes on her flesh.

A spotlight shone on the bright pink stage curtain. A prerecorded voice announced the first act.

"Put your hands together for the Sensual Shannon and her pot of gold!" the announcer bellowed. Out walked a tall redhead wearing a short, green plaid, pleated skirt. She bent over and exposed her red satin panties.

Movement to their left caught Gina's eye.

Finally.

Three of the Department's finest sauntered through the door, followed by a fourth who wore a cap that concealed his face. Everyone was dressed in the black leathers they'd been talking about so much. Thanks to the heavy beat of the music, she'd missed the noise of their Harleys arriving. Devon, the first one in, gave her a wink, and Gina turned her back to them. She heard a low whistle and didn't want to see who'd done it. She was fairly sure she was blushing.

The bartender was studying her. She knew it was important not to let on she knew them, but she had to admit she was thankful they'd arrived.

A familiar scent crowded close to her right ear. Her body instinctively softened for just a moment before reality set in.

Damn it. Sam. This wasn't supposed to happen. He was the last one she'd expected to be on the team.

"I'm remembering all the sheets we tussled in. I'm getting hard just thinking about it. Miss you, hot stuff," he whispered tenderly, so no one else could hear. A chill went down her spine while she couldn't help but remember those lost days and nights with him.

She forced herself to stay focused on the mission and what she was there to accomplish. It pissed her off that his casual attitude was throwing a monkey wrench into an already difficult situation, so it wasn't difficult for her to turn around and slap him. Then she picked up what was left of her drink and threw it in his face. He didn't move a muscle, but she could see his was furious with her, blinking through the strawberry liquid staining his face and dribbling down his light blue shirt. Little red paper hearts hanging from the ceiling twirled all around him.

The bartender handed him a clean towel and Sam quietly wiped his face, his eyes riveted on Gina.

The rest of the guys whistled, whooped and chuckled. They grouped around the two girls. That's when Gina figured out the guys had brought him along on purpose to rattle her.

That's right. I'm outside the network. I got the fuckin' message.

"You going to introduce me to your friends, Gina?" Mia was giving them long, thirsty looks.

At least that part of the plan was working.

"This one, he has a bad memory. Like the fact that he has a wife," Gina said jerking her thumb toward Sam, who still lurked behind her. "The rest of them, if they're his friends, I wouldn't bother." She ignored all of them, hoping they'd think twice before deviating from the plan again and fucking trying to upset her. She ordered another drink.

Little Shannon was keeping the boys around the stage busy. She was down to her panties, her kilt and small white schoolgirl blouse discarded on the stage. She swung her long legs around the brass pole, turning, writhing and riding it with her thighs, leaning backwards air-kissing the men closest to the stage.

Not that Carlos was watching. He hadn't taken his eyes off Gina, and it made her skin crawl.

Sam leaned into the side of her head, carefully. "You've drawn the right kind of attention, G-spot."

Gina's loathing for the situation flared into anger. "Keep your fuckin' distance or I'll have him call the cops." She shot a glance to Devon as if to say, '*What were you thinking?*'

The reference to calling the cops was supposed to be the safe signal, but only used in a blown operation. The group got quiet. The bartender spoke up.

"You boys want something, or are you just gonna ogle the customers for free?"

"Yeah, I'm not on stage yet," Mia turned around, leaning back, to make the most of her lush breasts temptingly exposed by a mostly-unbuttoned black satin blouse. The boys responded appropriately, giving Mia the reaction she wanted. Sam whistled as he brushed past Gina, making sure that they had a thigh-on-thigh experience on his way to snaking an arm around Mia's waist.

He thinks he owns me. She had fallen really hard for him, and fast. That was the part that hurt the most. She'd thrown caution to the wind. No questions, just a couple of nibbling kisses, and *wham*, she couldn't wait to get naked with him. And because he was a cop, she'd thought she could trust him.

Mia was cooing and enjoying the attention of four really big leather-clad guys. Gina noticed the long looks she gave the corner, like giving the gang the finger. Mia was going to be a big problem when she found out the guys she was getting cozy with were cops.

Little Shannon was really working her buttock muscles, shaking them faster than Gina thought was humanly possible. The dancer backed up closer to the face of one of the front row crowd and Gina felt herself shudder again. The gentleman had his forefinger rubbing up and down Shannon's rear, as he inserted dollar bills in the lacy string that held her panties together. When the supply of bills dried up, she moved on to the next customer, revealing a little more each time, letting the customers get a little closer, touch a little more inappropriately.

Gina wondered what it would feel like to do that on-stage for strange men. Could she do it if it was required? For the good of the mission? She decided the answer was a definite *no*. What difference would it make if you debased yourself for a paycheck from the Department or from a bar?

It was still wrong.

CHAPTER 2

NAVY SEAL ARMANDO Guzman was surprised his sister, Mia, was not answering her phone. That meant she'd lied to him again. Her 'evening at home with a girlfriend' meant a trip to a local bar hanging out with the wrong crowd.

So much for the surprise dinner. He liked to be impromptu with Mia, despite the fact that she accused him of spying on her. Well, yes…that was partially true.

Fredo was his constant companion these days, ever since Fredo's best friend, SO Calvin Cooper, had gotten himself involved and married to a cute little thing from San Diego. Libby had *encouraged* Cooper to find larger digs, rather than cramming them both into the Babemobile Coop had lived in down by the beach for the past three years. So they were currently house-hunting with the help of his team leader's wife, Christy Lansdowne, who was the Realtor for all the Team guys these days.

Armando also knew Fredo liked to hang out with him because the Mexican SEAL had the hots for his sister. At first, this had seemed like a bad idea, but Mia's terminal case of bad judgment kept escalating. Even Armando didn't think she could go wrong with any one of his Team buddies, but he'd never let on he felt this way. It was sport, needling Fredo to death at every opportunity, since Mia would have nothing to do with him. And the more she rejected him, the harder Fredo tried.

Gotta hand it to him. He's persistent. Fredo's short stature and powerful arms made him the best on the Team in wrestling. In fact, Armando couldn't remember a match the man had ever lost. The Mexican SEAL's prominent forehead, ruddy complexion and infamous unibrow did not, however, make him a favorite of the ladies.

"That's just not something a man should ever do, have his eyebrows tweezed," he'd told Armando that evening when they'd discussed his lack of love life. Although not as good-looking as some of his buds, Fredo had a heart the size of the ocean they had to swim in on a daily basis. Armando had never had a problem attracting women. Girls lined up for him ever since he was in junior high.

The pair drove to Mia's house to confirm what Armando feared. Fredo dove from Armando's Hummer, ran to the garage at the end of a concrete driveway, and quickly returned. "Her car's not in the garage, Armani."

"Let's take the groceries in so they don't get warm," Armando said. They'd stopped by the store they called *Whole Wallet* to get some organic steaks and salad fixings to make a meal he knew she wouldn't prepare for herself. Armando halfway hoped Mia had invited her cute friend Gina over. They'd have some wine, sit out on the patio, and watch the stars come out on this beautiful spring evening in San Diego.

"Where's the kid?"

"I'm guessing my mom's."

Armando had bought the house for Mia recently. He'd

also helped her fix up the two-bedroom stucco bungalow into a sweet little home for her and her baby. Mama Guzman had planted flowers that were just now beginning to bloom. They wouldn't match the psychedelic colors covering Mama Guzman's yard, but, given time, Mia's house would have a jungle in front of it, or their mother would die trying.

Buying the house for Mia had given Armando the right to a key, or so he'd told his Team. He promised never to barge in on her when she was entertaining, but tonight was different. She'd gone out of her way to say she wasn't entertaining a man, and Armando thought some face time with his tempestuous sister was warranted.

As soon as they stepped into the living room, Armando smelled pot. "Shit."

"Whoa. Can't believe it." Fredo said, shaking his head. "That's a fuckin' shame."

"What kind of a mother smokes around her son?" Armando swore.

"Armani, that girl's got some demons. Wish she'd choose me. I'd exorcise those spirits, love them right outta her."

Fredo got a sock to the arm that made the bottom of his bag drop out and the salad mix fall to the floor. Luckily the greens remained encased in their plastic bags.

"I know you have the best of intentions, but she's my sister, Fredo." Armando was more worried for his sister's state of mind than he liked to show.

"I feel you," Fredo began. "But while I'm waiting here, holding my dick and trying to be all proper, she's doing the down and dirty with half the scum of San Diego. And the only reason she's not with Caesar is that he took that little detour to San Quentin."

Armando pushed Fredo onto the couch. "That's enough. Shut the fuck up or I'll leave you right here." It didn't make sense she'd want to go back to that dickwad.

Some day you're gonna tell me, sis. Who hurt you? If he could just find out what the problem was, Armando was sure he could cure her of—whatever. It was unacceptable that any sister of his would be throwing her life away like this.

"I'll happily stay here, Armani. You go chase around and look for her. She'll come home eventually."

"I didn't mean that."

"So 'splain this to me. You save her life and the life of her baby. You buy her a fuckin' great house in a good area, you buy her furniture, and you help your mama, too. And she disses you like this? I'm telling you, those demons is not only gettin' bigger, they're having babies. What's next?"

"What's next is I'm gonna find her, bring her home, and cook her a fuckin' steak. And you're gonna be a perfect gentleman, hear?"

"Yessir. I get you."

After storing the perishables, Armando and Fredo stopped by Fredo's apartment to pick up his Parks Department four-door beater truck. No sense exposing Armando's black Hummer to the neighborhood where they'd probably find Mia.

Armando slid onto the torn leather bench seat and examined the contents of the cab behind him. The floor was nearly ankle-high with fast food wrappers and old milkshake and soda containers.

"Some super sleuth you'd make," Armando said, holding his nose. "All anyone would have to do is sort through all your wrappers and receipts. They could re-create your whereabouts 24/7."

Fredo rolled his shoulders and jutted out his chin. "Just because you got an obsessive compulsive disorder for specks of dirt, don't mean you have to insult a normal male with normal eating habits." Fredo didn't look back at him.

"That's not normal," Armando said with a thumb pointing over his shoulder.

They rounded a corner and the noise of displaced paper cups, balled-up bags and wrappers was unmistakable.

Fredo put on the brakes and nearly was rear-ended. "You wanna walk? You're usin' my petrol for your own devious little plan. I'm just along to make sure you don't get your ass busted."

Armando started to open the door and Fredo grabbed his shoulder. "Get the fuck back in the truck, Armani. I'm just messin' with you."

"Okay, then shut the fuck up." They rode in silence for a few minutes. Armando was twirling the comment Fredo had made over and over in his brain. He couldn't hold it in any longer. "Obsessive compulsive?" he demanded.

"No shit, Sherlock. Like you have to put plastic down on the couch yesterday before I could sit down."

"That's because you were working out before you came over. You were sweaty, man."

"Yea, well, don't you get sweaty balling all those coeds on your couch? You think I mind if I sit my ass down on some teenage cum?"

"They're not teenagers. You know that."

Fredo humphed. The silence continued. Then Fredo spoke up. "I clean my truck on the first of every month, and always before deployment."

"That's a very good thing. No telling what could grow in the back seat in six months unattended. Might have to have a HazMat clearance."

"That's Coop's problem, with all that Kambucha he drinks. I think it's disgusting to drink fungus piss."

"Well, hell's bells. We finally agree on something." Armando smiled at his Mexican friend and found Fredo chuckling as well.

They looked like a couple of guys looking to find some action as they cruised down across the tracks towards a run-down commercial district in one of the seedier parts of town. Fredo's truck was barely still green, it was so thoroughly covered with rust and scrapes. But everyone on SEAL Team 3 knew underneath the front seat was a container welded to the frame that could hold enough firepower to start a war in a small country. Normally there would be duty bags with special demo equipment and ammunition tossed on the second seat behind them. Tonight they were traveling light. Anyone who tried to mess with the box underneath the seat would be met with an electric charge strong enough to send him to the hospital, courtesy of Fredo's best friend, SO Calvin Cooper.

Armando easily spotted Mia's white Nissan glowing in the moonlight. He grimaced when he saw it was parked haphazardly, one wheel up on the curb. A variety of older cars and a few tricked-out, lowered ones with blackened windows dotted the nearly deserted alleyway. Fredo found a parking space nearby. A dark cat darted across the street and disappeared on the other side.

"Bet you bought her that car too, huh?" Fredo said.

Armando ignored him as he looked in the doorways of several clubs and saw women and an odd assortment of men lingering there. A string of Harleys that was way too nice for the neighborhood stood to attention right outside one particular bar. Armando thought if there was any kind of action at all, his sister would go for the bikers before the bangers.

Fredo continued, "You ever think that, like, maybe Mia doesn't want you going around interfering with her life? She's had that conversation with you, I know."

"Did that ever stop *you*?"

Fredo shook his head. "Not the same thing, Armani. I don't go check up on whom she's goin' out with. But I would, if you gave me—"

"That's not going to happen, Fredo. Mia's my responsibility."

"Except...what if you're pushing her away? You can't lead a horse to water."

"Depends on how fucking big the horse is."

Fredo laughed. Armando felt good having his Team buddy at his side, and giving him shit was part of the fun. They crossed the street and walked towards the entrance of Babes.

Guttural saxophone music blared from the pink wash of light spilling out from the opened doorway of the bar. A big guy with more exposed tats than bare skin was there to collect their ten bucks.

He saw the pink flash of a girl's rear end on stage just before the stage lights went out. The house lights came on, but it didn't help much. He eyed the skinny gang members congregated at the stage, noticing that several of them were weaving and glassy-eyed. At the counter, a bevy of beefy guys dressed in black were hovering around someone seated there. Armando had a sickening feeling that someone was his sister.

Fredo stepped in front of him. "Don't be stupid, Armani. I'm not into getting the shit kicked out of me tonight."

Armando noted that every single one of the guys behind Fredo outweighed him by more than forty pounds. They also were about a foot taller than Fredo. But Armando would take them on any day with one of his teammates on hand to back him, regardless of the size or weight difference.

"Dude," Fredo insisted. "No drama, okay? You don't need some asshole taking pity on her, 'kay?"

Adrenaline did a double tap to Armando's heart and he sucked in a deep breath. His hands made fists before he was conscious of it. He tensed his thigh and felt the knife strapped there. It was always like this in the war zone. Except he didn't have the H&K slung over his shoulder.

Relax, but be prepared for anything.

Without saying a word, Armando parted the crowd and wasn't surprised to see his sister sitting right in the middle. He *was* surprised to see her friend Gina next to her. The feeling must have been mutual, because Gina sat up straight, her eyes going wide for a second before she resumed that cocky attitude that matched her dress. Damn, but the lady was practically poured into that fuzzy red thing. Armando's body liked the view, the scent of her perfume all but sending him into a trance.

Down, boy.

Mia scowled when she saw him. "What the fuck are you doing here?" she demanded. He could see her cheeks flush red. A really big guy had his arm around her waist and pulled her even closer.

"I guess wanna ask the same about you," Armando began, slowly scanning the faces of the males in front of him, especially the big guy. "Fredo and I stopped by the house and were going to cook up some steaks, since you said you were going to be home."

"We changed our minds—right, Gina?"

"Damned straight," Gina said between chomps of her bubble gum. "She need permission or something? I don't see no dog collar."

Armando wanted to make her spit out that double wad of gum so he could grab the woman and lay a decent kiss on her bright red lips, but he quickly banished the thought when one of the bikers stepped between him and the girls. Armando watched the others to make sure they weren't also getting aggressive.

"These ladies are taken," said the man in front of him. "Now why don't you go get yourself some company elsewhere?"

Mia was grinning behind him.

"That's my little sister," Armando began. He hoped that's all he would have to reveal.

"I think we can handle this," the larger one said as he stood up. Then he pushed aside his friend and stared directly into Armando's eyes with a sneer. He suddenly broke out in a smile. "But you can try your chances with this one over here," he nodded to Gina. "If you can stand the competition, that is." He winked at Gina.

Armando looked at the stained blue shirt and decided to take a chance. "How could I trust my little sister to a guy who slobbers all over himself?" Armando pointed to several large rhubarb-colored stains on the guy's shirt. "Or did you get fresh with one of your buds?"

"You fuckin' punk. I think you need to leave," the giant said, taking the bait and stepping dangerously close to the two SEALs.

Armando was quick to grab the guy's collar and pull him so their faces nearly touched. "I'm not afraid of you, Gringo," he said to the giant. Armando could faintly hear Fredo give a light moan of disbelief. He released the big guy with a shove. The moose looked stunned.

"Shit, Armani. Wasn't planning on getting bloody tonight," Fredo muttered behind him.

Armando shrugged off Fredo's words, irritated he was being publicly reminded to stand down. But he knew it was the right thing to do. He just didn't want to.

Mia was on her feet, fire burning in her eyes. She tried to get in front of the leather-clad monster, but a beefy arm pushed her back behind him.

"Hey, pick on me, why don't you?" Armando added, "Or are you one of those guys that like to beat up on women?"

The big guy was thinking about something. Armando could see he was barely reining in his anger.

"Oh, stop it, you two," Mia said just in time. "He does this all the time," she said to her entourage.

The big guy stepped back but was still blocking Armando's access to his sister. The awkward seconds were broken when Mia added, "I can fuckin' take care of myself, Armani," she said from behind the man. This made the guy smile, his eyes narrowing as he tilted his head. Armando saw something dark and damaged in there.

"Like the little lady said," the biker began, "she doesn't need any help. We're here to take good care of her."

Armando's fists were itching to connect with the guy's fleshy cheeks.

"Just because they're SEALs, they think they can do anything," Mia muttered and started to get back up on the stool.

Mia had broken the unspoken rule, and Armando's anger flared. He also could feel a current of energy filter through the group. Someone inhaled sharply. He usually told strangers he was a UPS driver.

Fredo stepped close in behind him. There was a waver in his voice, "Wow. That was a stupid thing to say, Mia."

"Fuck off, Fredo."

"Honey, we're just looking out for you. You make your brother crazy—"

"Fredo, that's enough," Armando said. He put his hands on his hips. "I'm taking my sister home," he said to the group as he scanned their faces. His gaze lingered on the big guy. Fredo swore softly behind him.

"Like hell," Mia chirped. "We was just getting acquainted."

But Armando noticed the big guys did seem to back off slightly. Something had broken the tension in the room. He didn't buy it was entirely out of respect for his skills or that he was a SEAL.

"Another time, Mia." He reached for his sister but missed. Then he turned to Gina. "You need to come along, too. I'm not leaving you alone in here."

"And who appointed you king of my life?" she said with a sneer.

"Mia's told me you're smarter than that, Gina. Or you gonna tell me these guys are your type?"

Armando saw a little spark in Gina's face as her eyes darted to the big man. She broke into a full-on grin. "You're right about that. I have no intention of getting anywhere near him." She flashed white teeth and Armando found himself getting aroused.

Gina took Mia by the arm, sliding her friend's enormous purse up to her shoulder. "C'mon, Mia. I say we split. Testosterone is like perfume. Too much is unbearable. It makes me think stupid."

Armando watched the way Gina's buttocks quivered under the red, form-fitting dress as he followed them out of the bar. Her small waist accentuated her large breasts. He could imagine her naked in spite of the fact that it was a really dumb idea to entertain such thoughts.

CHAPTER 3

FREDO GRABBED MIA'S car keys. It happened so quickly, Gina knew it must have been a choreographed sequence between the two SEALs.

Divide and conquer the enemy.

Mia flustered and argued, but got inside her own car at the last minute, allowing Fredo to drive her home.

That left Armando holding the door open to the old beater truck. Damn, but the guy was cool. The happenings in the strip joint hadn't seemed to ruffle him one bit. He'd have been just as comfortable getting black, blue, and bloody. Gina wondered where he would draw the line.

Do I know where to draw the line? Well, his was personal. Hers was her job. But it was definitely fucked that her exboyfriend had to land himself in the middle of her professional world too.

But that's what kind of a choice you made, Gina. Always making the wrong choices when it came to men. In a way, very much like Mia.

She watched Armando standing there, waiting for her. The other car was waiting for her as well.

Never waste an opportunity to make another bad decision. Her roommate in college used to say that every day, while at the same time managing to bed most of the football team and as many of the soccer players as she could get. Gina always waited up for her, just in case she needed a ride or got too drunk. Just like she was now trying to do for Mia. It was the reason she became a cop. Another bad decision? Well, it certainly was something that had been locked and loaded way down inside her soul after she got the call from the police that fateful night. That night when her roommate became someone's victim and Gina had sat waiting for a call that would never come.

She wondered what would ruffle this man of steel, amazed that he could make choices so quickly as he had just now. Was he ever afraid in his job like she was in hers?

What threshold am I walking through tonight?

She leaned over to look around the SEAL, checking on Mia in the passenger seat of her own car. Of course she would be safe with the little warrior, a guy who would probably die trying to protect her, from what Mia had said. But this one standing in front of her, balancing on one hip, leaning against the door, his muscular arms worthy of any Popeye character, was dangerous.

To her heart.

"Do I have a choice?" she said to him, watching that smirky little smile and sexy eyes making fun of her while her heart did flip-flops. She'd been close to peeing on herself while she sat and watched her ex-boyfriend nearly call out the brother—the *SEAL* brother of the woman they were working. It had been wrong on so many levels, even the Pope couldn't dish out enough forgiveness.

"Get in." It was a command that made her tense, but the smile he flashed afterwards made her panties wet. Suddenly her ankles wobbled and she nearly fell, which would have been totally uncool. And damn, if he didn't reach out and put a strong, muscled arm around to steady her. He let her go after he gave her one hurried squeeze, just tight enough for her to learn he was aroused.

Another footnote to a perfectly fucked evening. Her mission was nearly blown. Why did she feel guilty for that? They were supposed to be hanging out with the gang by the stage. Well, she couldn't help it if Sam and the rest of the crew had decided to pull a game change on her. As she slid onto the torn leather seat of the old truck, she smiled at the recollection. It had been damned satisfying, slapping Sam and tossing the drink into his face. She'd stared right back at him when he showed his anger. And she didn't flinch or cower this time. She was filled with pride. She'd stood up to him, *finally*!

But now what? On any other evening, getting into a truck with a SEAL would be a no-brainer. Nothing wrong with a night of sex with a hot guy, if that was where he was headed. She wasn't completely sure, but she wasn't *that* rusty that she couldn't recognize a good, clean come-on. The fact that he was the brother of their party of interest and it was totally forbidden only heightened her anticipation. But decisions like that were never good ones. She had to put a stop to this somehow.

Tell that to my body. She watched him walk around the front of the vehicle and, yes, she squeezed her eyes shut and imagined him naked.

Get a grip, Gina. As much as she hated to admit it, something about the man set her insides on fire. He was all the right kinds of dangerous for her. A hero. Breathtakingly good-looking in that Latin Lover way she loved in men. Shiny black hair worn a little too long. Tanned complexion with just a hint of stubble. Body well-honed and disciplined. He knew what he wanted and wasn't afraid to go after it. And he loved his sister, which was the biggest heart-snag of all.

He got in the driver seat, slammed the rickety door closed and sighed.

Did all the air just get sucked out of the truck? It seemed like minutes as she watched him blankly stare through the windshield, his face illuminated by the red taillights of Mia's vehicle, now pulling away in front of them. Those dark eyes with long lashes and succulent, full lips. She shouldn't have stared so long, but she couldn't help it.

He tilted his head and turned in her direction. The eyes didn't lie. He had the fire inside that his sister had, but in all the right places, not the wrong ones, like Mia. She let him appreciate the red fuzzy dress with the scoop neckline. She didn't care if her chest got blotchy with nerves or if her cheeks flushed. And, of course, her nipples perked right up.

"So how is this going to work?" he asked. The words slid out like satin sheets.

"I'm not quite sure I know what you mean," she heard herself say in response. She made a point to beat the waver from her voice.

"I take you to your place, or to Mia's?"

"Mia's."

"Your car there?"

"No, I took a cab."

"And so how would you get home?"

"You assume I want to go home. Maybe I'm going to stay over."

"I don't see a pajama bag."

The crease at the side of his mouth dimpled and she

watched the tip of his tongue running across his bottom lip. The words "pajama bag" had never sounded so sexy.

She stuck her chin out, looking back at him with heavy-lidded eyes, and whispered, "I don't wear pajamas."

It was a dare. She watched him explore her face, roving from her eyes to her hair, her cheekbones, her ears. His gaze paused on her lips as his parted and he moved closer, then stopped.

Damn. It wasn't wise, but she knew he wasn't going to touch her unless she met him halfway. Her hesitation forced another smile from him as he waited, looking at her with the come-on-little-one-you-know-you-want-to   look.   And double damn, she was all in.

She bridged the gap and their lips touched. She expected him to be rough and urgent, but he took his time. She heard his little moan as he took another deep breath, then let it out and pressed into her harder. And yes, she wanted him, wanted him to find her with his tongue, wanted him to hold her face in his massive, callused palms like a delicate flower. His scent was laced with aftershave, but could not be masked.

The deep kiss came to an end. He'd not been wild with his hands, but he'd pulled her toward him. She'd put her arms up over his shoulders and laced her fingers through the hair at the back of his head. It was all feeling way too comfortable.

A loud bang on the driver's side window made them both jump. Sam's grimace was a thing of beauty. Like a multicolored piece of swirling blown glass, his face contained every emotion Gina could think of: rage, revulsion, envy and jealousy. The last one was best, she thought. Best thing about it, she'd hurt him, and she hadn't even been trying.

Armando was quick to start the truck and move them down the street, leaving the foursome faux bikers in a cloud of gray dust.

"I take it you two have some history," he said as he shifted into third.

"You could say that."

"Is it history or present?"

"Most definitely history. Sam's married, just didn't bother to tell me until after he'd gotten what he wanted."

"Ahh," he said as he leaned back in the seat but continued driving. "One of those."

"That's usually the type I attract." She couldn't believe she'd just said that.

"I disagree. I'm not like that guy and I'm definitely attracted." He kept his eyes on the road as the truck bounced along the dark road. If the engine hadn't been so loud she was sure he'd have heard her heart pounding.

Then common sense began to flood into Gina's head. She cautiously said, "Look, I'm not sure about all this." Her body was having a temper tantrum and using strong language too. But she pushed herself to complete the idea. "Perhaps you have me wrong." She halfway hoped he thought it was a joke. No doubt he knew exactly what kind of girl she was.

He turned and looked back at her, studying her eyes. "I don't quite know why my sister hangs around with some of the people she does, but you're the exception. You seem to have a lot more going for you. Ever thought about making different choices? It's dangerous down here."

Tell me about it. "You don't know anything about me."

"No, I don't. But I sense you aren't anybody's fool, either."

"Are you kidding me? You actually need an explanation as to why I want to spend time with her? She's your little sister, for Chrissakes. You saying she's too good for me or the other way around?"

"I'm going to make Mia turn her life around if it kills me."

"Well, it might just."

He paused, started tapping on the skinny black steering wheel. They'd come to a stop sign. "Which way? I know Mia lives to the right. Where are we going, Gina?"

The street dead-ended at the stoplight. Left would take them to Gina's apartment. He was going to make her tell him again, as if perhaps she was having second thoughts.

Hell, yes, I'm having second thoughts. "I said Mia's house. You heard me." She tried to sound defiant but it sounded stubborn.

"You going to sleep naked with my sister?"

"I never said anything of the sort." He was starting to irritate her.

"Well, how about I help you get those pajamas, then?" He turned and sent a smile she felt all the way to her toes.

"Why do you do that?" she asked.

"Do what?"

"Make me say stupid things. Make *me* make the decision."

"Honey," he leaned over and gave her another soft kiss. "*I've* already decided. But I'm not into forcing the lady, if you know what I mean. Up to you, no hard feelings either way." He fed her another gentle kiss.

No, there wouldn't be any hard feelings. But she knew she'd regret not taking him up on what he was offering.

Maybe just a little harmless sex wouldn't be so bad. After all, Sam and the boys had messed with her tonight and hadn't even been very nice about it. Just a little mind-blowing sex. Revenge sex. Sex without strings. There was something about this man she knew she could trust, if she would allow herself.

A car behind them honked at their lack of response to the light change. He didn't move a muscle, waiting.

"Left," she finally blurted out. His scent made her eyes flutter.

"Ah, she chooses wisely."

"That's rather egotistical, isn't it?"

He chuckled and shifted into second when the truck backfired. She jumped in reaction. "It's been suggested a time or two," he said.

"I'll bet."

"I like a woman who knows what she wants."

"Why is that?" She knew immediately it was the wrong thing to ask. Things were spinning out of control in a hurry. She halfway expected his answer.

"Because," he grabbed her hand and pulled it to his mouth, kissing her knuckles, "she won't be afraid to tell me what I need to do to please her, with or without the pajamas."

CHAPTER 4

H E KNEW SHE was aroused by the way her eyes widened when he'd kissed the back of her hand. He could see them having sex together, a satisfying and painful thought because of the Tomahawk missile between his legs. It was difficult driving the truck, reaching over the wheel to shift with his left hand because his right hand was entwined with hers. And as long as she hung on to him so tightly, he damn sure wasn't going to let go. She watched the tangle their hands made together as his fingers reached up towards her chest. He touched her with the backs of his knuckles right above the deep neckline of her fuzzy dress.

And best thing of all, she let him.

As he snaked one finger down her front, Gina closed her eyes and licked those bright red lips. Ordinarily, he'd want to wash off all the makeup she wore. He liked women plain but beautiful. But tonight, he knew he'd take her either way and her hot come-on looks were turning him hotter, which surprised him. He was as excited by her puffy crimson lips as the mounds of her breasts heaving under his fingers.

If a little rub right there made her shudder and moan, what would she do when he did something with his tongue?

He was starved for the taste of her. Suddenly he wanted to be planted deep inside, making her melt in his arms with ecstasy.

He was weaving over the roadway and knew it was dangerous, so he pulled over and into a deep shoulder, put the truck in neutral and yanked the hand brake. He'd forgotten to turn off the radio he and Fredo had listened to on the way over, and the crackle of the Eighties Mix made him feel just like he'd felt in high school. He was back on that infamous date with the Homecoming Queen, the one whose father wouldn't allow them to date afterwards because Armando was Hispanic and Mary Jo and her family were very lily white.

It had been years since he'd wanted someone this much He turned off the ignition and slid over, pressing her back against the passenger door, throwing a knee between her legs and riding her thigh as he kissed the soft places under her chin and behind her ear. He wished he could take his time with her, make love to her all night, but, if she didn't stop him, he'd nail her right here in the front seat.

He liked that she wasn't as urgent as he was. He'd half-way expected her to rip his clothes off, but she seemed to hold herself back. Her kisses were long, though. She inhaled his tongue and lingered against him everywhere they touched, which he took as a definite sign she was just as into him as he was into her.

He smoothed his palm up against her thigh and towards the center, rubbing up and down her panties. She arched back and raised her knees slightly. Unless he was completely misreading the situation, Gina wanted him to take her now.

"You want to do this here?"

She sighed, lacing her fingers through his hair, then,

tracing down his nose with one provocative finger. She took his face in her hands and breathed, "Anywhere."

A car passed them and honked. Armando figured it was someone who saw the steamy windows, the silhouette of two people beginning to get it on, and recognized Fredo's truck.

Another Team Guy.

"Back seat?" he asked, thankful for the four-door beater, but hoping she wouldn't notice the condition of the compartment. Before he could warn her, Gina was up over the back of the front seat, her luscious ass practically in his face as she dove to the bench behind. The unmistakable sound of hamburger wrappers and milkshake cups being tossed to the floor and crushed didn't dampen his ardor.

She crouched for a second, removing something from her bra, he thought, stuffing it in her purse. Up on the seat, she quickly slipped her dress over her head and shoulders and wadded it up as a pillow under her head. She laid there in her black panties and bra, feet still encased in the red spike heels, waiting for him to do the rest. And she held a little foil packet in front of her.

Nice. Because Armando had forgotten to replace the one he'd used.

Armando had a little more trouble getting over the seat back due to the size of his package, which hung like a lead weight next to his thigh. He must have been as big around as his arm. At least that's the way it felt.

As he covered her body, her fingers found his zipper, and he was glad she was quick, her urgency beginning to grow. God, it made him ache for her even more. He felt her fingers squeeze his buttocks as the cargo pants slid from his waist down to his knees. He kicked off his shoes and removed his pants the rest of the way. She lay back, putting one long arm under her head and letting the other rest on the back of the second seat, holding the condom.

Her flat stomach showed she'd worked to have that hard body. Her thighs and rear were fleshy, just like he liked them. Skinny girls were a turnoff. He liked women sexy, but not fragile.

He slid his palm under the top of her panties and squeezed her sex. Her chest made a beautiful bow in the moonlight as she gave herself to his hand, as she spread her knees apart and begged for penetration.

He put one finger inside her and she inhaled. Her legs were trembling as he heard their combined breathing, as the rush of passing motorists and car lights swooshed through the night air. He rimmed her opening and slowly dipped his head, pulling aside the lace trim of her panties and kissed the outsides of her hairless lips.

Gina jerked with each stroke of his tongue. Her moist slit tasted like honey. He watched her head thrash from side to side and her own hands squeeze her breasts together. He loved it when women touched themselves. He inserted his tongue fully.

"Oh, please," she said in a whimper. It moved him that she was in such need of tender touching and kissing. He kissed her again, rubbing his tongue up and around her clitoris.

She gasped. "More."

"Yes. Tell me what you want," he heard himself murmur.

"Inside."

"Yes, very soon. What else do you like?"

"I like this." She reached down between them and gently

guided his hand, pressing two of his fingers deep inside her. Her moan turned him to granite.

"Yes. Good girl," he said with difficulty. "Does this make you come, Gina?" His balls were on fire as he watched her writhe beneath him, helping him pleasure her with his two fingers.

"Almost." He loved watching her barely able to keep from coming apart. She was barreling over the cliff.

"Save it for me, okay?" He suddenly wanted to come inside her at precisely the same time as she did. For some reason, it was important.

"Can't wait much longer," she whispered.

He rimmed her opening when she removed her grip. She was reaching for his cock, smoothing the muscles of his lower torso. He watched her beautiful skin shudder in the diminished light and reveled in the need she showed him. He bent down and licked the long slit of her sex again and kissed her nub. "You taste so good," he said over her moan. He bent and laved her again.

"Please," she begged.

"Honey, I'm right here. I'm not going anywhere," he said. He watched as she gave him a sultry smile. She knew he was teasing her, making her wait. And he knew that the longer she waited, the harder she would come.

"Please." She grinned. "Fuck me, Armando."

He liked the sound of his name on her tongue. He usually didn't like women to talk dirty to him, but coming from Gina's gorgeous lips, he loved it. Leaving a finger inside her, he leaned over and kissed her neck, her breasts through the black lace bra. Then he found her mouth. He heard her muffled moan, when she must have tasted her own juices as they kissed.

Her sparkling dark eyes in the evening light called to him. He placed both hands next to her face and gently bent down and kissed her deeply. She wrapped her legs around his waist and rubbed her sex against his package. Without either of them using hands, his unit found her. They both paused as he poised at her opening.

He was overcome with the need to be careful with her, for some reason. He remembered the packet she held. It bothered him to break the moment, but he had to use protection.

Gina tore the top open with her teeth and had the condom coating him in seconds. She ringed his girth and fondled his balls, giving them a gentle squeeze that nearly sent him into orbit. Then she removed her hands, placing them above her head.

Again, his package found her. She arched to accept him, her chin extended and her lovely neck bared. He slid his left hand under her head and brought her face to his as he watched the pleasure of his entrance in her lovely brown eyes.

"Oh God," she said. "Oh…" Her voice bounced as he rode her slowly at first, then faster. He released her breasts with the front clasp of her bra and sucked hard on her nipples. His pace quickened as he thrust deeper and deeper, her legs squeezing tightly around his waist. He could feel her red high heels against his back. He was going to explode in a few seconds, but not before she did.

She clenched down on him and he began to lose control. "Come for me baby," he whispered and Gina screamed and began to shake. She pulled his head down and kissed him hard, moaning. Armando began to lurch as he plunged deep inside her. God, he'd never wanted to screw a woman ep, so full, so hard. For several delicious moments they

1 and writhed as he let his orgasm fuel hers. He caressed her skin and wanted to kiss her everywhere as she moved against him, as she gave herself up to him.

He never wanted it to end. He'd take everything she could give him.

And more.

In the hazy aftermath of their lovemaking Armando noticed that Gina's eyes were filled with tears. He kissed her cheeks, rubbing the streamers of saltiness away with his thumbs. He kissed her eyes and then lost himself in her mouth all over again.

"Thank you. That was incredible," he said as he came up for air. He never said that to women. He was used to hearing it, though, but Gina didn't say that. Instead she said,

"I want you in my bed."

Well, he wasn't about to deny the lady anything. After all, he'd just had the best sex of his entire life. It had been short, too short. And it had happened in an old pickup truck, not even in private, on a bench seat littered with Fredo's fast food wrappers. But it was still the best sex of his life. And he wanted more.

Way more.

CHAPTER 5

G INA COULDN'T BELIEVE she'd cried. In the back of a dirty pickup after scorching hot sex. Well, on the back *seat* of an old pickup. And with the hot guy she'd been dreaming about ever since she'd met him, that Navy SEAL with the training and the self-discipline she obviously lacked. What did he think of her? Even though he wiped away her tears, kissed her eyes, her ears and whispered things to her mouth she didn't understand…something in Spanish she didn't recognize. He must have thought she was a deranged, loose, unprincipled woman so hot for sex she'd do it in a garbage dump.

Her body started to awaken from its erotic sleep as he kissed her, cooed in her ear. The ache between her legs became uncomfortable again.

I'm embarrassed. God in Heaven. Was she really that desperate?

Something inside her made the tears already filling her eyes gush. She turned away from him and tried to bury her head in her wadded-up dress. What was this? It wasn't regret or shame.

What, Gina?

Armando's strong fingers lifted her chin and turned her

to stare directly into his warm brown eyes. Did she see pity there?

"What is it, baby?" He kissed her again gently on the mouth. He rubbed her cheeks with his thumbs, holding the back of her head, lazily making circles in her scalp with his long fingers, as he nibbled everywhere. "Did I hurt you?" he whispered.

What? How could he think that? Oh yes, the tears. He thought she was in some sort of pain.

Well, I am. Something deep down inside her had been uncorked, and now her emotions came out in a jumbled mess like clothes in a dryer. Reds, yellows, blues and whites all mixed together. Random. No order. And so frightening.

He nudged under her ear and whispered, after planting a delicate kiss, "Talk to me, Gina. I didn't mean to hurt you, take advantage. Baby, I'm so sorry."

So this guy was telling her he was sorry for releasing her inner siren, the one she kept locked up because she always got Gina in trouble? The one that fell too quickly for guys, especially guys who were masters at breaking her heart? Like this Navy SEAL.

And she'd told him she wanted him in her bed.

What have you done?

She'd been staring at the dog tags dangling over her, at the way the silver shone against his thick, tanned neck. His dark eyebrows and long black lashes, the fullness of his lips. She loved the gentle rise and fall of his chest, making the dog tags sway in the moonlight, touching her flesh, tinkling like tiny pieces of breaking glass. It was music. She saw the beads of perspiration caught in the stubble above his upper lip. That lock of hair that fell in a shiny loose curl over his smooth tanned forehead. This was a face she could fall for, dream about forever. This was the face of a protector, a hero. And worst of all, he was worried about how *she* felt.

His forefinger rubbed along her lower lip, bringing her gently back to reality. A small crease line had formed between his bushy eyebrows. A vein pulsed above it, disappearing into his hairline.

She pressed her palms against his pecs, resting against his warm flesh for a moment before pushing his hard body. He rose up and helped her to sitting position with one strong muscled arm. He sighed, looking out the windshield at the passing lights through the trees.

She had to explain, and hoped she could. "It isn't what you think."

The jerk of his right shoulder told her he wanted to put an arm around her and draw her close, but he'd stopped himself. He was resisting the urge to be tender with her. God, her heart was beating so hard she thought she might faint.

"The intensity. I'm not used to that much intensity." She took a chance and turned to look at his profile. The vein in his forehead disappeared. He started to nod slowly. Then she saw the crease form at the side of his lips, precursor to an unmistakable smile. As he continued to nod, she watched his chin arc towards her, his body shift. His arm wrapped around her shoulders as his fingers played with the hair at the nape of her neck. Firm fingers dug into the muscles at the top of her spine and massaged her there, making her relax.

His eyebrows tented as he seemed to have difficulty holding back laughter. "But you're okay with the sex?" His eyes sparkled as he searched her face, like he was memorizing every detail. The lips that had done wonderful things to her body just minutes before drew back and she was completely dazzled with the most gorgeous smile she'd ever seen.

"I'm good with the sex." She matched his smile.

"Outstanding, because, sweetheart, I'm just getting warmed up."

Oh, God.

"That invitation still open?" he asked.

She frowned, not sure what he was talking about. He leaned over and kissed one of her nipples, sending it into a delicious little knot. He held the side of her neck with one hand as he kissed her all the way up the other side.

"The part where you said you'd show me your bed," he whispered. His warm breath gave her a little tickle she felt all the way to her knees and beyond. Then his fingers eased their way toward the aching place between her thighs, but she kept them pressed together.

"I love the way your body moves," he whispered. "The way your body tastes."

She relaxed her knees and allowed him to slip a finger into her opening. Their heat level was rising fast. She giggled. "Can we do it without the trash?"

He jerked for a second, pulled back to study her expression and returned the chuckle. "That was a new one for me too. Why don't we get dressed and you take me to your place? I'll see if I can introduce you to some more intensity, but only if you want to. You tell me when to stop, okay?"

He held her chin with his fingertips, placing his forehead against hers.

"'Kay," was all she was capable of saying.

THE RIDE OVER was uneventful, except for the way she

needed to sit close to him, their thighs touching, his hand smoothing down hers, up and down between her knee and her hip. Her body missed his warmth when he had to pull away and shift the gears on the truck. She felt as if she were in high school, with the soccer player she'd fallen in love with who always drove her home after games. They'd detour down a country lane for some beautiful sex before he'd take her to her front door. He used to drive his father's old landscaping truck, but it mattered little to her.

She'd lost her virginity to him that summer. It was a simple, quick affair before he was to ship out overseas. There were no promises made, but she knew she'd wait for him to come home. He was the son of Mexican immigrant parents and had been proud to sign up to do his duty for the adopted country he loved. The uncomplicated, simple ways he showed his gentle affection for her became something she depended on. When he left for Afghanistan, she'd found herself in a funk until the day his father called and told her in his broken English that his son had been killed.

Something inside her died that day.

Gina thought perhaps all the other brief relationships she'd had afterwards, the horrible choices she'd made in the ensuing years, had been an attempt to find him again in the arms of her new lovers. But no one compared.

Until now.

Now she was about to let in someone she had no business being intimate with. She'd let him fully have his way with her. The brother of their person of interest. Were her personal feelings getting in the way of her job?

Hell, yes.

So, maybe that's why she'd been crying. Maybe this was the way it felt, just before you get your heart broken. Like the body knows before the head does.

She watched the jewel sparkles of the colored evening lights against the raindrops on the windshield in front of her. The music was playing some tune she recognized, but didn't want to recall. Like it was something she'd have to forget later on. The warm familiarity with which his hands caressed her, how she fit right inside the stretch of his arm, how good it smelled to lean her head against the bulge of his shoulder. Even though she was headed down a one-way, dangerous tunnel, for some reason she felt safe.

They pulled up to the condo the Department had rented for her. All her stuff was in storage, since this assignment meant she had to let her other apartment go. Like her life, everything familiar and part of her past was packed safely away under lock and key. Her family photographs, year-books from college, and special cards she'd saved were all hidden.

Only her public persona for the job, the "cheap" Gina, who was the best friend to the lady they were using to get info on the gang activity—that Gina was the one who lived here.

But that Gina had snagged this man, this perfect night. So why deny herself? After all, wasn't this just like all the other guys she fell for? Guys who left her? Wasn't it about time for her to take charge, allowing herself to enjoy something, just this once? Then she'd be the one to do the leaving. Wouldn't that be good self-care? Break his heart before he could break hers? Then it would be back to business. All cop, the real Gina. The Gina who was tough and could function in a man's world of crime, death and abuse.

She'd been leaning against him, and when he turned off

the motor and pulled the brake, she was reluctant to leave his side. They sat for a moment watching droplets collect and stream down the glass in front of them. No sense rushing if this night was all she would have with him. She knew that whatever was coming next was going to change her life forever.

Armando looked down at her. "You okay?"

Gina nodded, but didn't pull away.

"You sure? Now is the time to stop it, if you got some reason—"

She reached up and pulled his head forward, kissing him. The heat and the fire between them ignited again. The once-tentative kiss became all consuming. Their hands flew over each other's bodies.

A sharp whack on the driver window from the outside shattered their aroused stupor. Gina knew instantly who it was before she saw Sam's tense outline under the light of the streetlamp. His twisted face was red with rage.

Armando was out of the truck so fast Gina almost fell into the driver's door. With a couple of kicks to Sam's fleshy midsection and one to his face, the SEAL had Sam on the pavement groaning, and then suddenly he went limp.

"You fuckin' animal. Now you got a fight." Armando straddled him, yanking Sam's arms up. But Sam was beyond caring. Gina slid out quickly and tried to stop Armando, but he pushed her off.

"Get inside, Gina. Lock the door and call the cops."

"Armando, don't hurt him."

The smirk Armando showed her broke her heart. His face was full of a question he probably didn't want to ask.

"I can handle this," she began. "*You* shouldn't get involved," she pleaded. It was true. Sam wasn't really a threat to her, because she would call the Department and complain, probably bring paramedics to look Sam over, which would give Gina protection. But if Armando did some permanent physical damage to a member of San Diego's finest, he'd be in a whole lot of trouble. And with a blown cover, so would she. Armando had to be convinced to leave.

"Go. I'll be okay."

"I can't leave you alone. Here. With this guy," Armando shot back.

"You have to. Don't worry, I'll call the cops. But you don't want to be involved. Just disappear. I promise I'll call the cops right now. If you get involved, you risk your career, Armando. He's not worth it."

Armando stood up. Sam's blood stained the front of his shirt. His fingers combed his hair and then he put hands on his hips, breathing heavily. "But you are," he said.

"No, Armando. I'm not. Please, just go."

"So it's going to be this way, huh?" Gina noticed the bitter squint in Armando's face.

"Not what you think. All he wanted was to break the two of us up. He's done that. Let me get some medical attention for him and get the police to haul him away. I'll say I did this."

Armando frowned at the suggestion. "Like they'll believe you that you beat this piece of shit up? What if he presses charges against you?"

"You think he'd risk the ridicule of his biker buddies, saying he was slapped around by a girl? His ex? Leave it, Armando."

Sam started to groan.

"Please. I don't want you getting into trouble on my behalf." Gina practically got on her knees to plead.

"Why don't you let me worry about that?" he said, wiping sweat from his forehead with his arm.

"Because I have a gun and I know how to use it. Trust me, I'll be okay."

Armando adjusted his clothes and rolled one shoulder. She could see anger and confusion cross his face, but at last he shrugged and came closer to where she stood.

"I'm sorry. I thought—"

"He didn't care anything about me until he found me with someone else. Remember what I told you? He's married. He has no right…"

"Gina, all the reason I shouldn't leave you alone with him."

"Mr. Smith and Mr. Wesson would disagree. Trust me when I tell you I'm quite safe. If I felt otherwise, I wouldn't request you leave."

"Then go inside. I'll wait here until I know you're inside. What if his friends are just lurking around some car here?" He made a sweeping motion with his hand.

"No. Absolutely no. You get out of here."

"Why are you protecting him?"

"I'm not. I'm protecting *you*. This could go on your record. He's not worth the trouble he could cause you."

"I can handle myself. Worse badasses have come after me before and I did just fine."

"Yea, with the rest of your Team. This is different. You're going to have to trust me on this, Armando. Please! Just go. I'll be fine."

Sam coughed and spit up blood. She was running out of time. She pulled her weapon out and held it down, legs apart in the stance she'd been taught. She got out her phone and dialed the station.

"I've been attacked. I'd like some police protection over here right away. I'm in danger." As she listened to the voice on the other end of the line, she motioned for Armando to leave. It hurt that he nodded his head and, without taking her in his arms, walked back to the truck, opening the driver's door. Before he got in, he removed the rest of the window, kicking it with a swift upward jab with his right foot. Glass was scattered all over the street. Shards sparkled like diamonds in the night.

In a cloud of gray smoke and one large backfire the truck disappeared into blackness.

She prayed it wasn't the last time she would see him.

CHAPTER 6

ARMANDO CRANKED THE steering wheel and screeched around the first corner he could find. He'd double back and make sure she was okay. Gina was right about one thing. He could get his ass in a sling for tampering with the local riffraff. Didn't matter that they were the scum of the earth. As a SEAL, he was required to take the high road, even if that meant it cost him his life. He was used to risking his life. He wasn't used to risking the career he felt he was made for just so he could get into a fight with a lowlife biker at a gang bar. Not the way he'd envisioned his discharge happening.

And that's why this was so freakin' hard, to leave her alone with a cretin who clearly had no boundaries and had trouble controlling his rage. That sort of dude deserved worse than a kick to the gut and a broken nose. Armando had no room in his "decent zone" for bad guys who liked to beat up women and kids.

For a street urchin, Gina sure knew how to take care of herself. Surprisingly well put together, he thought. Carried a concealed firearm, which was against the law in California. But she didn't appear to be fazed. So maybe Gina was tougher than Armando thought. Maybe she was one of those GI Janes who got booted for bad behavior. Cavorting with the wrong officer or married man. Yet he couldn't see her being that kind of a slut. She'd already been hurt, she'd said.

No, there definitely was something more about Miss Gina. His traitorous body part was enthusiastically looking for another close encounter, in spite of the fact he'd been sent away—at gunpoint, no less. Didn't matter if the gun was aimed at the ground or at the beefy asshole who interrupted them.

He slowly pulled around two more streets, through a one-way alley and then parked perpendicular to Gina's street, shutting off his lights as he did so.

Motorcycles rumbled down the street and soon three Harleys parked beside what must have been Sam's bike, propped in the shadows at the edge of the complex. He'd been stupid not to notice the vehicle. He'd been distracted by the feel of her skin as he ran his fingers down her arm, the way her perfect breast warmly caressed the right side of his torso as they drove. He loved the way she smelled, all spicy and almond, not like the cheap perfume he'd scented on hookers and other girls who frequented this neighborhood.

This evening, as he'd looked down at her, with those big brown eyes and dark hair splayed all over Fredo's second seat, he'd felt as if she was his first woman. Like it was her first experience too. This resembled a sweet high school thing he'd forgotten about. Something innocent and good, the way she made love to him. It was clean and dignified. Took his breath away how much he wanted to please her. Go slow. Make it last forever. And fuck! She'd cried, for Chrissakes. At first, he'd thought he'd hurt her. But no, she was overcome.

Overcome? When had that happened to him before? He checked his memory. Was she a virgin and he didn't notice?

He discarded that thought. He gripped the door handle, ready to bolt from the truck when he heard the police sirens.

Thank God.

A short tussle ensued, and tempers flashed between two uniformed officers in the first patrol car and the bikers. Flashlights darted everywhere, accentuated by strobing red and blue lights, waking up Hell itself with the commotion. So much for low profile.

An EMT van arrived, but Sam was up on his feet, kicking the dirt with his black boot and probably swearing like any crusty sailor would if he got an anchor dropped on his foot. At one point Sam groped for Gina's arm, lurching his huge body forward, but the uniforms separated them. He earned a huge push, which sent him on his ass in the road. His face was red, made redder by the flashing lights, as he stood, arms waving in the air. The three buddies grabbed him in a huddle, but Sam wasn't having any of it, not at first. He got talked down in the end, though.

Two uniforms escorted Gina safely to her condo. A second patrol car pulled up. After determining it was safe to leave, Armando put the truck in reverse, careful not to grind the gears, and backed up slowly, then turned around when he was out of eyesight of the little conclave.

He headed to Mia's house and hoped Fredo had been able to hang on long enough that he could take his buddy home. He needed to think up a good explanation for the missing truck window.

The rain that had fallen earlier returned. He watched Fredo's wipers do a piss-poor job of removing the wetness from the dusty windshield. He made a mental note to have the wiper blades replaced when he got the window done.

The little yellow house with white trim glowed from within. Mia must have turned on every light inside. He knocked on the front door, hearing Mia in the middle of a frank discussion with Fredo, as the baby cried in the background.

"You fuckin woke up the kid, Fredo," Mia said as she stalked towards the front door. Armando's signature knock had alerted her as to who was waiting on the porch.

"Yea, well, I don't care. Mia, you gotta start listening to people who care for you. You're throwin' your life away, babe."

"I'm not your babe," she snarled as she opened the door without enthusiasm. Without a "hello" she turned her back on her brother and disappeared down the hallway to a back bedroom.

"Took you long enough." Fredo's prominent forehead and bushy eyebrows were even more prominent and wrinkled. "I'm over here trying to make nice with this she-wolf and you're out there doing God-knows-what with that little dish. I hope she was worth it, man."

Armando wanted to say something, but decided to zip it instead. Mouthing off to Fredo and then telling him about his injured truck might not be the smartest of ideas.

"Had a little trouble over at Gina's."

"What kind of trouble?" Mia held little Ricardo in her arms. She'd changed into skin-tight black leggings and an oversized T-shirt. A rhinestone-studded clip held up her dark curls. The baby's face lit up when he recognized his uncle Armando.

"Mia," Armando said as walked with his arms outstretched to take the baby, "how well do you know Gina's ex, that Sam character?"

Armando loved Ricardo's fresh scent. He rubbed tears from the baby's chubby cheeks and let him pat his face, pull on the hair behind his ears.

"Met him for the first time tonight." Mia leaned against the hallway doorframe, and crossed her long legs, almost sending Fredo to the ground with a gasp. Acting as if she took no notice of the Mexican SEAL, she folded her arms across her nonexistent belly and sighed. It pushed up her breasts and Fredo abruptly turned his back to her and swore in a whisper.

"She never mentioned him before." Mia delivered a half-lidded who-the-fuck-cares look straight back at her brother.

This surprised Armando. "So then I have to ask you, how well do you know Gina?"

Fredo slumped on one of the leather chairs and waited for Mia's answer.

"We're friends. We hang out at places together. Go clubbing. We're good for each other, checking up on each other, texting when we pick up guys. You know. To be safe."

Fredo was swearing in Spanish again, lecturing the floor, but kept it low.

"She pick up lots of guys?" Armando winced inside that he'd asked her that question.

"I never know. I think so." She uncrossed her arms and stood erect. "Why, am I supposed to go follow my girl-friends around and see who *they* go home with like you do to *me*?"

"I don't do that, Mia."

"Fuck you, Armando. What do you call tonight? We

were having a good time with some new acquaintances and you go all Navy SEAL ballistic on them. Ruin our evening."

Fredo inserted himself. "Mia, those dudes were going to ruin your night all right. Girl, you sure know how to dredge the bottom for the worst scumbags"

"You forget one thing, Fredo. The bikers were *Gina's* friends. Not mine. Not sayin' I didn't kinda like the big one, though." Mia flashed her toothy smile and batted her eyes directly at Fredo while she delivered the kill shot. "I like big guys. Big, *tall* guys, with lots of tats and muscles."

Armando saw Fredo bunch his hands into fists. His breathing was long and labored, but in control.

God bless you, Fredo. You are a fuckin' saint. Armando could not say the same for his sister. He looked at little Ricardo wiggling in his arms. He vowed to be very prominent in his nephew's life. With or without Mia's permission. He'd make it his personal mission. No way was this little boy going to grow up Mia's way as long as he was alive to alter it.

"You know what, Mia? You just insulted the man who saved my life more than a dozen times." Armando was saying it because it was the truth, not just to give Fredo a shred of the respect he so richly deserved. "You just hurt someone who only wants the best for you. The more we try, the meaner you get. Mama, Clark, Fredo here, and all the rest of the Team—everyone cares about you, except *you*."

She walked up to Armando and snatched the baby from his arms, retreating to the corner of the living room. "Well, now that you've gotten this all figured out, get the hell out of my house," she spewed. "Just because you bought it for me doesn't give you the right to come in here and tell me how to live. I can take care of myself. What about *that* don't you understand, Armani?"

Armando could do nothing but shake his head from side to side. Fredo had lost interest, staring down at the ground. He could tell that the Mexican SEAL wanted to be anywhere but here.

"C'mon. Let's go." He got a nod of agreement from his shorter Teammate. Armando felt like a complete douchebag for getting Fredo involved in the first place. And then to have to stand there and hear him get abused by his own sister. Not to mention the shit he and the rest of the Team had been giving Fredo over the past year.

Before they could close the door behind them, Mia shouted out, "And don't go trying to use your sexy ways to turn Gina against me. You stay the hell out of my life, hear? No rescue needed, or wanted, thank you very much. And stay the hell away from my friends."

Outside, Fredo held out his palm for the keys and Armando ignored the gesture.

"Fuck's wrong with you, Armani? Give me my fuckin' keys."

"I'm gonna fix the window."

Fredo walked over to the driver's door and swore. He kicked the truck, creating a small dent to match several other ones. "That asshole do this?"

"I'll fix it, I said." Armando was getting weary of the drama. What he really wanted was a cold beer, some smack talk, and then a hot shower and bed. He could still smell Gina's scent on his shirt. He still felt her silky skin beneath his fingers. He was getting hard all over again. But he was standing here talking to one of his best friends about his broken window. And he was still getting hard.

What kind of animal are you?

Armando released the keys and Fredo drove them over to the Rusty Scupper. Lieutenant Malcolm Jones, Cooper and a new guy, SO Marc Beale, all from SEAL Team 3, looked up from the table outside where they had parked their butts, warming themselves by the fire pit in the center. They were alone since the place was wet from the rain. Armando noticed the three Teammates were wet as well.

"You guys know it's been raining?" he asked them after he gave his order to the waitress.

Beale made a *ribbit* sound like a frog.

Cooper grinned. "Hell, Armani, I was just thinkin' of going for a swim. You up for that?"

Jones had wrinkled his nose.

Fredo had noticed too, and added, "Jones, you gotta understand, this is a tradition. We love our midnight swims as much as we love our midnight HALO jumps. Right guys?"

There was a general mumbling in the affirmative.

Fredo continued. "We do this at least once a week. I do believe it's been about that, maybe even two weeks since our last midnight swim."

"I don't like it much in the daytime, or anytime for that matter," Jones said. With his dark complexion, all Armando could see was the LT's white teeth. "Growing up in Mississippi, I stayed away from watering holes and such. Good way to get bit by a water snake or get yourself tied to a tree by some frisky white boys."

"Frisky white boys?" Fredo asked.

"We're talking Mississippi. Not many Mexicans there when I was growing up, not that it would have made much difference. Things are different now." Jones took another sip of his beer. No one was going to touch that comment.

Marky Mark turned to Armando. "Lannie say where we was goin' next week, Armani?"

"Nope," he answered. "I asked him, do we take our fins and trunks, our gloves and parkas, or our cash?"

"Guess we'll find out the evening before," Coop concluded.

"Roger that. We's on a Need. To. Know," Fredo said.

Cooper crunched down ice from his mineral water. He uncurled his lanky, six-foot-four body and bowed to the group. "Well, I need to be going home and get some face time with the wifey. Got a big day tomorrow. Moving into our new house. I promised Libby I'd be home early to help with the last-minute packing."

"Why?" Fredo asked. "You can put everything you got in that Babemobile in the back of my truck. And everyone here knows you aren't gonna get any sleep tonight."

Armando chuckled.

Fredo shot his heels up into the air. "Oh, Cooper, let me push against this wall so you can get deep. Oh. Oh. Oh. Ooooooh!" Fredo crooned. Beale and Jones began rocking in their chairs as if the motorhome Cooper lived in was rocking under them.

Cooper's enormous frame cast a long shadow as he came to tower above the little group. "Shut. The. Fuck. Up."

No one heeded his warning.

Cooper tried again. "That sounds like you banging one of your professionals, Fredo. You listening in for pointers when I'm not paying attention?"

"Hell no, Coop, we can hear it all the way to Ducky's. We sit out there and lick our cones while you're getting your dick polished off," Beale inserted.

"Well said, Marky Mark. You a legend, Coop." Jones

appeared to be glad the focus was off the swimming.

Cooper made a gesture like he was loosening his hips, doing a slow, gyrating hula for everyone to admire. "Tough job, but someone's gotta do it. I'm working on a little Cooper. Sort of a housewarming present for my new bride."

The group broke into laughter and several Teammates whistled their approval. With the tension reduced, Armando watched his supersized Teammate walk down the street to the motorcycle parking. He put on a flowered helmet that belonged to Libby and kick-started a red Vespa. He looked ridiculous, hunched over the handlebars, riding the lawnmower motor off into the night.

"He still hasn't bought a truck? He's been talking about it for weeks now," Fredo barked.

Beale leaned forward and received his new beer, winking at the waitress. "Libby's dad *gave* him a new truck for a wedding present. He doesn't like the gas mileage."

Armando leaned back in the chair and looked up at the stars. He wished his family problems were about trucks and gas mileage and a wife who wanted to get pregnant. He wondered if life would ever be that normal for him.

But good for Coop. If it can happen for you, buddy, maybe there's hope for me after all.

CHAPTER 7

N EXT MORNING IN the squad room Sam showed up in the same foul mood he'd had the night before. Gina watched him bang into chairs and bluster, as if every movement involved great effort or pain. He ignored his other UCDs, who in turn eyed him carefully, trying to avoid the bull in the china shop. She didn't doubt he *was* feeling pain, and secretly relished the thought that Armando had done this to protect her.

Wanting to be prepared, she ran several scenarios over and over in her mind, deciding she was going to push back just as hard as he did. She thought the other guys would pile on if Sam started going after her, so she'd have to do it smart. If she got lucky, maybe Sam would go off on one of his legendary tirades in front of the brass. As she watched him bite his lower lip and devour the stubble growing just below, she knew he was close. Very close. It wouldn't take much. Everyone in the room was watching him.

After the initial group chastisement for a mission almost blown, she and Sam were asked to stay behind and talk to their sergeant in private. The glass door was closed, but long looks from the bullpen didn't give her any feeling of privacy.

Suck it up, Gina. You're a big girl. Wanted to play in the big leagues? This is how it's done.

Wasn't going to be anything easy about this.

"There a problem here you two can't handle?" Sergeant Kozinski had a walleye and Gina wasn't sure whether he was looking at her or at Sam.

"No, sir. I'm good." Sam spoke up first before Gina could respond. Like hell he was good. He hadn't been good since the day after he'd charmed her into his bed. That Sam she never saw again after Night One.

"Gina?" Kozinski asked.

The quiet pause in the room highlighted Sam's laborious breathing. She could tell he was suffering and had probably spent the night getting shit-faced. She was hoping Kozinski noted the bloodshot eyes, the stench of alcohol a fresh shower and a pint of aftershave couldn't mask.

"Sir," she began. She adjusted the little girl voice that wanted to come out first. "I don't want Sam working on this case. This is my undercover detail. I'm the one in jeopardy. Wasn't expecting him to do anything on this but run his snitches. Didn't know until last night he was part of it." She looked at her sergeant. "And I don't like it one bit, sir."

So far, so good.

Kozinski nodded. "It wasn't something I approved. Sam used his own judgment, under the circumstances. Ton of Scorpions at the bar. Backup was needed. At least, that's what I was told."

"But *I* didn't call for backup, sir, and it would have been *my* call to make." Gina was going to keep tossing hooks out there, hoping one of them would snag Sam. "And even if I did, he'd be the *last* person I would request."

Her jab began to work as she heard Sam's quick inhale

and the squeaking of his steel-toed lace-up boots.

"Just who the fuck do you think you are, Gina? A rookie pulling rank?" Sam was red-faced, and exactly the right kind of belligerent to make Gina's case to the sergeant. She could have kissed him, she was so happy at the display.

"Hold it, Sam. Back off," Kozinski warned.

"Maybe you better tell Kozinski about your little lap dance in the back seat with the SEAL?" Sam spewed, ignoring his sergeant.

"You have no idea what went on in the back seat, Sam. I'm working the case the best way I can." Gina tried to sound calm, but she was feeling the ground falling out from under her.

"What's a SEAL doing here? Someone talk to me," Kozinski asked as he shifted his gaze from Gina to Sam. He finished eyeballing Gina. "Gina, what the hell'd you do?"

"Nothing, sir. I was playing the part I was asked to play. We noodled around a bit. Nothing I can't handle. And we're both adults. I'm single. So is he." She glared at Sam and could see her gaze left its mark. She glanced down at his left hand and noticed his wedding ring was gone. "It won't be a problem, sir."

"This SEAL the brother of Mia Guzman?" Kozinski asked.

"Yessir," Gina and Sam said in unison.

"Wish the hell he'd butt out. You best get unfriendly with him in a hurry, Gina."

"Easier said than done, sir." She could feel Sam's intense stare. She could smell his anger brewing.

"Well, then your cover will be blown, Gina. And that will be on *you*," her sergeant answered.

"Understood, sir."

"Honestly, sir," Sam began, "I think we should get another officer to do the detail. Gina has shown a total lack of objectivity."

Gina's blood boiled. Her few minutes of Heaven were being tarnished by an abusive ex-boyfriend who had about as much objectivity as a man dangling from a rope in a climbing accident.

"Sir, that was an unfair comment. Sam is the one who inserted himself and almost cost us the entire mission last night. *He* is the one who needs to be removed. He is jeopardizing all the efforts I've made so far."

"Bullshit, Gina. You call it *effort*, screwing that SEAL—"

Sam's voice carried into the bullpen. Several heads on the other side of the glass turned in their direction.

Kozinski muttered obscenities to the floor. "I'm going to have both your badges in about a minute. Jee-ZUS officers! Get a grip. I feel like I'm talking to a couple of kids who got in a fight on the playground in junior high."

They both apologized. Gina worked hard not to smile. Victory was nearly in her grasp.

"If Sam stays on this case, then you won't have to replace me. I quit." Gina couldn't believe she'd just said this. Her insides were cheering.

"I sure hope you know what the hell you're doing, Gina." Kozinski paused to look at Sam. "And I could say the same for you."

Sam started to object and he suddenly faced the palm of the sergeant's hand. "Save it. You're off the case, Sam, except for working with the informants. You've done some damned good police work here. Let's not screw with it, okay? I'm going to back Gina this time. You're to physically stay out, unless otherwise requested." Then he turned a wizened eye on Gina. "Young lady, you better not fuck this up."

Sam left the office, without being granted permission, leaving the door open. Gina knew Kozinski was about as fair as they made them. He'd let Sam sulk off this time, but if there were a second time, Sam would get something that would show up in his file.

"I'm sorry, sir. You know we have a history, right? He doesn't seem to want to let it be." Gina felt perhaps the sergeant might have compassion for her under the circumstances.

She was wrong.

Kozinski had quietly closed the door to his office and stood, his hand on the doorknob. "Hell, Gina, the whole department knew about your torrid little romance. You honestly think I'm that dumb?"

"No, sir."

"We're all adults here. Takes two people to fuck each other's brains out. You could have always said no."

"But Sam was senior to me. At first I was worried—"

"God dammit, Gina. I wasn't talking about *Sam*. I was talking about the SEAL."

ARMANDO AND KYLE, LPO for Team 3, were waiting for Gunny to open the gym. The retired Gunnery Sergeant was getting slower and slower. He'd been the father confessor to all the young SEALs from Team 3, especially Kyle, the Team's LPO, and his crew. Armando and Kyle had been inseparable all throughout the BUD/s training, and they'd deployed together three times.

Gunny had a hand in helping Kyle, Cooper and Fredo rescue Armando from the Mexican gang who had kidnapped him after abducting Mia. For this Armando would be eternally grateful.

Kyle had told him privately Gunny wasn't in the best of health. He sported a scar going from his belly button to his neck where they'd opened him up and then stitched him closed. He'd refused further treatment for his lung cancer. Everyone knew the only reason the cancer wasn't growing faster was because Gunny was just too damn ornery.

The older Marine wheezed and spat a wad of something thick and dark before he set his shaking hands on the keys, trying to thread the lock. Kyle looked worried.

"You're here early for a Saturday, you two. Have a frustrating sexual encounter, boys?" Armando could see Gunny's attempt to change the focus fell flat.

"Shut the fuck up, Gunny. How was your night?" Kyle asked.

The front door opened, tinkling the tiny brass bell over the doorframe. Gunny punched a combination into a newly installed keypad nearby. The gym had nothing but rusty old equipment, but a string of vandalisms had Gunny trying to protect what little he had invested there. Duct tape repaired the display case, which now stood empty. The thieves made off with the T-shirts and a case of bottled water, leaving the old gym equipment behind.

Gunny coughed up more phlegm and spit it into a tissue behind the display case. He discreetly dropped it into a trashcan. "Watched Dancing on Air last night. Double elimination. Reba, the one with the big boobs, made it, so all's well."

Armando smiled and slung a towel around his neck as Kyle headed for the bathroom. "I shoulda come over and kept you company."

"Gee thanks. Nah, all you boys got your own lives these days. I'm starting to feel like a third tit on a stripper."

Armando felt the sadness and knew Gunny wouldn't be around long enough to see him married and starting a family of his own, like Kyle and Cooper were doing. It made him a little sad.

"So I take it you feel like shit, then?" He kept his back to the older man, working his first rep of free weights. He ended his set by throwing the dumbbells down on the rubber mat, which was the standard protocol. Placing them gently on the ground would get you tossed good and proper from the gym.

"That pretty much sums it up. But I do have some good news." Gunny was staring out the front plate glass window.

"What's that?" Armando asked as he began his second rep.

"Got a son coming to see me all the way from Thailand."

"No shit? When?" Armando threw the weight down again as Kyle came back into the gym.

"Next week. Says in his email he wants to meet me. He's twenty-two."

"Didn't know you had a son," Kyle added as he walked over to pick up the barbell Armando had thrown.

Gunny chuckled, which turned into a full-on hacking cough. "Well I knew the odds were 50-50 there'd be a son. He found me on Facebook through the gym. I sure as hell enjoyed knocking up all their mothers, and I understand I'm a virile son of a bitch." He spit again into a tissue. "Just never met any of them."

"Well, timing's good. We got a few days off before we go on the training mission."

"Yeah? Where to?"

"I figure Alaska, Mexico or Vegas, baby. But they don't tell us until just before. Sucks, but it doesn't really matter. We're always ready."

"Right you are," Gunny said as he wiped down his rusty old equipment.

"So what day is it, and we'll come back you up."

"Wednesday. Probably scare the shit outta the kid, a bunch of SEALs showing up at the airport."

"Yup. That would be scary as hell. Not like meeting his crusty old dad for the first time. Nah, that would be a piece of cake compared to meeting the likes of us." Kyle winked at the retiree.

That got a snicker out of Gunny. "Not nearly as scary as the time I showed up with his mother in the wedding cart. First time most of her relatives met me, and I'm not so sure I left a good impression. Kinda happened real fast-like."

"Love has a way of doing that to a man, doesn't it?"

"You've never taken the plunge, even got close, have you, Armani?"

"I've had relationships that have lasted longer than your marriages, Gunny."

"That's not sayin' much."

Armando knew in his heart that he wasn't the marrying kind. He loved women and all the exciting sex play, but he wasn't a good one for commitment, since he was really married to the Navy and his SEAL brothers. But Kyle and Cooper had found theirs, so perhaps…no, he had to change his train of thought right now or he'd fuck up his day.

"So Gunny, your wife was Thai?"

"Yes. Beautiful girl. Only knew her for about a month before we shipped out."

"Time enough to get married. Get her pregnant."

"Always time to get married. But then, I don't believe in divorce." He slapped Armando on the back as the dumb-bells hit the mat again. "I just figured it out the other day. I've been married six times, but never divorced."

CHAPTER 8

A FEW DAYS later, Gina met Mia at the coffee shop around the corner from Mia's house. She noticed her charge looked unusually weary. Something was bothering her. The baby was sleeping in his stroller.

"You been out for a run, Mia?"

The girl stared back at Gina looking annoyed "No. You know I don't do that."

"I hear you. Don't much like the exercise either," Gina lied.

"Girl, I know when I'm being sold a story. Your arms are as buff as I've ever seen on a girl. You mean to tell me you don't bust your buns at some gym somewhere?"

Gina blushed. Confusion and the sense of *Uh-Oh* descended like a blanket, wrapping itself stubbornly around her. She shivered. It had been a stupid remark, and she should have known her physical conditioning wouldn't be lost on Mia. She'd almost crossed the line again and revealed too much. The girl noticed everything, and Gina's cover depended on no slip-ups.

Gina masked her fear as best she could. "Had a friend once who was a body builder. Now *that's* what *I* call working out."

She got a sneer in response. "Nah, that's some freaky shit. I mean, getting man titties and having your unit climb up into your belly, and then look like some hairless baked potato dude in your 40s. No thanks."

The baby began to stir. Mia picked the fat toddler up and nuzzled him.

"Lunch is on me," Gina said, happy to change the subject. She loved the way little Ricardo's fat hands reached for Mia's hair, her jewelry and anything else he could grab. Despite Mia's poor choices in men, the baby looked well cared for.

Mia turned Ricardo facing out. He gave Gina a big smile. Mia eyed the menu absent-mindedly while the baby's arms moved through the air, looking for something he could grab. "You sure you can afford all this breakfast and lunch stuff, Gina? For a girl who works in an office, you sure spend a lot of money eating out."

Gina noted Mia's observation as another crack in her disguise. Was she questioning their relationship? "Just trying to be nice. You've had a pretty rough couple of days. I can start meeting you at McDonald's, or just show up at your house, but I know how you like your privacy."

The comment worked. Mia chuckled as she tried to keep the menu from Ricardo's stubby fingers. She fanned herself, which made the baby reach for it. "Privacy. My fuckin' brother won't leave me alone," Mia said.

I wish that were my problem.

"I think Armando is a good guy, Mia. Maybe he's just trying to protect you. I can understand it."

"Well, why doesn't he get his own woman, then? He could order *her* around and have a hissy fit, and judge all *her* fuckin' friends. Not me. I'm his sister. I don't want *or* need it."

The thought of Armando ordering Gina around and being possessive was actually very enticing. She remembered the feel of his kisses on her flesh. She hadn't been able to get enough of him. The man was pure sexual eye candy. The fact that he cared about how she'd felt afterwards made her miss him terribly. More than she should.

How the hell am I going to complete my mission while I'm melting like a schoolgirl for the wrong guy?

Gina decided to do some digging. "He doesn't have a girl? I'd think a guy like that would have his pick. Ladies in San Diego throw themselves at SEALs every day. He must be some kind of celibate priest."

Mia spit out her coke. "Excuse me while I barf."

Ricardo started giggling, sounding like a kid in the back yard who'd found a sprinkler.

The waitress brought a rag over and cast a critical eye at Mia, who appeared to be oblivious of the effect her outburst had on anyone else.

"Armando had a girl he really liked in high school," Mia started. "He was the goalkeeper the year we went to the soccer State Championships. He could kick the ball downfield, or pass and dribble and then run like hell, and he used to score, leaving the box open, he was so confident. He had some moves."

You're telling me?

"Ginger. I think her name was Ginger. Her dad was an Irish cop, and she had the red hair and a temper to go with it, just like her dad. God, Armando loved that girl, and she treated him like shit. I mean, she got with other guys on the side, and he was the last to know. Get my drift?"

"I do."

"They broke up. He had to. She was making a fool of him. He sulked for weeks. And then, she was killed in a car accident, along with a couple of others. They'd been drinking. Armando began the dark period again."

"Again?"

"You think Caesar and his guys are bad dudes? You should have seen the guys Armando used to hang out with when we first came here from Puerto Rico. Only difference, he wouldn't let them touch me. I was eight or nine at the time."

"But he changed."

"He fell in love with soccer. It was like he was married to it."

"Bet your mom was pleased."

"Answer to prayer," she said. "Mom prays about everything. Obsessed with it."

Gina wanted to ask more about Armando's second "dark period," after the death of the girl, but thought it wasn't safe.

"So Gina, your big friend Sam stopping by tonight?"

Gina cringed at the thought. "I don't trust him."

"Why don't you let *me* be the judge of that, or do you still have some flame for him?"

More like the fires of Hell. "Mia, we're done. But he's not a very good dude. I wish you wouldn't get mixed up with him." She recalled Sam and how much he loved bondage sex. She knew he had to work very hard to control his temper, keeping it within what she thought would be acceptable parameters befitting a cop, but under the right circumstances it could explode. Part of her had found it exciting. The other part wished she'd never met him. That was what she and Mia had in common. Both had hooked up with the wrong kind of guy.

"Who said anything about not liking bad dudes or getting mixed up? Just want some good times. Dancing. Make them spend money on me. I like that. I like to tease the shit out of them and then look for the next one before I drop this one for that one. The badder they are, the more fun for me."

Gina forced herself to laugh at Mia's dangerous posture. Inside, she was sad for the beautiful woman sitting across from her and wondered how she could possibly be Armando's sister. It didn't fit. Armando was such a decent guy. He willingly protected his mother and his sister, and without complaint.

"You got something you hate about good guys?" Gina asked.

Mia looked away immediately. When she drilled back at Gina, her eyes were cold, black, and filled with malice. "There are no good guys."

And there it was. Mia had a dark period too, except, unlike her brother, she was still living it.

Gina thought about it all afternoon and over the next couple of days. She was supposed to get cozy with what was left of Caesar's old gang, the Scorpions. But both the girls would be safer with the Department guys running backup. Sam could give them intel on the gang's illegal activities, so Gina could get snagged up in one to be able to testify to bring them down or make the arrests herself. Except that plan wasn't safe at all for Gina because she knew Sam would have a hard time staying out of it. And the really safe guy was one she wasn't supposed to have anything to do with.

What a messed-up world.

Gina felt as if she was at a fork in the road. She had

some serious decisions to make about the future of the investigation and how she was going to be able to successfully carry it out. As much as she considered it a bad option, she had to talk to Sam. No way around it. She needed Sam's expertise and his informants. She just hoped she could convince him to reel himself in.

Kozinski called her one morning to request she mend her fences with Sam because it was getting to be a "thing" in the Department. That meant Sam had been lobbying for position with anyone who could listen, enlisting allies.

With a gut full of second thoughts, Gina called him.

"Hey baby, I knew you'd call me."

"Don't get your hopes up, Sam. I've had a good workout today and a couple of days to think about everything, and I need to make a truce with you."

"Thought you wanted me off the case."

"I want you off *my* case."

"But baby, we were so good together. You remember how it was."

"Sam. It's not going to happen. Never. Understand?"

"Never say never, baby. Think of how much fun it would be playing the part of my girlfriend, and all the teasing you could do. Makes my dick hard just thinking about it."

"Fuck you, Sam. I knew this was a mistake. Thanks for making the decision easier for me."

Gina hung up. God, she wished she had other options. Now she had to try to make nice with her boss. She knew the sergeant would be pissed.

A FEW DAYS later the girls met again at Babes. Carlos Compos had taken up position near the stage like he did every night. Gina wondered if he had a woman or a home to even go back to. Or perhaps he had an apartment behind the stage. He noticed them immediately as they slid onto their perches at the bar.

Though her stomach felt as if it were crawling with lice, she managed a sultry smile in Carlos's direction, and that was all it took. The smooth-skinned, newly elevated gang leader with the pencil-thin beard and well-oiled, slightly curly black hair chewed on a toothpick as he made his way across the room towards them like a prince descending from a throne. This time he was all over Gina. His eyes roamed, lingering on her chest and the space under her butt where her legs had crossed. She tried to put Armando's face on the man to make things easier, but what little success she had was dashed when she smelled cheap cologne that had literally been poured down the man's chest. The gold chains he wore were wet where it mixed with the man's sweat.

Disgusting.

Carlos gave Gina his version of bedroom eyes while he snuck a hand up Mia's skirt. Mia leaned into him to smash her pubic bone against his knuckles, cutting off his advance but giving him a good feel anyway.

The girl had balls.

"I didn't give you permission, Carlos," Mia whispered, but Gina could see she was secretly excited by the attention.

"I'm not feeling you. I'm feeling your friend," he said as he removed his hand and continued to gaze at Gina. "Honey, can I go down on you right here? I got a nice hundred dollar bill and something else if you want it."

Gina tried not to shudder, but she had to look away.

"Sugar. No need to be shy. I'm good with the ladies. I'm not, like, this bitch's guy."

"I'm not Caesar's bitch," Mia protested.

"Except you have his kid. No one gonna touch you while Caesar's alive." Carlos gave Mia a greasy grin. "He's in a cage, but he's still alive."

Mia turned to the bar, giving Carlos her disgusted shoulder. She ordered a Margarita from the bartender, who was watching everything carefully. He had a hopeful expression. "You gonna let guys get a touch, you might as well dance for me, ladies," he said.

Carlos used Mia's distraction to zero in on his prize. Gina could see in his eyes that he intended on having her any way he could. He put a forefinger on her shoulder and drew it down her arm, then down her forearm to the back of her hand. He peeled her fingers away from her drink and gave her palm a tender kiss. Inside she shuddered at his touch, but she worked not to let it show.

"I'll bet you taste real nice," Carlos's words oozed out with syrupy sweetness.

Two other gang members entered the room just before the next dancer began her gyrations. They were enthralled with the skinny girl on stage, who looked all of fifteen years old and was scared to death. Her slender thighs had bruises on them she'd tried to cover up with makeup. Gina knew she was probably a young runaway and a drug user.

Making a mental note to have the girl's ID checked, calling it in, Gina focused on Carlos again. He looked pleased to be the recipient of her attention.

"How about it?" he asked.

"Sorry."

"Are you, really?" Carlos looked between Mia and Gina. "You fancy chicks?" he asked Gina.

"No. I'm just not in the mood," she answered. It was the

truth.

"I can fix that."

Gina made a mental note to watch her drink. She knew Carlos would find a way to slip something in on her if she wasn't vigilant. She had no intention of getting that close.

Mia came to Gina's defense. "Hey, get away from my friend. She told you no. What part of that don't you understand?"

Carlos licked his lips. "I just want a little taste. Or maybe she might like to give me a little something." Carlos wiggled his eyebrows. Then he turned his face to Mia. "Darlin' I need a mouth on me quick or I'm gonna spill. You guys got me all bothered."

Mia pointed to the dancer, "She looks like your type."

The young girl bent over, giving the sparse crowd a view of her quivering buttocks bifurcated by a silver G-string. Carlos smiled and backed away from the two girls until he got close to the stage. While looking at Gina, he took out what looked like a one hundred dollar bill and placed it under the elastic of the teenager's G-string. He leaned over to the offered soft flesh of the young girl's rear and gave her a lick and then a kiss. He rubbed himself and closed his eyes. When he opened them, he was staring right at Gina.

Adrenaline pumped through Gina's chest as she resisted the urge to run away from this, from the police work, this seamy undercover stuff, from Mia and Sam and even Armando. It wasn't the work that bothered her.

It was that she felt like bait.

CHAPTER 9

G UNNY GREETED HIS son, Sanouk Wattanapanit, at the San Diego airport with Kyle and Armando at his back. Armando felt like they were standing in on the old former Marine's wedding procession or an official award of valor citation. The tall well-muscled boy of twenty-two was handsome, with Eurasian features and smooth light brown complexion. But his ears identified him as one of Gunny's offspring. The protuberances stood out and were probably as useful as large, flat handles on a bowling ball.

Gunny's first words were, "Holy shit. You look just like your mother."

Armando noticed the boy's embarrassment as he bowed slightly and gazed down at his supersized feet, encrusted in torn canvas sneakers without laces. When he finally looked up, Sanouk's smile became heartbreakingly respectful and contrite.

"Father, I have been waiting my whole lifetime to meet you." His English was perfect, flawless, with just a hint of accent. He'd been well schooled, Armando thought.

"I'll be goddamned," Gunny blurted out. "I thought we'd have to be, like, doing sign language, and I was wondering how that was going to work out."

Armando shared a smirk with Kyle, and knew his Team Leader had entertained the same thoughts. The sign language obviously hadn't stopped Gunny from knocking Sanouk's mother up, after he married her, of course.

As the awkward seconds drifted away, Gunny finally asked his son The Question. "So, how is she?"

"*She* is named Amornpan, and she is well. I have a step-father she married soon after you left."

This brought a scowl to Gunny's face. He grunted acceptance and stepped back a bit when the boy came forward to give him a hug. The young man towered over Gunny by several inches, and though Gunny stiffly accepted the gesture, the boy tenderly held his biological father and patted his back. "Thank you for my life," he whispered over Gunny's shoulder.

Armando knew about the loss of a parent. His own father had been gunned down in the line of duty in Puerto Rico shortly before his mother moved him and his sister to L.A. Being the surviving family of a murdered cop wasn't especially safe in Puerto Rico. Armando struggled with the loss all during his teenage years, years he did things he wasn't proud of. He made it into manhood with an overwhelming need for revenge, and a desire to protect good people. It was stashed away in the back of the SEAL's psyche along with his lost childhood. But, as limited as his own father's time had been, he couldn't imagine not having known his father at all, like this boy.

Gunny's hacking cough interrupted his son's hug. He pulled out a handkerchief with trembling hands, placing it over his mouth. "Sorry," he mumbled, trying to hide bloody remnants of an earlier coughing attack.

Sanouk eyed the red stain on the handkerchief with

alarm, and then drilled a worried look into the two SEALs. "You are my father's friends?"

"Glad to meet you," Kyle said as he extended his hand. "Perhaps you can talk some sense into your father. I'm Kyle."

"And I'm Armando." They both took turns shaking the boy's firm grasp. Gunny continued to cough.

"You are unwell?" Sanouk asked his father.

"Rot of the flesh. Nothing more." It was Gunny's standard answer whenever he didn't want to explain himself to a stranger. Armando hoped the coming days would give Gunny a new reason for living. He was hoping the boy could convince Gunny to go back to the doctor for treatment.

Crowds from the arriving planes were shifting all around the group. Sanouk picked up a computer case and slung it over his right shoulder. "I have bags," he said as he started to follow the signs to baggage claim. Obviously, the boy was used to traveling.

Father and son walked next to each other in awkward silence as Kyle and Armando trailed behind. Sanouk carried himself like an athlete. His long limbs appeared powerful despite the lithe gait. Unlike other Thai men Armando had met, Sanouk had a western frame, not only in height, but thickness too. And from the shape of his broad shoulders and long arms, Armando could tell he was in perfect physical condition and probably worked out on a regular basis.

"He's not at all like what I expected," Kyle whispered to Armando.

"No shit."

"Thank God he must take after his mother," Kyle continued.

"Yeah. Except for the Dumbo ears."

The two SEALs chuckled, causing Gunny to turn and give them a worried frown.

Armando thought it odd Gunny was suddenly lost for words. He noticed the side-glances the older man gave his son, checking him out whenever the boy looked elsewhere. Since Gunny had always been a loner, it was odd to see the early forms of attachment, the fatherly bonds Armando knew were unfamiliar to him. He'd spent years making wisecracks about the women he had married and children he must have fathered.

The baggage turnstile coughed up Sanouk's bags like one of Gunny's attacks. Armando was surprised the two bags consisted of an overstuffed black duffel and a set of golf clubs, which Gunny tried to pick up but Kyle grabbed away from him.

Everything was piled into Kyle's black Hummer. Sanouk rode shotgun admiring the vehicle. He was every bit the typical American kid, and when Kyle turned on some hip hop, Sanouk began to make some dance moves.

Gunny was breathing heavily as he sat next to Armando in the back seat. His eyes watered from the coughing or something else welling up inside. Armando guessed it was the latter. The old Marine couldn't stop staring at his son.

Armando gave the thumbs up as the Hummer wound its way back to Coronado. Gunny's expression was somewhere between shock and meltdown, that look Armando sometimes saw on young servicemen after they'd taken their first hit and were being medevac'd out.

A short time later they pulled up to Gunny's gym. A small crowd of former and active SEALs, as well as other military and civilian personnel, had gathered inside the place. Someone had brought a couple of large tubs of ice with water bottles and long-necked beer stuffed inside. Three large delivery boxes of pizza were stacked up on Gunny's duct-taped, empty display case. Several of the Team guys had brought their wives and babies. Kyle stood behind Christy and their kid and wrapped his arms around his family.

"Welcome to San Diego, Sanouk. We've sort of adopted your father, here," Kyle said.

Gunny searched the audience and nodded his appreciation for the turnout, but Armando had never seen him so uncomfortable. He fisted and un-fisted his ham-like hands, rubbed his palm up over his forehead to wipe the sweat away, and seemed to totter whenever he walked. His labored breathing was of most concern. Armando slapped him on the back.

"You okay, Gunny?" he whispered in the man's ear.

"Right as rain. I'm just wondering who's gonna clean up the mess," Gunny said, deflecting the conversation.

"I'll get you some water. You go introduce Sanouk to the group," Armando suggested. Gunny nodded.

"Everyone, thanks so much for coming. Sanouk here came a long way to check out his old dad, and I appreciate the turnout. I hope you'll help me show him around, but keep him away from the ladies, and let's temper the barhopping, okay? My only requests."

The group erupted in huzzahs and waters and beer bottles were raised. Several older SEALs came forward and slapped the young Sanouk heartily on the back, buffeting the young man back and forth as he tried to smile and address each one of them. Armando could see the boy's eyes widen with admiration, and it made Armando proud, too.

After all, Gunny was one of their community and any offspring, no matter the roots or origins, no matter if he'd been created in a steamy jungle because of his father's fondness for Asian women who didn't speak English, he was still family. To them all.

GINA CALLED IN the runaway she'd spotted at Babes, and Kozinski promised he'd have two child welfare workers stop by to check on her. Then he asked if she'd buried the hatchet with Sam.

"Not yet, sir. I know we need him. I just don't understand why he has to show up when I'm on duty. It places the operation and me at risk. Can't you see that, sir?"

"Look, I go back nearly twenty years with Sam. I don't have any reason to question his judgment…"

"Except for the little stunt he pulled with me," Gina blurted out.

"From the way I hear it, you were about as hot for him as a lioness in heat. Sorry, darlin', but I take Sam's side on this one. He's only a man."

Who thinks he's God's gift.

"He was a married man. He never told me. None of you guys did."

"Take that as a compliment, Gina. Take it to mean we think you can handle yourself. Not like the first time anyone in the department has gotten involved in an affair outside of work. It's ruined a lot of careers. You guys handled it well. It was over before I had to do anything. Now I want to just forget about it."

"But Sam won't."

"I think you're reading too much into it. Roll with it,

Gina. He thinks he's acting a part that works. So part of it is true. So what? Use it."

"But I don't want to play his girlfriend."

"Okay, but let him tease you a bit. Let him be the jilted one. Work it however you want to, but work it. These guys will be the only ones to bail your ass out of a really bad situation if it goes wrong. Remember that. The Scorpions kill people for petty, stupid reasons. You're dealing with some dangerous dudes. Be grateful."

That last comment grated on her more than all the rest.

Grateful? More like enduring. So, it was going to be a test. She'd used up her allotment of complaints and anything further would be just perceived as whining. She was on her own.

GINA DECIDED TO try one last time to reason with Sam. Though she'd written it off as a very bad idea, the near-confrontation at Babes with Carlos caused her to reconsider. She needed Sam's intel. Tito, one of Carlos's runners, was a kid Sam had busted earlier, and he had given the task force everything they needed to catch the gang in a couple of sting operations. But Carlos had always eluded them, and he was the prize. Gina knew it would be nearly impossible *not* to have Sam involved and still complete the mission.

If he could just stop making references to their shadowy past, there was a part of Sam she thought she could still trust. But his need to totally control her, confine her, stop her, was getting in the way. That, and her own fear.

Thinking back to their hot involvement last year, she remembered Sam had not *physically* hurt her, but had refused to let her leave his room, demanding she stay in his bed until he had fucked her multiple times. He was rough.

He'd wanted to tie her up.

And, she was ashamed to admit to herself, there was a dark part of her that had liked it.

God help me, am I one of those people?

At the time she could have grabbed a phone and called the Department. She could have struggled to get away, or screamed. But she'd stayed. She'd let him screw her over and over again. She'd submitted to him and found something there that was arousing. Gina tried to put it out of her head, but she couldn't.

No, best to stay away from him completely.

But how?

They still worked in the same department. It would be impossible to avoid him altogether. She'd had high hopes when he returned to the force after his messy trip to New York. But at their first meeting, there was no denying the sexual attraction he still felt for her. The outburst at the strip joint was the first time Sam had stepped over the line since his return. Maybe the insertion of the SEAL brother had thrown Sam off guard, or maybe he'd been drinking. Could this be just one isolated incident?

Surely the sergeant's warning would make him wake up to what he was risking for all of them. Now that he knew she didn't want to play along, maybe there would be a way he could control that demon inside him so they could work together.

Time to prove she wasn't afraid of him any longer. Whom was she doing this for, though, herself or Sam? In any case, she hoped to God this meeting worked. Gina was running out of options and in danger of blowing the whole operation. Because of the rocky start they'd had, she was also in danger of losing her badge.

Sam had agreed to meet her at one of the outdoor cafes along the Strand. She wanted lots of people around her, and the protection of daylight hours. She also knew this area was not one that Mia would frequent.

She flipped her silverware back and forth as she sipped on her iced tea. Sam's huge frame soon shadowed her table. He wore his black leathers, coming in the disguise he'd agreed to wear whenever she met publicly with any member of their task force. He sat down without being invited. He knew he looked hotter than hell.

Damn the man. He still pushes my buttons.

Sam's cool blue eyes looked clearer than the last time she'd seen him, when they'd been blustering and bloodshot. His mouth was twisted in a smirk, and she could see he wasn't making much of an effort to look or act civil. Still, it could work, as part of the undercover act.

"Thanks for coming," she said and then examined her ice tea. "You want to order something?"

He grabbed the small cardboard menu stuck between the napkin holder and the salt and pepper shakers. He ordered a burger, fries and a milkshake from the young waitress who stopped by. He didn't reel in his gawking at the waitress's ample chest.

Some things never change. You think I'm jealous? I'm so far away from seeing anything in you I even like. She had a job to do, so she donned her emotional disguise. She had to play nice with this cretin or she'd never get anywhere.

He was watching the waitress's ass sashay down the row of tiny tables. "Sam, this is really difficult for me to say, but I do need your cooperation." The words almost stuck in her throat.

"Damned right, Gina." He finally pried his eyes off the

waitress.

"Can we just be serious here for a second?"

Sam smiled to the wall next to him, giving her a profile view of his reddened face. She'd not noticed how ruddy his complexion had become and knew he'd been way too cozied up with alcohol recently. It was going to be a problem for all of them, she decided.

He leaned into the table and drilled her with his cold blue stare. "I got the touch. I know where you itch."

Gina turned red. Sam winked. Suddenly the need to bolt from this meeting became overwhelming. She began to hyperventilate. She grabbed for her herbal iced tea and began to gulp it down, but managed to spill a wide ribbon down her shirtfront. She felt it trickle over her bare breasts beneath the shirt fabric. Sam noticed her natural perkiness and his eyes flashed. He looked like he was having a good time at Gina's expense.

What was I thinking?

"Thank you, baby." He was staring at her nipples, which tightened for him in spite of herself.

"I'm not your baby."

"I know what you like. I dream about it all the time, Gina. Don't you?"

"No." She said it so loudly that several customers looked over.

Sam began to chuckle. "You're one messed-up chick, Gina. I know how to fill all those cracks. You know I do."

She tried to put the scenes out of her head. Sam with the handcuffs. Sam with the velvet-encased rope. Taking her from behind, in the rear. She rubbed her temples, temporarily erasing the erotic images.

"Being involved with you nearly cost me my badge. But

you were the best piece of ass I ever had, Gina. You must know how I feel about that."

That? He's thinking of my ass. Not me.

She was left with the sickening feeling he would never let her go.

Now what have you done, Gina? Why didn't you report him? Now it's too late. And you thought you could work with him now?

Gina gasped for air as anger exploded in her chest.

Sam continued to pursue his direct. "I sacrificed a lot for you, baby. Left my wife. Almost lost my job."

He was actually blaming *her* for his career blunder? For their affair?

She had to jump in. "You wouldn't fuckin' leave me alone, Sam. *You* came on to *me*." She lost her ability to control her own temper as her insides boiled.

"Little Miss Hot Pants Flirty-Flirty, 'Oh, I didn't do anything but flaunt myself in his direction and he just came after me,'" he said in falsetto. Lowering his voice, he hissed, "Gina, you know you wanted it. If I'd had enough time with you, you would have begged me for it."

An army with pointed helmets was jumping up and down her insides. Droplets of sweat traced down her spine. "Shut up, Sam. When are you going to wake up to the fact that you *hurt* me? You lied to me, abused my trust. You didn't tell me you were married, and you physically…" Gina felt the hot tears welling up inside. This was not going the way she wanted it to go. She wrestled with being truthful. How much of their affair had she secretly wanted? Even after she found out about his wife? Didn't she find herself daydreaming about him sometimes? Thank God she got out way back then, before he would consume her. Just in time. It had taken everything she had, but she threatened to tell the sergeant if he didn't leave her alone.

Sam grabbed her forearm, instantly shifting her thoughts. "Because I cared for you."

Gina extricated her arm from Sam's thick fingers and folded her hands together under the table. She stuffed down the worry. She welcomed the crowd around her, feeling safer in their midst. "You're so wrong, Sam. I am not your possession. Don't you get it? I never belonged to you. Why can't you just leave it alone?"

"What if I've moved on?"

Gina wasn't convinced. "Really?" She crossed her arms and waited for him to explain.

Sam wasn't going to give her the satisfaction as he ground ice with his back molars, staring at her impassively.

"I was sorry to hear about your divorce," she inserted, going for kind. The man had paid a heavy price for his own indiscretion. "I never wanted that to happen, even after all this. I feel like I owe an apology to your wife, for God's sake. But not to you."

"Nah, you were just the excuse we needed to separate. We hadn't been good for some time. But I left her because of you. You do know that, don't you?"

Gina could see the fierce honesty in his eyes. The man was a wrecking ball of emotion. He was totally damaged goods, but she didn't feel an ounce of love or compassion for him. And whatever he thought he was feeling towards her, she was sure it wasn't anything close to love, either. The only thing that mattered right now was her job. She needed to complete her first mission to get her career jump-started. If that meant making "nice" to Mr. Awful, well, she'd just have to. She was working in a man's world and she'd made some mistakes. Why should that be front page of the *New York Times*? Who hadn't made mistakes in their past?

"Look, Sam. It doesn't matter now. None of that matters. We're not going to ever be an item. You've got to understand that, Sam."

It was Sam's turn to cross his arms.

Gina added, "I need you to honor that boundary, if you can. And if you can't—well, I'm going to have to pull out and regroup somewhere else. This mission is what I've trained for. I *wanted* this job. I *need* this job."

He was searching her face, examining her hair and shoulders, her arms, being careful not to check out her chest. She could see he was trying to be decent.

"Sam, I came to ask for your help. Your cooperation. You need to tell me if you can do this."

"Glad to see you've come to your senses. Or was it your decision?"

"No. But the way I see it, I have little choice. I think you're a good cop, not that I trust you personally as far as I can throw you. You've got Tito and all the other informants you've cultivated over the years. I'm no fool. We need your connections right now. Professionally, you know more things about the job than I'll probably ever know. I need you to put the personal side of 'us' on the back burner. Better yet, take it off the flame entirely." She searched his face for a trace of empathy, something to convince herself he could be the man she knew he had been at one time. "Can you do this for me?"

He leaned back in the chair as the waitress brought his order. He looked at Gina's empty place setting.

"I'm not hungry," she explained, which was the truth.

He picked up a fistful of fries and stuffed them into his

mouth. With his jaw muscles working overtime, he watched her staring back at him. Gina tried not to put any emotion into her gaze. Nothing he could latch onto or be hopeful about.

He sighed and began to pick up his burger. "I think I can do that." He said it to the burger and didn't look at her as he took an enormous bite. The burger erupted with drips of sauce, oozing forth a tomato slice, which plopped onto the plate below. Sam wiped his lips, his hands and absent-mindedly scanned the side of the wall next to him. Gina could see he was thinking something over carefully.

"Sam," she continued, "I *do* need your help. I don't think I can do this mission without you. I come to you as a colleague, as one professional to another. I want to keep it that way, if you'll agree."

Exhaustion was becoming a factor in their little meeting. Her self-control was waning. She had to get this over with. Hopefully with his agreement, or the knowledge that she had to walk away from a job she thought she could do with a little help.

"So you want me back? On the mission, I mean." he said.

"Because of Tito and the others you've turned. Also, Mia likes you. You've worked the gang task force for ten years. You trained me in undercover work. And Koz wants us to work together."

Sam's eyes brightened as he aimed a huge smile and another wink at her.

"Look, Sam, you're a big, strong guy. But I can still have you removed from the case if I say one word. I got assurances on that," she lied. "Because…" She almost choked on the words. As much as she hated to admit it, this part of her story was true. She finished, "…because you also know me. You'd know when I'm in trouble."

Sam's eyes got deep. Something dark hovered there for a second before he blinked it away. Gina remembered the lost afternoons of sex and desire. She remembered how she'd needed those afternoons like air and water. When she wanted the dark side of sex.

Why?

She saw Sam want to reach for her, but hold himself in check. She could feel the pride swelling in his chest about being needed, being told he was big and strong. It was the core identity of every good cop she'd ever met. Sam might still have some remnants of it after all.

"I'll help you. This isn't exactly easy for me, though."

"I understand." She leaned forward and, without thinking, clasped one of his callused hands. "It isn't easy for me, either. I'd like to think I can trust you. You need to tell me, Sam. Can I?"

His large thumb rubbed over her fingers before they could escape while he watched their hands entangled on the formica restaurant table. Her stomach crawled with something oily and dark.

"I hope so, Gina. I surely do." He smiled. "You ever think maybe when all of this is over with there could be a chance—you and I, together?"

Gina wanted to run, suddenly getting a chestful of the *uh-ohs*. What had she done today? She had no business asking him to get involved in her first very dangerous mission. What was she thinking? What part of that was a good idea?

But if she'd ever believed him, perhaps now was the time to put that worry aside and go forward instead of dwelling on the dark past. If she was going to ask for his trust, she'd better start being honest. And if Sam refused to help her, she ran a great risk of failure.

"Sam, I honestly don't know. I can't go into this with you expecting or hoping this will happen, because I really don't know." She did a pretty good job of delivering that lie, and she didn't care. She knew she was taking a huge risk by getting him involved in the operation.

Sam nodded, watching his thumb caress her fingers. Watching as she didn't pull away from him.

Gina added, "Let's just start being co-workers on a case. Let's learn to trust each other first, and then let's see where it leads. That's the best I can do, Sam. No promises. And I make no demands on *you* either, except to leave me alone."

That brought a smile to his lips as he nodded again. "Well, sweetheart, after you, I'm kind of wrecked for anyone else."

The soft side of Gina was winning over, but just slightly. She couldn't afford for it to show right now. Her eyes watered. *Am I like a moth to the flame?* She knew she couldn't trust Sam. Not yet. Perhaps never. "But you have to, Sam. You have to forget there ever was an us."

Then she remembered the look Armando gave her as he had bent down and asked if she was okay. As he whispered things to her in Spanish, as he delicately told her of his craving and need for her. She knew she'd never have to worry about being safe around Armando, and if she'd never met him, her response to Sam might have been different.

But what was important to remember was that Sam was in lust with the girl she used to be, and Armando was attracted to the woman she was becoming.

With her tears subsiding, she gathered her wits about

her and removed her fingers from Sam's grip. "Come on, I'll buy you some ice cream to wash down that burger."

He winked at her. "Whatever you say, boss. I'll do anything you like. Anything."

CHAPTER 10

ARMANDO LEFT THE impromptu gathering at Gunny's Gym as soon as he noticed he was one of only three SEALs without a female escort. He'd even gotten some hazing about it, since there were usually at least one and occasionally two women on his arm most weekends. He knew it was the reason the younger SEALs liked to hang out with him. He was the luckiest man he knew when it came to finding female companionship.

But there was only one girl on his radar these days: Mia's friend, Gina. Something about the woman made him stare off toward the waves while he recalled the way her body rose to his touch and fell as he pressed inside her. He'd loved hearing the little whimpering noises she made as he pumped her. Their bodies just plain fit together like two pieces of a puzzle, like what he was giving her with their lovemaking was something they both needed. He'd never felt that way with anyone before, not even Ginger.

He was on his way back to base to check out some equipment he'd special ordered when he saw Gina and Sam walking down the sidewalk next to each other, eating ice cream. They weren't holding hands, but Armando noticed Sam's large thigh brushed against hers from time to time, and, although she adjusted away from him carefully, she didn't complain or ask him to stop. Or look perturbed.

Armando almost hit the car in front of him, which had stopped suddenly. He'd been so focused on Gina and that big biker dude. His disappointment, coming on the heels of the warm feelings he'd been experiencing earlier, left his insides cold.

He whipped around the block and parked so he could watch them walk on the opposite side of the street. Gina's red tank top was getting all kinds of attention from the military personnel who sauntered by her in groups of three or four. Her frayed blue jeans with the white fuzzy worn patches on her left butt cheek was a real turn-on. If she'd looked behind her she would have seen the reactions of the passing men. He watched Sam's confident grin as the biker made eye contact with every male who went by. *'She's mine,'* he was saying. No mistaking the fact that he was enjoying the walk and the challenges.

And Gina seemed oblivious to anything going on around her. Her forehead was wrinkled as she worked on that ice cream, musing over her private thoughts. Armando got hard just thinking of what those cool lips could do to his fat erection. But he also didn't trust what he'd just seen with his own eyes.

Careful about the emotions, the lusts. Keep your focus, stay in control. That's how you keep yourself safe. Stay alive. He'd seen unbridled pride or jealousy kill Teammates before. So he decided, just decided, he wasn't jealous.

Armando was a pretty good judge of people. Years walking around in the back alleys and bombed-out buildings in Iraq and Afghanistan had given him a sixth sense when it came to sorting out the bad guys from the good guys. Well, not exactly the truth. He had learned to separate the *really* bad guys from the *maybe* good guys. He didn't care about the petty thieves and wife beaters as much as he was tuned to identify the ones who wanted to die and take a bunch of Americans with them. The ones who could kill a dog or child with a high-powered rifle just because a US serviceman or woman happened to stop and pat them on the head.

He thought about the day his Teammate took his shift at the clinic so Armando could have a prescheduled phone call home. Mia had gotten into trouble again and his mother was beside herself with worry. After he talked to both of them, Armando had fallen asleep on his cot. He awoke to sounds of an explosion and discovered the entire triage tent had been blown to the heavens, his buddy along with it.

Armando had considered leaving the Teams then. But in the end he decided he wanted to stay in, even if it was to just tip the scale a bit and do some payback for those who'd cost his buddy his life. He knew the following weeks and months of deployment were his atonement for his lapse of judgment, but he couldn't afford to dwell there until he got home. In Afghanistan, he needed his wits about him if he was going to do the good he'd been sent there to do. He wore his pain silently, buried inside layers of steel. And he didn't take another nap for the following four months, not until he came stateside. He was finding that masking technique useful right now.

His thoughts turned back to Gina and her ex-boyfriend, standing in the late afternoon sun. He saw something other than a couple in love. He saw a couple forced together by some circumstance. And the guy was enjoying it more than the girl.

Of course, he could be wrong, but he usually wasn't.

His cell phone rang. It was Fredo.

"You sure ditched out quickly. Up for some poker?"

"Later. I'm over at the base checking out my material order." Armando had a small cottage industry making specialized vests, ones with hidden pockets and straps, for other Team guys who wanted to customize their gear. Everyone liked to carry their ammo clips and other enhancements in different places other than what their normal uniform allowed. And no two were alike.

"Stop on by about eight, okay?" Fredo replied. "I think we're gonna teach Sanouk some poker."

Armando chuckled as he watched Gina and Sam stop by Sam's huge black Harley. "If I'm not mistaken, that boy will be fleecing all of you tonight. He's dumb like a fox."

"A real testament to ol' Gunny, I'd say."

"Roger that, Fredo."

Sam started up his bike and half the street turned to watch the source of the rumbling noise. Gina stepped back and deposited the rest of her cone in the garbage can nearby, and waved to the leather-clad giant, yet the man didn't leave. Sam revved his bike several times as if waiting for something.

There was no goodbye kiss.

"Wow. That sounded familiar," Fredo said.

"Okay, I'm on the strand and bought an ice cream. That satisfy your curiosity?" He felt a little bad about the sharpness of his tone. He could hear Fredo bristle over the phone.

"I'm not checking on you, Armani. I feel your need for privacy. Doesn't happen to have anything to do with a certain girl, now does it?"

"Nope. It's just ice cream."

"You're full of shit," Fredo said and hung up.

Armando slipped the phone in his pocket and shrugged off Fredo's remark. The Mexican SEAL was also good at reading all of Armando's moods. Sharing life-threatening events tended to do that to a guy.

He watched her linger next to the biker as she stuffed her hands into her cutoffs. He knew he shouldn't be interested in an explanation from her. She'd lied to him about the ex. What else had she lied to him about? Was it all an act? It would be better to just walk away and forget about her, about her lies, but he couldn't for some reason. Well, he could. He knew he could. He'd been trained to do the unthinkable. But he didn't *want* to. And this was the good old U.S. of A., where things were supposedly "normal" and "safe."

And then Armando started thinking again about what those succulent lips of hers could do.

As Sam's rumble faded, Armando watched her walk aimlessly down the concrete, then cross the street and move towards the beach not more than four cars ahead of his parked car. As she sandwiched through a narrow gap between vehicles, he saw her lift her suntanned arms in the air, holding her stomach in, revealing her bare midriff and just a taste of her muscled abs underneath the skimpy red top. He knew what she looked like with her jeans unbuttoned, knew what kind of panties she wore, and what it felt like to slide his fingers carefully into the juncture between her legs and touch her there. He also knew what her face tried to hide, that she needed his fingers inside her, she needed to be loved hard but cherished. That she liked it intense.

And he was just the man to satisfy her. Intensity in

women was always a danger signal. Armando liked uncomplicated fun. He loved women who were sure of themselves and had good energy. Gina was all those things and more. Something dark lurked just under the surface of her skin. He thought he just might have nicked it a bit that night in the pickup truck. He'd never had sex in front of a highway full of cars before, even if they had been behind a small grove of trees. This relationship, especially now with Sam's appearance this evening, was getting very complicated.

Sounds of the surf pounded in his ears as he followed her to the edge of the beach. He tried to will her to turn around and see him, but she was in heavy concentration. He wanted to be discovered. But she never turned, just kept walking toward the water's edge. A few feet safely short of the waves she stopped and removed her sandals, then sat down.

She was like a beacon for him and he couldn't help but follow her. Was this stalking? Would she be afraid if she suddenly saw him? Would she even want to see him after what he'd done to Sam?

Walk away. You have no business getting involved with her. You never question your inner guardian. Why start doing so now?

He decided to ignore his better self, the prudent self that kept him out of danger and saved his life on many occasions overseas. Wasn't this just as important? Wasn't he crossing through a doorway of no return if he continued to follow her?

He sighed and decided that, yes, he could handle whatever it was he was going to find out. Right now, he needed an answer.

Armando stopped behind her seated form, then walked

around her, standing to the side, but within sight. She started at first and began to get up, so Armando immediately sat down next to her.

"Saw you cross the street, and, yes, I followed you here. Something I never do. Why am I doing this, Gina?" He faced the water's edge but could feel her eyes on him. Then he turned and saw the worry in her face, the crease at the top of her lovely brown brows, the way her lips formed an O. Several strands of curly hair blew across her neck and chin. He wanted to smooth them back, but squeezed his fingers into the warm sand instead.

"How long have you been here?"

Of course she wanted to know how much he had seen. He wasn't going to pussyfoot around if he could help it. Armando forced himself to focus away from her face and squinted at the ocean's bright late afternoon sunlight. When he turned back to her, he nodded, saying, "I saw him."

Her eyes got wider for a second as she quickly looked down at her knees. Her swallow was strained.

He wasn't going to ask her. He wanted her to tell him without asking.

"Things with Sam are complicated," she began. It was a good start, but not a strong one.

What's complicated about an ex? Or is he her ex?

"Didn't take you for one of those," he chose to say instead.

"One of those?"

"Women who keep going back to a guy after he's been violent."

Her back straightened. He'd hit a nerve. That was a good thing.

"I'm not one of *those* women, thank you very much."

Armando rubbed the back of his neck. She was lying to him again. Did the woman know the difference? "Do you even know the truth, Gina? Why can't I get a straight answer out of you? You got a thing against being honest?"

Gina stood. "Screw you."

Armando stood as well. "You already did, Gina. We fucked like bunnies in the back seat of my friend's beater, remember?"

She turned away and started to march off towards the road. Armando wanted to grab her arm and stop her, but he knew that wasn't the right thing to do. Her arms swung at her sides, her steps deliberate, ridiculously beautiful the way the flesh on her ass jiggled with each stomp. He placed his hands on his hips and decided that if she was walking out of his life, he'd better enjoy the view.

To his surprise she whipped around and came at him. She started yelling before she was within earshot, so all he heard was, "talk to me that way. You are a fuckin' bastard of the first order."

"Oh, the first order. As opposed to the second or third?" he quipped.

She scowled at him, huffing her displeasure. Along with her anger, she was a swirling tornado of other emotions, too, and he reveled in seeing her struggle to get a handle on her situation. Armando was grateful he'd been trained not to react. Let her work it out. He knew she would. He loved watching her fury.

"Who in the devil do you think you are?"

He smiled down at his feet. He was getting a serious hard-on. Dang it. This would make things more difficult. All he wanted to do was take her down and love the livin' crap out of her. He raised his gaze to her beautiful face, with her mahogany hair flying all around in the ocean breeze, her fingers bunching into fists and then extending. All scrunched up, her lips were so damn kissable, he licked his and uttered a line he knew he would pay for later, but he couldn't help it. "I'm the one who made you come so many times you could hardly walk afterwards, sweetheart, and you wanted more. At least, that's what—"

She slapped him. Well good for her. Yup, he clearly deserved that. He'd gone over the line a bit with that comment. But damn, even her slap was sexy. He wished she'd do it again. He wished she'd let him hold her until she stopped squirming, but that was out of the question. Didn't mean he didn't imagine what that would feel like, though. He was drawn to her high-octane energy.

Careful, you dog. You're gonna get into trouble.

"You have no right to talk to me like that," she shouted. "What we did was a mistake!"

Armando looked around the beach area to see if they had attracted attention. It was nearly deserted.

She was still angry, but she didn't leave. Perhaps she wanted to pick a fight. Well, she was playing with the wrong person for that one.

"Okay, Gina. I get that it was a mistake. What's with all this big drama?"

"What you said."

"What *I* said. Seems like—" he squinted his eyes as he thought better of what he was about to say. "Never mind. Erase that thought." He shoved his hands into his pockets. "You think it was a mistake. Okay, so be it. I'm totally hands-off from this point on. I see you, I say and do nothing. That what you're asking for, Gina?"

That one got to her. He could see her eyes widen. Unless

he was totally mistaken, her anger had flared, and that wasn't the reaction he expected.

She sizzled a bit, turning and sighing in frustration, and then she added, "Fine." Her delivery was followed by a speedy turnaround and exit toward the parking lot.

So here we are again in sunny San Diego, enjoying the view.

But he could tell she really didn't want to run away from him. And that was kind of exciting on all sorts of levels.

CHAPTER 11

*D*AMN THE MAN!

Gina was furious with him for his obvious lack of manners. But she was more furious with herself for being so flustered and not knowing exactly what to do. His words reverberated in her ears. *I'm the one who made you come so many times you almost couldn't walk...*or something to that effect, anyhow.

Awful part of it all, she thought as she arrived at her car, was that he was right. She steeled herself to not look back at him.

Why?

What if he wasn't watching her drive off? What if he was?

What the fuck difference does it make?

Her boss had asked that she cool it with the SEAL. Well, she'd just poured a gallon of ice water on that gorgeous hunk of man candy. The guy who'd shown her more rockets than the Fourth of July.

She started her car and began to edge out from the curb.

I'm not going to look. I'm not going to look.

And then she looked. She got a glimpse of him running down the beach, waving to someone south of him. So, he wasn't looking. Did it matter?

That's when the car coming from behind hit her.

Fuck!

She put her head in her hands and rested it on the steering wheel. Talk about control. Lack of control, rather. She'd just wrecked the right side of her car, because she'd been thinking about screwing the SEAL in the back seat of some dipshit old pickup instead of watching where she was going.

Where is your head, Gina? Think!

A young college-aged boy knocked on her driver window. "Are you all right, ma'am?" she could hear him say through the shattered glass.

This wasn't helping. *Ma'am? Am I that old?* She rolled down her window, which crumbled and fell in shattered pebbles all over the pavement. She stared at the damaged right side of the boy's car, and then over to her rear driver side. The tire was flat, the wheel well concave a full six inches. Her car was not going to be drivable.

"I'm so sorry," she began, and then tears filled her eyes. "I'm fine, but my car…" Cars were weaving around the accident. She was suddenly the center of attention as frustrated motorists and onlookers glared at her.

I'm an airhead of the first order.

ARMANDO RETURNED TO his Hummer after his run on the beach. It felt good to get the tension out of his system. He'd found Marky, Kyle, and Jones and he'd dovetailed into their run as easy as pasting a stamp on a letter. Seamless, that's how their friendship was. Simple. Uncomplicated. He liked uncomplicated.

He was going to join Kyle at the store on base so he could finally pick up his long-awaited order. The Velcro was not exactly the width he wanted, but it would work. The plastic hooks and fabric were perfect.

Kyle was taking over Brandon duty while his wife, Christy, showed a house. Armando saw the three of them walk in just as he was about to check out.

"Hey there, little man," he said to the baby, who was strapped backwards to Kyle's massive chest. The baby's fat arms and legs bicycled as he started an excited bouncing routine when he saw Uncle Armando. "Hey, gorgeous," he said to Christy as he gave her a kiss on the cheek. She was dressed to the nines.

"Watch it, Armani," Kyle growled.

"You let her strut in here all dressed up like that? What the fuck you thinking?" he teased his LPO.

Christy beamed. "At least someone appreciates high heels and tight skirts. This one prefers me barefoot and pregnant."

"Workin' on it. Workin' it hard," Kyle said while Brandon flailed his arms and legs. "Okay, Babe, go make us millionaires today," he said as he kissed his wife goodbye.

Armando was happy for Kyle and Christy. He was happy for all the guys who met women who were strong enough to handle their intensity. Gina was a pistol all right, but she had a hair emotional trigger, which was one thing in the bedroom, but entirely another one when it came to living in his world. He forced himself to focus on what he *did* have.

"What you up to?"

"Gotta go talk to Chief Timmons for a sec. You wanna tag along? We got that poker party tonight."

"You going to expose your son to that? A little soon, don't you think?" Armando said as they walked to the parking lot.

"No choice. Christy's got a company dinner and I had the choice. Go with her and get a sitter, or go with you guys and bring the little dude along with me."

"You let her go out to those functions without you, man?"

Kyle shrugged. "I'm the one she comes home to." He started to unstrap Brandon. Armando protested. "Leave him be. I'll drive you over there."

"Watch out for those Navy regulars or you'll get a ticket," Kyle said as he took up position at shotgun.

"And my millionaire friend will gladly pay it too."

"Shit, I wish. It's expensive being married. We couldn't do it without Christy's income. She makes more money than I do now. Isn't that fucked up?"

"Nah. I look at her and I think you got it pretty damned good, Kyle. Wife, baby, and she brings home the bacon too. She doesn't happen to have a sister, does she?"

"Brother, but they're not close. Gunny said you was getting cute with that friend of Mia's."

"Thing of the past, I'm afraid."

"Sorry to hear it."

"Happens. You know that."

"Roger that. Guess I was just lucky Christy couldn't read house numbers." He'd met his wife when she'd entered the wrong home to hold an open house for a fellow agent. Armando's home.

"Well, she was smart enough to marry you. I'd say you both got lucky."

They pulled up in front of the brick single-story building that housed command offices. Armando wondered what the reason for the visit was. "Everything okay here?"

"Wanna find out about our training, see if I can get the

skinny on where we're headed. Christy wants to plan a vacation, and if we're going to Mexico, well, I might do an extension and meet her somewhere nearby after our training."

"As opposed to Alaska."

"That girl would never go to Alaska. San Francisco's about as cold as she's willing to be."

TIMMONS WAS LOOKING even more tired than the last time Armando saw him. The chief's desk was covered in papers, even though he'd hired one of Daisy's friends, a woman who was a "specialist." Half the Team guys thought for a while that maybe he'd kicked the bucket, his desk and office had been so clean. But now the attractive bookshelves with the neat rows of forms, like cornrows, were covered over in plastic banners, jackets, rolled-up recruiting posters and a box of donuts that was still there from a month ago. A broken paper shredder with its electrical umbilical cord snaking over the top sat in front of the bottom two shelves, partially obscuring the contents.

The chief's retirement was coming up at the end of the year, and he'd been in a disagreeable mood ever since it was announced almost eight months ago. He looked up from an inch-thick wad of papers held with a silver binder clip. The eyes said it all. Though tired, he perked up when he saw little Brandon. It was well-known he loved children and tolerated his wife.

"Well there's our newest frogman. How you doin' there, fella?" He let the baby grab onto his forefinger. "Wow, he's strong. Been working out at Gunny's?"

"Yeah. He's going for everything these days. Started pulling himself up at six months," Kyle answered.

Armando looked at the frog statue behind his LPO. The replacement one for the first replacement. The green color was off.

"So, what can I do you for?" Timmons asked.

"Was wondering if you know where we're doing our training."

"Afghanistan."

"No shit? No way, Timmons." Kyle was livid.

"Just messing with you. Looks like the Nevada desert. Doing some coordination with the drone druids, and we got a new 50-cal we're trying out."

"That's a shame," Kyle said. "Was hoping for Mexico."

"Be patient, my man. It's kinda ugly, but Nevada has its perks."

The baby was beginning to squeal, so Kyle unstrapped him and hiked him over his left shoulder. Armando could smell the full diaper Kyle hadn't noticed.

"Well, that's just too damned bad. Can I tell some of the guys?" Kyle hitched the squirming Brandon a little higher. It was too high.

Brandon reached for, and got, the frog statue by the thigh. Before Kyle could rescue the Team mascot, purchased in honor of Timmons on occasion of their graduation from BUD/s, and replaced now twice, the statue went crashing to the floor. Shards of bright green glass scattered everywhere.

Brandon knew he'd done something wrong and stared into the face of his father without moving a muscle. He put one finger in his mouth.

No one said a word.

THE POKER PARTY was just the kind of thing Armando needed. Fredo's apartment already smelled of cigars, sweat and beer by the time he and Kyle arrived. Gunny was having a serious discussion in the kitchen with his son, the kind of discussion a man wasn't supposed to overhear, but both Kyle and Armando knew it was advice about women.

Kyle leaned closer. "Does he not realize he's talking to the son of the woman he knocked up?"

"You know how Gunny is. I'd say he's trying to make up for the years he doesn't have left."

Kyle looked down at Brandon, who was now fast asleep, having received a change of diaper and a full bottle. "I could never do that, man. Abandon my kid."

"Those were different times, my friend. Gunny knew he'd never settle down and get domestic. He knew the Marines were his family. And we are his offspring. I can't think of where I'd be if he hadn't driven my ass home some of those early days."

"That's for sure," Kyle agreed.

"Besides, I think the kid grew up just fine. Probably better with her than with Gunny. Can you see that old fart getting old in Thailand?"

They both laughed.

Armando thought about all the dirty ports and third-world countries Gunny had waded through in his quest to find exotic love and bury his demons. The sea was a good place for burying things. Deep and cold, it never gave back what it was given. God bless the old fart, Armando thought. All he wanted was a little excitement, some loving arms and a warm smile. Gunny's needs were simple. Maybe like his own.

If he hadn't made it into the SEAL Brotherhood, would he have done regular Navy and traveled those same ports looking for pieces of himself all over the world?

Armando knew the wharf in San Diego where the nice yachts were moored. He imagined the collection of million-dollar vessels that occasionally cavorted with their Navy boats out on maneuvers. He'd seen the smart attire of the rich and famous as they pretended to get out in nature's elements while the SEAL recruits did dives and long swims in the oily waters of the bay.

It was also the favorite place to dump a stolen car, or what was left of it after it had been stripped. Growing up, he'd known *that* life was not what he wanted, but he hadn't yet learned what he *did* want. He'd take dates to the pier to watch the sun set and pretend he was one of those rich boys who commanded their father's yachts.

Then he discovered soccer. He even toyed with pursuing a professional career, but didn't have the money for the private lessons he needed to make a top team and get noticed by college coaches. His grades were good, but not exceptional, so the chances of getting a college scholarship were nonexistent.

Then one day he had a talk with the Navy recruiter who came to his high school and from that day on, all he wanted was to be a SEAL.

He thought about the string of warehouses they'd used a time or two when it was a big thing to steal a fifth of Jack Daniels and spend the night getting drunk and attempting to get laid. At fourteen, his prospects were slim, but the ladies liked him anyhow, and if he was drunk it didn't matter how old they were or if they weren't very pretty.

Thank God I found the Navy. He'd been a good swimmer in Puerto Rico, and someone had suggested the swim team in high school. He could out-swim everybody, but he would never show up for practice, so he was booted off the team. Soccer became his new passion, and half the guys never showed up for that, either, since most of their players had part time jobs after school, so it worked for him. He began to feel the pride of playing on a winning team, and saw himself with more of a future. Stealing cars and getting into trouble didn't have the pull it had before.

But swimming got him noticed in BUD/s, and helped make him a SEAL. He'd finally found something he could do all day long and not regret it the next day. He could work like a dog and get up again the next day and *want* to do it all over again. Being a SEAL was something he truly was made for.

"And where the fuck have you been?" Kyle asked.

Armando shrugged. The card game was stalled, waiting for his response. He didn't like all the bloodshot eyes peering into his private thoughts.

"Anyone tell you thinking about things is dangerous?" Fredo added like the Father Confessor he tried so hard to be.

"Thanks, Fredo. Glad you got my back," he answered as he threw down his worthless hand.

Just then, several retired SEALs entered the apartment. The testosterone level was threatening to blow the place up, Armando thought. Winning at poker wasn't as important as when you left the party. You were a pansy if you left first, especially if it was because you had a date.

Armando wouldn't have that problem tonight.

JUST AS ARMANDO had predicted, Sanouk displayed an uncanny knack for playing poker, and winning. The more shit-faced the Team guys got, the more he won. Fredo took a drink of the young Thai's vodka collins, and discovered it was mostly collins.

He had faked his way into picking up some enormous pots when the rest of the guys thought he was too inexperienced. The lesson was painful in terms of pride and costly in terms of nickels. They never bet big stakes, unless they were in Vegas. Somehow the idea of losing to a casino wasn't as abhorrent as losing to one of your buds. No one wanted to be the one to make it so a Team guy couldn't pay his rent.

Kyle had put Brandon to bed in Fredo's only bedroom. Gunny was passed out in Fredo's lounger. He'd been watching some nudie flick on the VCR. The film had allowed Sanouk to sneak peeks while the guys were distracted. It was important for the men to make comments about the size of the actor's dicks and the skanky girls with mullet hairstyles. The reddish cast to the films indicated they were nearly a generation old.

"Fredo, you get these at a Mexican garage sale or something?"

"No. If they came from there, they'd be in Spanish, or didn't you notice?" Fredo quipped back. His eyebrows scrunched in a serious cluster, resembling a giant tarantula.

"Well, you *do* know they make some really nice ones now, all artsy. They touch them up," one of the older guys commented.

"I like these just fine. They get to it. I don't want to be teased. I want to see it happen. In gory detail," Fredo answered, unmoved by the comment.

Armando laughed. "If it puts Gunny to sleep, that should tell you something, Fredo."

"Each to his own taste, I say."

"There it is," Beale commented. "The professor of sex."

Fredo was mumbling to himself when Sanouk declared

himself the winner of the largest pot of the evening. Since it was midnight, everyone mutually agreed it was time to go home. Everyone left except the five from Team 3.

Kyle peeled Brandon from Fredo's bed and the baby took one look at the room full of SEALs and former SEALs and lay back down against his daddy's chest, falling asleep again.

"Since Coop's not here, who's not drunk?" Mark asked. Cooper was usually the designated driver since he consumed no alcohol.

No one raised their hand, but everyone looked in Sanouk's direction.

"You got a driver's license, kid?" Armando asked. "You can drive my Hummer, but you'll have to walk from my place."

"Yes. My license is good here for thirty days."

"Armani, everyone lives around here. Why don't you have him drop you off at Mia's? He can come back here to crash and go home in the morning with Gunny, unless the old guy wakes up," Fredo said.

"Sounds like a plan."

MIA'S HOUSE WAS fully lit. Armando could hear the music inside before he got his door open. He turned to Sanouk with a word of caution, "Don't fuck up my car or I'll have you on the next plane to Thailand, hear?"

"Yessir, Mr. Armani. I'll be most extremely careful of your vehicle. You need not worry."

"He's good," Jones chimed in.

"Keep the keys with you. I have a spare set hidden on the truck," he said to Sanouk.

"No problem."

Armando said his goodbyes and headed up Mia's walkway. He figured his mother had been coming over lately, because there was a nice collection of bright dahlias blooming in the front yard. He heard Mia speaking with someone else in the house. A female voice.

Gina.

That was unfortunate. He looked down the street to try to flag the boys down, but they were already nearly out of sight. Instead of walking in or knocking like he usually did, he rang the doorbell.

Mia swung the door open. She was dressed in a pair of skin-tight pants and a big shirt. Her hair was atop her head in a rhinestone-encrusted clip. Armando heard the music turned down and saw Gina in the distance.

"Now what?" Mia said to him.

"I need a place to crash."

"Something wrong with your place?"

"I'm a little drunk. Was looking for a place closer by."

"Then call a taxi. You're not welcome here, right, Gina?"

"Sorry to bother you. I'll just—"

"Oh, it's okay. Let him in," Gina said from inside the room.

Mia pulled the door open wider and allowed him to enter. "You just can't seem to leave me alone for one night. You gotta come meddling again. You insult my friends, try to tell me who I can and can't date…" Mia began, picking up steam for a rant.

Mia's chattering was background white noise. Armando had locked on Gina's eyes and wouldn't let go. She was trying to avoid him, but each time their eyes found each other, there were sparks Armando could not deny. He wanted her in the worst way, even though he knew it was unwise.

Mia left to attend to Ricardo, who was crying in the back bedroom.

"You want a glass of water or a soda?" Gina asked.

"Sure. Water would be perfect."

He followed her to the little kitchen and leaned against the countertop while she got a glass down and filled it with cold water from the fridge. He could stand there and watch her all night.

"Didn't see your car out front," he said.

"Yea, well, that's a long story." She handed him the cool glass.

He sipped his water and enjoyed the view as Gina went back to the sink and rinsed some dishes. "My car's in the shop. I had an accident shortly after I left you at the beach."

Armando stiffened, set down his water glass and crossed the room to be at her side. "You sure you're okay?"

Gina looked at the ceiling and exhaled. "I'm fine. It's been one hell of a day."

"What happened?" He grabbed her right arm, drawing her into him. She seemed to dissolve into his chest. Her arms wrapped around his waist and she began to cry. "Hey, it's okay," he said as he stroked the back of her head while she sobbed.

"Well this is a pretty picture," Armando heard Mia's words behind him.

Gina abruptly pulled away and wiped the tears from her cheeks. "Don't sweat it, Mia. My fault entirely."

Armando was grateful for the minute of space Mia gave them. She didn't react, but stood watching them carefully.

"Okay. So, I think I should call a taxi," Gina said as she

brushed the hair from her face.

"I'd offer to take you, but I was dropped off," Armando said.

"Where's your car?" she asked, frowning.

"Sanouk has it, along with several of the Team guys. I'm in no shape to drive tonight," he said.

"Sanouk? Who's he?" Mia asked.

"Gunny's son," said Armando. "Came all the way from Thailand to meet him."

"And you just gave this guy the keys to your Hummer?" Mia gave him the what-were-you-thinking look. "Gina, he wouldn't even let me take it to the store when he first got it. And now he lets a strange kid take it…"

"He's not just a strange kid. His English is better than most grunts on base." Armando added, "Besides, Marky and Jones are with him. They wouldn't have let me drive. I'd never make it home."

"That makes two of us," Gina said.

"Gina stay," Mia pleaded. "Stay here tonight. Tomorrow we'll get your car stuff handled. I'll take you to work if you want."

"No, I'm fine. I'll rent something in the morning." She opened her purse, extracting her cell phone. Armando could not miss the snub-nosed .38 tucked neatly to the side, and it worried him.

After Gina called the cab they sat. Mia went into the kitchen.

"You're packing tonight."

"Yes. I always do these days."

"Except that it's illegal here. You know that."

"I have a permit." Her eyes were unflinching.

"You want to explain that?"

"Nope. None of your business."

"You bring a gun into this house, in front of my sister and my nephew, and it's none of my business? How dumb do you think I am?"

"It isn't what you think."

"So a lot of things aren't what I think. Like your ex. He isn't really your ex, is he? You just cheated on him with me. He's still your guy."

"He is not my guy."

"Well he *thinks* he is. I can recognize that."

Mia came flying out of the kitchen. "Stop it, both of you. You'll wake the baby. And when that taxi comes, Armando, it's yours. I want my privacy, got that? I told you earlier I don't want you coming around unannounced, harassing me, my friends."

Armando thought about revealing to his sister what he'd learned about Gina, but he decided not to. When they heard the honk of the taxi in front, he quickly turned to Gina.

"I want a quick word." He nodded to his sister. "In private."

Mia's eyes got huge. "What the fuck's going on?"

Armando grabbed Gina by the arm and pulled her outside on the front stoop. He motioned to the taxi driver to wait.

"Give it to me."

"No."

"I'm not asking. I will not leave while that gun is in my sister's home."

The standoff was as electric as their embrace in the kitchen. Her face shone in the moonlight, lips moist and pouting. Her defiance of him turned him on. His hard-on was painful and made absolutely no sense.

"Then you're coming with me. We share the taxi. No way I'm leaving you here with that weapon, and I don't care how many stories you tell me." His voice was husky with need. He could see she was in complete shock, bristling under the command he'd given her. He turned, jogging back to the front door to explain to his sister he was taking Gina home.

It gave Gina just enough time to get in the taxi and take off.

"You're losing your touch, brother," Mia said as she leaned against the doorway. "Now you're scaring them off."

"I always scare them off." Armando whispered as he watched the taxi barrel down the street.

IT WAS THE right thing to do, of course, but the pit of her stomach clenched and Gina thought she might vomit. The cabby was looking at her with a scowl in the rear view mirror.

"You sure you're okay, miss?"

"I'm fine," she said, which was a total lie.

There was no denying the chemistry between them. Even now, with all the obstacles that separated them, she could feel her heart trying to claw its way out of her chest, trying somehow to crawl back to him like she was tethered.

I'm blowing it. I'm blowing the whole operation. She was supposed to be getting information about Carlos and what remained of the Scorpion gang who were responsible for a significant number of crimes involving guns, drugs and girls. With Caesar in prison, the operation was to get Carlos and his lieutenants before they had a chance to organize and beef up their security.

She wasn't doing anything she should not be doing, but she'd not been spending as much time on her job as she should have, and walked the line between wanting to tell Armando the truth to gain his trust and help, or just breaking off their relationship completely. Problem was, if she had to go through Mia to get to Carlos, that meant the SEAL was going to be right next to her. It was too close.

Maybe her involvement with Sam had so infected her moral compass and shaken her so much, she would never be good at any of this undercover work. She could not reel in her emotions. She was making way too many mistakes.

If I'm not careful, someone could get killed.

It was one thing to blow a mission, but quite another to risk the life of an innocent.

But Armando wasn't exactly an innocent. He was a veteran of more bloodshed than most people on the force saw during their entire careers. And his hardwired DNA made it so he would not give up on his sister. What was she going to say to him to get him to back off? What *could* she tell him?

She needed advice, but knew if she went to her captain he'd pull her off the case. Sam would be of no help. Who could she trust?

You wanted this, Gina. You wanted to prove to yourself you could do this. Suck it up and deal with it. She had to figure it all out by herself.

Since the meeting with Sam had gone fairly well, she decided to set up a time tomorrow to see Armando. She had all night to think about it, come up with a plan. Maybe she could reason with the SEAL.

If she could keep herself from jumping his bones again.

CHAPTER 12

D ETECTIVE CLARK RIVERTON got a call on his cell phone just at the wrong damned moment. Daisy's plump little ass was centered on his lap, her love tunnel fully available to him in spite of the handcuffs. Her tan Ranger Rick child's shirt had hiked up, exposing smooth swaths of the flawless tanned skin up her back. If his hands hadn't been restrained, he'd be snaking his way up her spine with his fingers, and then around to the front of her to squeeze those drool-worthy tits big enough to make a girl fall forward. He was hard as a rock, even after the phone rang for the third and then the fourth and last time. His cock was always right, in matters of priority, but damn, he'd been waiting for two days for that callback. Tomorrow would be the weekend.

"Daisy, honey. I have to take that call."

"But Captain Cock, I think a few minutes wouldn't hurt. Just put it in a little and then we'll stop." Her lilting voice sounded so logical. "Or, I can babysit it while you talk in your cop voice. I love your cop voice."

Yes. He knew all about that.

Of course, he would just put the head of his penis inside her wet opening. And of course he wouldn't be able to stop until he'd completely satisfied both of them. They both knew that.

"Fuck it."

"Oh, exactly, Captain Cock."

DAISY'S PROPS AND costumes were folded and carefully stowed in her pink bunny bag. But she hadn't bothered to put any clothes on, except for the Ranger Rick shirt with the ridiculous beaver character stitched onto the breast pocket, so of course he couldn't concentrate, looking at the crescents of her enormous tits and tight little butt with the red handprint where he'd spanked her. His phone rang again, and this time, distracted or not, he was going to answer it. It wasn't the call he was expecting, but he was satisfied enough to let duty call.

"Riverton."

Daisy chose the opportunity to kneel before him as he sat on the edge of the bed. She found his withering cock and proceeded to give him his third oral of the day. Her teeth scraped along the underside of him and then she sucked in his balls, causing him to hiss into the phone.

"Clark? You okay?" It was Detective Mayfield. Riverton could hear Mariachi music in the background. Mayfield had moved in with the attractive Señora Guzman.

"I'm fine," Riverton forced out between his teeth as Daisy pulled and sucked forcefully on his ball sac.

Jeez. You're gonna suck it right off of me, sweetheart.

Riverton snuck a peek at the dimples of her derriere while her blonde head worked overtime in his lap. He nearly dropped the phone.

Mayfield continued, "Listen, we got notified about an undercover operation going on. I'm kinda related to the party in question. It's Mrs. Guzman's daughter, Mia. I can't involve myself, due to—well, you know how it is, Clark."

"I understand." He laced his fingers through Daisy's blond hair, squeezing the back of her neck as he ground deeper into her mouth. The woman was a master. She could get come out of a 90-year old, he thought. "Is there some kind of a problem?"

"Thought perhaps we could talk it over, say, tomorrow sometime? Not over the phone."

"I—I understand." It took everything he had to even respond coherently. Moaning into the phone was not an option, and, dammit, he'd nearly forgotten even that small courtesy.

"Meet me at the Scupper around noon? I'm buying since I need a favor."

"Will do."

Riverton pressed the end call button, then examined it again to make sure. Once he hadn't been careful enough and the squad room still occasionally played the message he'd inadvertently left, thinking he had hung up. He'd earned the nickname amongst the younger guys as "Sexy Grandpa," though Riverton never thought of himself as old enough. He didn't mind them thinking he had a healthy sex life.

Daisy looked up at him, her lips wet and her lipstick smeared. One false eyelash had started to come off. On Daisy, it looked sexy as hell.

"I fixed the plumbing problem, Captain Cock. Is there anything else you'd like me to do?" She stood demurely in front of him, the ridiculous shirt only covering half her breasts and not reaching her navel. Her hands were folded over her sex.

"Get your hands off there," he pointed.

Daisy complied, extending her lovely arms and hands to

the sides, then up to her chest. She leaned over, which made her double-D-cup breasts come pillowing out from behind the shirtfront and between her fingers. She presented them to his mouth.

Before he could lock onto her she pulled back and squealed, "Wait!"

Riverton stroked himself, reassuring his member that good times were shortly at hand as he watched her pull a tube out from her pink bag. That would be the cherry stuff she liked to use. He didn't have the heart to tell her he hated that crap.

But watching her rub it over her nipples, making them glisten and pucker, while he stroked and kept himself on the ready, he decided the cherry gel wasn't all that bad. As she bent over and gave him a taste, he decided he actually could grow to like it. Maybe he could take her to one of those shops and they could pick out something more to his liking. But this, right now anyway, was working just fine.

His tongue rolled over her left nipple and then he sucked her hard, making her scrunch up her brow and put her lips in that little O-shaped pout she did when she was coming. He could explode at any moment, just seeing her bending over and letting him have his way with her tits.

He removed the tube of gel from her hand and ran a line of the pink liquid down his cock. "You're a quick learner, Miss Daisy. Perhaps a little treat?"

"I got something better than a treat," she said as she straddled him. Then with one sensual stroke, she sat on his cock. His face was buried in her chest again, which was only the second best place it could be.

Thank God he didn't have to do anything until noon tomorrow, unless that damned FBI agent called him back.

MAYFIELD HAD ORDERED a salad and was stuffing his face when Riverton showed up a whole five minutes late.

"What happened to you?" Mayfield asked.

At first a quick smile darted out, then Riverton reeled himself in and got serious. "Not sleeping well these days."

"You look like hell. We're not young anymore, Clark. Gotta take care of yourself."

Riverton nodded. He noticed Mayfield had lost about twenty pounds. "The Mrs. got you on a diet?" he asked, pointing to the salad.

This time it was Mayfield's time to break out in a chuckle.

This also amused Riverton. "I get it. She's hot for gringos," he teased, playing along with the fun.

Mayfield sighed and stared down at his salad. "No, she's just hot for me." He wouldn't make eye contact.

"Must be nice. I'm glad to see you finally happy."

Mayfield's head rose to attention. "I am. Truly. I am."

"Well, sir, that makes two of us, although mine isn't full time."

They laughed in unison. The waitress took Riverton's order for a green salad and a diet coke.

"You're a cheap date," Mayfield snorted.

"I've been told that a time or two. Money's hard to come by these days. I'm thinking your little lady may be on to something. Maybe if I ate rabbit food I'd sleep better." He presented a lopsided smile back to Mayfield.

"Well, Clark. That depends."

"On what?"

"On *who* you're sleeping *with*."

Riverton's salad arrival broke up the laughter. He liked the big San Diego detective, who was fair and honest. The man was one of the last good guys on the force, and would be retiring soon, which was a damned shame. Riverton was also hoping to take early retirement and go into real estate with the savings he'd stashed over the years.

"So, you got a call," Riverton primed.

"Yes. There's an undercover operation going on involving Mia Guzman. My lady's daughter. You know her son, Mia's brother, Armando, one of the guys on SEAL Team 3?"

"Okay, so that's the connection. Yes, I remember him. Handsome sucker. They call him Armani, right?"

"That's him."

"So, what's the problem?"

"He's trying to interfere with the operation. He's very protective of his sister. We need him to butt out for a bit so the undercovers can do their job."

"You're gonna tell him about the operation?"

"Nope. I can't." Mayfield drilled a look that went all the way to the back of Riverton's skull. "You are."

"And under whose authority? I could get in a shitload of trouble here."

"You didn't hear this from me. You overheard it from someone else on the force. You know Armando. You know he is a good guy, and you don't want him involved in something that could jeopardize his career. Trust me, you'll be doing him a favor."

"And what makes you think he'll decide to stay away?"

"First, he's supposed to. He's not to get involved in civilian things stateside. That's hard for them to do when they come home. But if he got caught up in this operation, especially if he blew the operation, the Navy'd hear from my superiors, and people would demand action of some kind. You know how jealous regular law enforcements are of these SEALs."

"Yup. I'm well aware of that." Riverton was thinking it over. "You have an address or phone number?"

"I'd best not give you his number, but I have it if it's an emergency. Just file that one away. I think it would be best if you act like you've run into him casually." Mayfield pulled out a slip of white paper from his vest pocket. "And here's his address. They hang out at Gunny's, and the tattoo place—"

"I know those places," Riverton interrupted. Daisy's tattoo parlor was where all the SEAL Team 3 men had theirs done. He thought about her slender pink fingers working over their flesh and he was jealous. But not jealous enough to keep from getting another hard-on just at the thought of her. Just like he'd gotten a hard-on this morning when he dried off with the towel she'd used before she left for work.

"Okay, then. I'm off to some meetings. We good?" Mayfield asked.

"Not promising I can get with him today or tomorrow, but I'll work to get through to him soon. You got a deadline, has the operation started?"

"Oh yes, been going on now for a few weeks, but the insertion team is in place as of a couple of weeks ago. It's important."

"Gang task force?"

"That's right. Mia has some connected friends she can't stay away from. That's why Armando has been interfering."

"Protective."

"They all are. But if he knows we're on the case, I think he'll back away."

"Not if he thinks she's in danger."

"She's not."

"With a host of gang friends? You blowing smoke up my ass?"

"Idea is to get the bad guys together and have a tea party for them in the Graybar hotel. Armando doesn't have to duplicate what SDPD is already doing."

"Got it."

"Thanks. I owe you one."

"Nah, just doing the right thing," Riverton answered.

But inside he wondered if the SEAL would think of it that way. Or if he would be able to stop the man from doing something he felt was right. It was going to be a challenge getting through to Armando.

He also had to be careful not to take calls in front of Daisy, since she knew them all. As Cooper's ex-girlfriend, Riverton knew she'd always be loyal to the Brotherhood, no matter what it cost her in bed. That was saying a lot for the little lady most people underestimated. Though she was a little on the kinky side, which was just to Riverton's liking, Daisy was a good girl through and through, and intensely loyal. He didn't want to say or do anything to make her think less of him.

This would be more complicated than he'd originally thought.

CHAPTER 13

A RMANDO SAT AT the rear coffee table, in the dark. It was where they always sat as a Team, when they had to plan something and didn't want to be disturbed or overheard. Even in the dark everyone wore sunglasses. Just part of the uniform.

Well, this was sort of a private meeting, too. Gina said she wanted to explain some things. Another story? The truth this time? Why didn't it bother him more?

Perhaps this is what I deserve. God knows he'd told his share of lies, especially to women. He never told them he loved them, though. But he told them all kinds of shit to make them feel better about themselves. Or at least, that's how he justified it.

Truth was, he didn't feel like much of a catch. He recognized the signs of PTSD all right. Inappropriate behavior. Unwilling to let go of things that normally wouldn't bother him. Having the need to intervene in other people's lives. He'd been the Teflon SEAL, Mr. Armani, the slick Latin Lover who didn't like drama and left women satisfied, but never called them again. Oh, no. Calling would have meant a relationship and a commitment. Hell, he didn't know where he'd be in a few months. He was damned sure it was the wrong time for something more. Not until he healed. And he knew there were a fair number of his Teammates who never healed, going from wife to wife to girlfriend to wife, leaving a litter of kids all over the country, just like Gunny. Now, since the news that Gunny had asked Sanouk to stay and help him run the gym, Armando was feeling more alone than usual.

That wasn't what he wanted. He would never knowingly father a child out of wedlock, and hadn't that he knew of. That wasn't fair to a kid, or a woman either.

He closed his eyes. Across his internal screen paraded the faces of women, children and the elderly, their lifeless death masks haunting him. He saw those faces of innocents killed by their own people every time he pulled the trigger to send some bad guy to hell for all of eternity. Some days he had as many as twenty kills. And he knew there were some days he just wished he could kill all night long, too, not even stopping for food or sleep.

That's what happened when your mind started to unwind, he thought. He'd worked on himself to be able to pull the trigger to take a life, convinced it was to save a life. He believed that with all his heart. The time to question that decision was never on the battlefield. The time to question it was in the training, or in the workup to deployment, or in the downtime after a bad run. But when he was suited up with all his gear, he became the man, the most feared sniper in his squad. The man who could do the impossible shots. He'd once blown the head off a tribal thug who threatened to kill his own child to avoid capture. The man got his wish. And the little boy ran to his mama afterwards, unharmed.

He was glad he was trained, qualified expert sniper. So much easier creating death when you didn't have to stand right next to it. He'd never killed with his bare hands before. Chances were, he'd have to do that before getting out. But he knew he would do it if called upon.

Some young coeds were trying to catch his attention. Did they know about the blood and carnage parading through his head? Did they know how desperately he wanted them to never see anything but the insides of shopping malls and houses by the beach? To spare them the level of death and destruction some women their age endured overseas. He'd sacrifice his life to keep them from having to experience the things that lived in his head. It was sometimes what gave him strength to do what he did. Just so the folks at home could have a normal something.

So he gave the girls a subtle, practiced wink and they tittered their way out the doorway into the sunlight. Young. Innocent. Oblivious to all the dark forces out there. All the hell on earth others had seen. *So what the hell am I doing here?* For an instant he forgot where he was. Then he remembered. Waiting for Gina.

He'd even showed up a full ten minutes early. Now Kyle and Fredo would have some definite opinions about that.

Sunday morning was usually a busy time at the Scupper. Of course the tourist crowd was totally different from their evening group. Parents of Navy recruits haunted its walls, remarking on the memorabilia, the pictures of the fallen heroes over the bar, the polaroid of Saddam Hussein in handcuffs, looking small and helpless after his capture.

Armando couldn't fault people for wanting to pay homage to his brothers in arms. But a part of him thought it got in the way. Too much hero worship could lead to blind spots. He knew all too well that there were living disasters in his community, walking time bombs. Their job was to do the things they were trained to do and then come home and have a normal life.

What the hell is normal?

He'd heard the stories about how some of his brothers couldn't sleep. Couldn't let a woman touch them. Couldn't hold their kids. They'd seen things they shouldn't have in their short twenty-something years on this earth. And just like the motto they lived by, "The Only Easy Day Was Yesterday," it wouldn't ever get better. Maybe some of the pain would fade in time. But one never forgets fallen comrades or the faces of the innocents caught in the crossfire.

It was hard to admit he'd made some decisions he wrestled with late at night. He saw the face of one young wife of a terrorist who had attempted to protect her husband from Armando's kill shot. He'd gotten them both with the same round, but hers was the face he remembered. Even though he'd seen more faces of pure evil, it was the women and children he couldn't get out of his thoughts. They were the people he was supposed to protect, or at least try to spare if he could. Even when they chose the wrong side. They were supporting and defending their men in battle. And the children had no chance at all.

His first tour had gone on like a party. He was a newbie SEAL, a fledgling. They wouldn't trust him with the important stuff. His job was to get out of the way and let the varsity guys do what they knew how to do. His job was to observe, to learn, and try not to do something stupid to get them all killed.

Somewhere along the line he became the guy who was giving instructions. There was no official rank change in his file. No difference in pay. No difference in the way he felt.

But there was a subtle change, a new mantle he wore. It was now his responsibility to watch over others like he'd been watched over.

He gazed at the young portrait of Lance Grissom, the kid from Indiana who wanted to be a doctor. When the young medic took the IED intended for him, Armando knew there would come a day when he could no longer do this job. But it wasn't that day, and it wouldn't be tomorrow. However, there was one thing that happened to every SEAL who ever served in this elite force: that day always came. He just hoped it came without too much blood and gore or collateral damage. That he could walk away with all his body parts in working order, and that he could leave knowing he'd done all he could to protect and defend his country. Maybe then it would be okay to just walk away.

One of the older Team guys told him that as soon as a man started thinking that way, he was on his way out. Armando wasn't sure about that. Just like he hadn't been sure he would make it through Hell Week in BUD/s, as he watched others drop out and he was still there. He found, after a time, he had no opinion about it. He was just there. He'd just continue being there until he wasn't. That was all there was to it.

Mia had worn a huge hole in his heart. She was as attracted to the dangerous life as he was, but the difference was she was attracted to the wrong kind of danger. Armando had taken the path of his father, that one good cop, surrounded by too few other good cops in Puerto Rico. And like his father, Armando knew if he was just vigilant, he could outlast all the evil in the world while it was his job to do so.

But as hard as he tried to help, Mia would not walk the

straight and narrow. Perhaps she, too, had some internal flaw, some place she went where she didn't think she was good enough to live a life of goodness and light for her son. If he had a son, he'd do everything in his power to keep every shadow of evil away from the boy. Mia seemed to want to take the boy down with her. Armando couldn't let that happen. What would it take? He wondered.

Then he began to think about Gina. He expected her to come through the doorway any second now. There was something about her that was different. He couldn't quite figure it out. Part of him worried she was a bad influence on his sister. But part of him thought perhaps it was the other way around.

Or, was he looking for that pony in there somewhere? Was he looking for what he *wanted* to see, or was he being objective? He didn't know anymore. He just knew that the touch of her skin was something he did dream about at night. It helped him sleep, knowing that there still was a soft part of him that could feel those things. Something that wasn't dead.

So, is that what it was? Love?

Probably not. Probably all he wanted was to just relax with someone. Maybe in time it would happen for him like what happened to Kyle and Cooper. Maybe his day would come, if he was vigilant. If he continued to just show up. Because he still believed in a better world, even with all the evil he'd seen. That there were more good people than bad people. And that every new child he saw born healthy and brought up in a good, stable home had a chance to help save the world. And he'd be there to protect them until they could wear the mantle. And so it would go throughout history. The fighting man's legacy.

And that's what he was. He would always be a warrior. It was what he was made for, and, God willing, it would be something he wouldn't have to die for. But he could do it. He signed up for this.

So it should be easy to talk to Gina today. He tapped the table with his fingers, aware that the anticipation was feeding an erection at a damned inconvenient time.

You dog.

Forcing himself to change his thoughts, he looked at the mothers and fathers with their sons and daughters in their fresh uniforms. He gave thanks there were still people willing to do their part. Families who knew to support a son or daughter who wanted to serve. Because the whole family made the sacrifice. It wasn't something that could be explained. It was something that had to be lived.

Maybe Gina could help him with Mia. If he could just think straight around her. She might be the key. God knew, he was completely out of options.

And, speak of the devil, there she was, a fresh vision of heaven right in front of him. She breezed through the doorway without knowing how Armando's heart raced. He took a deep breath and stood for her. He could do this, if he could just keep his dick in line.

Her flowery scent fell over him, and it was everything he could do not to take her in his arms and ask for a do-over. Could they just hit the reset button and start all over again without all the mistakes? The lies?

He pushed away his concerns and focused on just listening to her. She had something she wanted to say to him. And he knew it could be something like, "I'm done. Moving away. I never want to see you again." It would be like her to finish it off clean, bold. She had it in her. He knew she did.

And even if he didn't like it, he would have to accept it.

"Thanks for coming." Her little smile showed her shy side. That was almost as attractive as her wild side. "How's your head this morning?" she asked.

"Nothing a good strong cup of coffee can't cure. You got a car?"

"Yes, thank God for good insurance. Just came from the rental agency."

He could tell she was nervous because she kept rubbing the back of her neck and looking around.

"Expecting someone?" he asked. He tried to make it sound cool, but the asshole Sam was stomping his feet and yelling at him from inside his head.

"No," she said. "I came to see you."

He liked her steady stare back at him. Unafraid. Something had shifted. She'd faced a demon and she'd won. Good for her.

"I'm all yours." It was true in more ways than one, but that was all he was going to say or do right now.

She ordered the seafood scramble, so he ordered the same. The waitress refilled his cup and gave one to Gina. Over the top of the steaming mug she closed her eyes and blew the aroma right to him. She wasn't totally relaxed, but she wasn't angry.

Thank God.

He could tell she was trying really hard to adjust for him. Perhaps playing another role? What role? And why?

He could have made some snarky remark but he just watched her.

Vigilant. Be vigilant.

Her eyes opened and he saw her need there. Was this a trap? Did it matter?

Fuck it. Here I go.

"I feel like I need to be completely honest with you, Armando."

Oh, no. Am I going to like this?

"Okay."

"I have a lot of respect for what you do. I always have."

"Okay. Why do I get the impression there's a 'but' in there somewhere, Gina?"

She smiled and toyed with her coffee mug rim with her forefinger. "I think you have me wrong."

"How?"

"I have a job. I think it's an important job." She glanced up at him and he caught her checking out his mouth. "I'm a very responsible person. I manage a lot of paperwork for some important people."

"Mia says you work for an insurance company."

"Yes, I do." She wasn't looking him in the eye. "Sometimes we can't tell our clients everything about the process we go through. And that's not comfortable for me, but I do it because it's for the good of the people I work for."

"So far, so good. Did you not think I could understand this?"

"I thought maybe you would. I think you do the same in your job. You do things you can't talk about. You are specially trained to conduct yourself on a higher level than most, and that's what I respect so much about what you do."

This wasn't going where he thought it would.

"I'm going to tell you something, and I think it will explain some things to you. I don't want you to be angry with me."

"You were a guy."

She laughed. It felt good to see her throw her head back

and laugh. The smooth flesh under her chin was especially delicate and called to him.

"No. I'm not a guy. I'm a woman."

"Whew. Because that would have made me angry, even though I would have tried not to be."

Her dimples framed her plump lips. "Good. I'm glad we got that out of the way. No, you don't have to wonder about that with me."

"So, why am I here, Gina?" Inside he winced. Was this too direct?

"I want to explain my relationship with Sam."

"Am I going to like this?" he asked.

"I don't know. But I think I need to tell you anyway. Seems like the right thing to do." Her eyelashes fluttered down as she examined her forefinger doing the racetrack of the coffee mug again. "It's about the gun, or rather, the reasons for having one."

"Okay." He sipped his coffee and watched her struggle for the words.

"Sam…did things to me." Her eyes checked out his reaction. "He was into some bondage stuff. At first it was just a little, and I was okay with that. I actually enjoyed some of it."

Armando let his eyebrows rise. "You said at first."

"Well, he escalated into other things. He wanted to bring in other men, other women." She leveled a gaze at him that went straight to his heart. "I just couldn't do that. That isn't me. Not that I'm knocking it. Just not for me."

How could Sam have wanted to share her? He'd have killed anyone who tried to lay a hand on her. If she were his.

"He scares me, Armando. I'm just trying to ease him down. He keeps turning up and following me."

You have no business hanging around him, Gina. Was there something about the dangerousness of this guy that she liked?

"I'm afraid if I just end it, he'll come after me and hurt me," she added after another silence.

But Gina, why don't you stay away? Why don't you get protection?

"You have a gun. Have you been to the police?" Armando couldn't understand why she was willingly playing with fire.

"I don't like cops," she said, looking away. Armando heard a waver to her voice. "I want to handle this on my own." Suddenly he saw a scared little girl in Gina's place.

"Not smart, Gina. Guys like that get off on hurting women. And they get away with it because no one turns them in." He made eye contact and she quickly looked away. What was she hiding? "You should go to the police. Make a complaint. You can't protect yourself against guys like him. I've seen bullies like that before. They never give up. They have to be stopped."

The pain in Gina's face scared Armando. He leaned forward, placing his hand over hers.

"Did he hurt you?"

"No. Well, not physically."

"You don't have to live this way, Gina." He wanted to say more, but his feet were sliding into quicksand. Her smooth skin and the scent of her warm, sensual, places flooded his head with fantasies. She leaned back to take inventory of his face while their fingers entwined. He found her pink lips ripe and waiting for him. He'd been dreaming about those lips for the past twenty-four hours. In a careful move, he kissed her palm. She leaned forward and kissed him.

She. Kissed. Him.

He slid his tongue along the crease and was rewarded with her opening to him. The whimper she exhaled as their tongues mingled nearly set him on fire. The woman was dangerous, but he wouldn't be able to stop.

The delicious slide into the fires of arousal slammed shut all the what-ifs bouncing around his head. He turned his back on his own advice; the words he heard whispered in some distant corner of him, telling him to be careful. To go slow. And far from taking things slow, he found himself urgent to be inside her.

He scanned the room, looking for someone who was too interested in their kiss, but found no one.

"I'm sorry he hurt you. You didn't do anything to deserve that." He delivered this while watching one tear trickle down her right cheek. "You deserve to—" He looked down at their entwined fingers. He drew them to his mouth and kissed her knuckles.

"Can you take me home?" she asked, her eyes full and moist. Her innocence took his breath away. The idea that she wanted to make love to him in his bed suddenly sent him into full arousal. He had not brought a woman to his inner sanctum since he became a SEAL.

Of course he would take her home.

CHAPTER 14

THEY LEFT HER rental car parked and he helped her into his Hummer.

"I like this one better," she said, admiring the shiny black paint job, so unlike Fredo's beater, and the fact that the smooth leather seats and dark interior smelled like Armando instead of fast food wrappers.

He reached behind her to strap her in, and she couldn't help but touch the thick muscle at the side of his neck, following it up with a kiss.

"I'd like to make it to a bed, if you don't mind." His bright white smile dazzled her insides. The anticipation of what was to follow gave her butterflies. She was short of breath.

"I don't mind." She let her fingers trace down around the front of his T-shirt, coming up the other side, and then drifting into the hair behind his left ear. Armando's dark features reminded her of delicious milk chocolate. She watched his lips come towards hers, and respectfully catch a nibble. She rode the crest of his scent as she squeezed his curly hair between her fingers. Then her palms came to rest on his chest as he leaned into her touch.

He was pure sexual candy. And he was going to let her

indulge as much as she could handle.

Am I ready for this?

She knew the answer to her question as the door closed and he walked in front of the truck on his way to mounting the driver's side. She knew his sure hands that started the vehicle, shifted the gears, and gripped the steering wheel would play her body like an instrument. His lips and tongue would find her in all the ways that mattered. She would give herself completely to him in every sense of the word.

Except tell him the truth about what she did. That part she had to keep to herself.

The pulsing down low under her panties warmed her as her sex felt swollen. She watched his face in profile as they threaded their way through streets she didn't recognize, until they drove down a narrow, tree-lined street bordered with bungalows featuring Spanish red-tiled roofs. That's when she noticed the sliver of a view of the ocean beyond. In the distance, foamy water spray danced and played with the sparkling white beach.

She followed him up a red concrete walkway to a rounded front door with a metal cross-grate over a tiny center window. He stopped. Even the way he inserted his key into the lock was sexy, as he stood with one hip cocked, his muscled arm—the one with the frog footprint tattoos extending from inside his wrist to the bend in his arm. He opened the door a crack and turned to her.

"You sure about this?" His smile was far from angelic.

"Absolutely. I like your house already."

His answer was to take her in his arms, press his lips to hers and devour any niggling hesitation.

Once inside, he closed the door quietly behind them as she examined the rough-hewn beams of the living room's vaulted ceiling. It looked like a home from a 1930s movie set. He snuggled up to her backside and warmed her, nibbling her neck and saying something in Spanish in her ear.

Armando's palms swept from her thighs up under her shirt, sliding it up over her head in a very smooth move. He kneaded her breasts as she leaned her head back onto his shoulder. She liked being able to feel the steel of his massive arms and the hardness of his abs.

"You should know better than to go braless when you're near me."

"Note to self. Show up naked as often as possible," she whispered as she turned, balanced her arms on his shoulders. She felt his arousal as she pressed her lower torso against him. "Now let's have this off you," she said as she slipped off his shirt and pressed her already-tingling breasts to his chest. She ran her hands down the sides of both their bodies, feeling the connection of her flesh against his.

Her body melted into him. His hands grasped her ass and pressed her into his groin. She slid her fingers down his waist and worked on his button fly. He let her find him inside, and she squeezed him gently, surprised to find him commando. He slid her pants down her hips while she stroked him. His jeans dropped and he removed them and his shoes quickly. He stood before her completely naked. She still had on a pair of pink lace panties.

Armando quickly kneeled and pressed her knees apart, seeking the warm, wet juncture between her legs that so desperately wanted to be kissed. He slipped his tongue under the elastic of the panties' thin fabric and easily found her opening. With lazy movements he stroked her up and down, darting for a deep taste between long probing movements. Her quivering sex was ultrasensitive as he buried himself deeper between her legs. Her knees began to vibrate.

Still on his knees, he watched his fingers slowly remove the panties covering her. Armando sat there absorbing the sight, then began tracing one forefinger up her inner thigh until it found her folds and, with the same lazy motion, he impaled her.

Gina braced herself on his shoulders, spreading her knees wider, and then drew his head toward her belly. She squeezed the back of his neck as his fingers worked their way to fill her. The glorious feeling of his hands on her in the most intimate of ways filled her with ecstasy. He dipped his head lower, and now his tongue joined his fingers as he lapped and sucked her lips, pulling her soft tissues gently with his teeth. She felt her body lying in wait, anticipating his huge cock. A rolling orgasm took hold of her, sending her floating.

When she stopped shuddering, Armando stood and took her hand. He led her down the hallway to a light-green-colored bedroom that was sparsely decorated. The king-sized bed was covered in a black satin coverlet. A filigreed steel bedframe and footboard looked oddly feminine in the otherwise masculine room. Several hooks at the side of a closet door were filled with jackets, backpacks, pouches and straps.

He dropped her hand to spread back the coverlet. He helped her into the cool white sheets underneath. The pillows her cheeks brushed against smelled like him. Her thighs smoothed over the cotton until they found his warm legs. He moved over her as he pressed himself against her.

He handed her a foil packet. He watched her face as she

sheathed him, kissing his pecs and squeezing his cock.

"Thank you," she whispered.

"My pleasure."

Back and forth he slowly moved his cock until his head found her. He stopped pressing and took her face in his palms, kissing her from her shoulder up to her mouth. She moved her torso up to meet him, pressing his buttocks with both hands, spreading her knees to the sides.

Armando began the rhythmic motion in and out, stroking her body with his girth, pushing deep inside until she saw stars. His long lazy strokes became more intense. She wanted him deeper. She wanted him to fill her. She needed to feel the size of him stretching and loving her insides. Gina never wanted it to end. They said not a word to each other.

The glow of their silent joining was shattered when she cried out as her body twisted and clutched under his, desperate to feel his enormous size deep inside her. She reveled in the way his strong arms held her as she arched back and gave herself to the orgasm that crashed over her. She tasted his sweat as she nipped at his shoulder, feeling the urgency of his own climax. For a few seconds he held her close to him while their bodies shuddered in unison.

She could still feel him spending inside her. It suddenly seemed important to take every bit of him he would give. She squeezed his buttocks and pressed him hard against her for those final seconds of his release.

AN HOUR LATER, when she woke up to find him asleep but still inside her, she looked down at the muscled torso and smooth flesh of this warrior. She'd found some scars, as she'd loved him, things she hadn't seen or felt in the truck the first time they had made love. He had an inner thigh wound, a scrape over his shoulder blade and a scar on his left bicep that had been mended with stitches. His chest expanded and contracted, pressing her deep inside the bed's foam mattress and then releasing her to catch her breath. Her fingers lightly skipped along his strong upper thigh, onto the round buttock muscles that were firm as steel.

She found the scar below his right eye worrisome, as well as a long, healed slice to his right upper lip. God willing, she'd be able to kiss away those scars and in time they would heal soft as a baby's bottom. If she kissed him enough. If he would let her tend to him, take care of him. His one arm was underneath her back, the thick fingers of his right hand grabbing for the flesh at her waist even in his sleep. He was possessive, didn't want her to leave without him knowing.

And that made her hotter than hell, and ready for round two.

MUCH LATER, OVER chowder at the Crab Pit, Armando thought he'd bring up the subject of his sister. "Can I ask a favor of you?"

"Sure."

"We're going on a training this week. Will be gone until Friday night. I want to ask you to look after Mia while I'm away. Can you keep her out of trouble for me?"

She frowned at his request.

"I know we haven't talked about it—"

"It's fine." She patted his hand. "I'd be happy to look out for her for you."

"Thanks." He wanted to ask more. "How did the two of you meet?"

"At Babes," she avoided his eyes again. He knew she'd

lied.

"*You* went there?"

"Why, you think I'm too good for Babes?"

"Absolutely you're too good for Babes. Bad crowd there."

"I can handle it," she said. She was avoiding eye contact with him again.

"You know, I just don't get you. You're way too classy to get caught up with the guys who hang out there."

She reached for his hand. "Armando, let's not talk about it. Let's not spoil this perfect day."

But Armando couldn't let it go. "Why do you go back there, to that place inside yourself? You're not the type of girl who belongs there."

"Oh yeah? Where do I belong, besides in your bed, of course?"

"Well, not in that cheap strip joint. I don't know. I don't understand you, that's all."

"Nothing to understand. I'm a simple gal."

"But you could have so much. You have so much going for you, Gina. Why are you throwing your life away like this?"

She was getting annoyed. "I'm not throwing my life away. I have a great job. I found you, didn't I?"

"Yes, but I was going to ask you not to go to that bar anymore. Those guys are dangerous, Gina."

Her eyes glazed over. "And you're not?"

"No, I'm—" he struggled for the words. "I'm a different kind of dangerous. Not like Carlos and those creeps."

"I think they're headed for a fall."

"How would you know that?"

Gina was thoughtful and then answered. "Just a hunch.

Come on, Armando, give me a little credit. Don't you trust me?"

And there it was. He was forced to say that yes, he trusted her, to keep Mia on ice until he could figure something out. He had to trust her because there weren't any other options.

CHAPTER 15

FIFTY MEN FROM SEAL Team 3 stepped into the military transport and flew to an abandoned, dusty airfield somewhere in the Nevada desert. There were no structures visible for miles, but Armando knew there was a whole surveillance complex just ahead. The "buildings" looked like foothills and cattle sheds. Most of the structures were underground.

They gathered up their gear and jumped into seven unmarked dark-covered trucks. The back was open to the desert air and all they had was a hard bench to sit on.

Cooper, Fredo, Marky, Jones and Kyle all sat next to each other. Cooper and Fredo were discussing the pros and cons of married life, not that Fredo was any closer to it. Armando had to hand it to him, though. The little SEAL never stopped trying.

"The fuckin' movers, man," Cooper began, "mixed everything up. I went to unpack the kitchen box so at least we could prepare our first meal in the place, and found Libby's underwear."

Cooper caught hell for that one. Several other men from Team 3 started laughing. Leopold was a tall Mormon boy from Pennsylvania, nearly Cooper's height. "I'd take that one as a sign. Breakfast in bed. All I'm sayin'."

"Libby was not in the mood. She was so pissed she almost ordered me out with the movers. Like it's somehow *my* fault. *She* labeled the fuckin' boxes."

"Welcome to married life, son," Kyle said. Though they were all close to the same age, their LPO liked to dispense advice about home life and domestic harmony almost as much as Gunny.

"I believe the term you have yet to learn is, *yes, dear,*" Armando added.

"You best learn that or yo' mamma gonna hold her knees together real tight. You got twenty years of purgatory minimum," Jones added with a smile.

Fredo had to jump in on that one. "That's when you get some professional advice," he said as he stood and gyrated his hips to the sounds of oohs and ahhs from the audience.

"And then you get that damned letter from the lawyer," one of the other men said.

They'd been driving for nearly an hour and the bench seat was getting hard. The background chatter was comfortable, working like white noise. Armando thought about his glorious morning and afternoon on Sunday with Gina, and couldn't wait until Friday when they'd reconnect. He'd be so ready for her he got stiff just thinking about it.

"You're kinda quiet, Armani," Kyle said as he shoved his shoulder into him. "Everything right?"

He smiled back at his best friend and BUD/s swim buddy. If it weren't for the fact that Armando had a minor infraction stemming from a bar fight, he'd be the same rank and have his own platoon, but he preferred being Kyle's second enlisted any day of the week. That fight had cost him almost $150 a month in pay, but it had been worth it at the time.

"I'm good. A little stir crazy."

"Me too. But hey, we got about half a mil worth of ammo to go expend the next few days. We got more to use this week in training than whole platoons use overseas in a year."

"Well, that's the point, isn't it? Use it in training so you don't have to later on?"

"Yup. Being prepared definitely keeps you alive," Kyle agreed.

"Also makes you a great lover," Marky Mark added as he winked.

Several laughed. Armando thought about being in training with Gina, and damn, it was getting hot in there. He definitely was obsessing about her soft flesh and that pouty mouth that tasted so sweet as she shattered under him. Seeing her climax was going to be the highlight of his day when he got back. Every day.

What the hell am I saying?

"Fuck it," he mumbled under his breath.

"Yeah?" Kyle had picked up on it. "You sleeping these nights?"

He knew Kyle was fishing for signs of PTSD. Lord knew they'd seen more than their fair share of screwed-up operations and things gone wrong. Team guys killed.

"I'm thinking about one little lady who's gonna make sleep a luxury," he whispered back to Kyle.

"Roger that." Kyle patted him on the shoulder. "About time, Armani."

"Nope. Not quite that far. But I'm having fun."

"Love 'em and leave 'em, until one snags you and you have no choice. And then you say, *yes, dear.*" Several others overheard the conversation and had joined in the refrain.

THEY RAN EXERCISES in the dusty sand of the high desert, shooting and blowing things up. They used hand-held drones like one of Cooper's to coordinate positions and identify targets. Armando found shooting the new .50 caliber M2, Ma Deuce, which mounted like a gargoyle on the back of a jeep going at sixty miles an hour, the most challenging. He familiarized himself with the quick-change barrel system and what to do in case of a jam, which they said would never happen.

A couple of manufacturer's reps were on standby to instruct them during the week. Because of Leopold's Mormon faith, his nickname was Moron, but that had nothing to do with anything that would describe the big kid. His girlfriend was going to meet him in Vegas after their training, and he planned to propose to her. He'd been practicing his proposal over and over again. If it didn't work, at least they'd have a very romantic weekend at Caesar's.

On Friday, after a hard week of long dusty days in the high desert, they were rushing to get all the equipment off the trucks so they could make their plane and touch down in San Diego while there was still part of an evening left to waste. The Browning was a heavy sucker, and the barrel was still hot from all the rounds they'd rammed through it. Someone pulled the lever on the stabilizing arm and the sucker dropped straight down on top of Moron's forehead. It knocked him clean out.

Cooper worked on Leopold furiously, making sure he regained consciousness quickly. The hole in the middle of his forehead was partly singed from the hot steel of the barrel. There was no question it was going to leave a ring, and would need stitches.

"Fuck!" Leopold screamed as he came to.

"Guess we don't have to worry about whether or not he's all right," someone said.

"It coulda knocked some sense into him," Fredo added.

Blood was streaming down the cut, covering his lips and teeth. He sputtered and coughed, in between his invectives toward the heavens and anyone else who stood around to watch.

"You gotta hold still or I'm not going to be able to patch this up," Cooper said calmly.

"Fuck!" Moron shouted again so loud it reverberated across the desert. He was trying to stand, but Coop outweighed him. He was the only SEAL who did. Coop finally sat on the big kid so hard it nearly knocked his breath out. The two skinny advisors looked worried but said nothing.

Kyle made an announcement. "So you see? That's what happens when we rush things. This is what gets you killed, gents. You pay attention. Who pulled that pin?"

A short wrestler-type build of a man, a recruit from Latvia named Dimitri stepped forward. "I am sorry, sir. I didn't see him there."

Kyle grunted, but Armando knew he wouldn't write it up unless the guy hadn't confessed. "We can die by enemy fire, or we can die by friendly fire. Or a training accident. We use this to remind ourselves to be careful. Being careful is what keeps you alive. Some days it is the only reason you stay alive. Don't assume anything."

Cooper had begun trying to stick butterflies over Moron's bleeder. He finally had to resort to a gauze pad and a wad of athletic tape wound around the kid's head several times to get the bleeding to stop.

"You're gonna have to go to the hospital back in San Diego, Leo."

"Fuck that. I'm meeting my girl here at Caesar's Palace."

"I can't stay. You gotta be seen by someone."

"Just stitch me up. Go ahead."

"I got nothing to deaden the skin."

"I don't fuckin care. Just stitch me up so my girl doesn't have a heart attack when she sees all the blood."

"You're gonna have to have her wake you up every hour. You could have a concussion."

"Shit, he's not gonna sleep all weekend, are you, Moron?" someone said.

"Maybe not now," someone else added.

"Shut. The. Fuck. Up." Leopold was still in a hurry.

Cooper looked to Kyle. "Your call."

"Your ears ringing?" Kyle asked the kid.

"Nope."

"Would you tell me if they did?"

"Nope. But they're not ringing. I got a headache, though."

"I'll bet." He turned to Cooper. "Give him something for pain after you do it."

Cooper nodded.

"Make it hurt. If he passes out, he comes with us," he added in a whisper.

"Roger that."

With an audience around them standing in a tight semicircle, Cooper put twelve stitches in Moron's forehead like he was appliquéing a quilt, and the boy didn't flinch. True to his word, Cooper made it hurt. But no one would have known until it was all over. Moron got up, looked at himself in the steel mirror and then punched Cooper in the jaw.

"You did good, kid. Now, no alcohol this weekend, hear?" Kyle admonished him.

"Fuck's up with that, LP? You know I'm a fuckin' Mormon. The only thing I *can* do is screw."

CHAPTER 16

G INA USED THE week to dive into Mia's world. They explored other bars some of Mia's lowlife friends frequented, under the guise of looking for hot dates willing to spend money. But Sam and a couple of the other detail followed them around, seeming to have an uncanny knack for showing up when they least expected it.

Carlos gave them a generous offer to work for him, which was a break for Gina since she got it on audio. He gave a rather lengthy description of how he used girls and youths to send messages, occasionally delivering money. Gina allowed herself to be talked into it, over Mia's objection. She was pleased Mia was beginning to recognize the dangers of being involved in the wrong crowd. Something had shifted.

Gina met several of his couriers at the palatial home overlooking the ocean in La Jolla on Wednesday. Carlos was on his very best behavior. But she knew from Sam's snitch that they'd just purchased a warehouse full of military equipment, including some state-of-the art firepower. There was a race for time to find out the location before it could wind up in Mexico.

"I would treat you like a queen, beautiful Gina with the

perfect body."

She let him think she found that attractive. Mia tried to act disinterested, but Gina picked up on her friend's unease.

Even as she played up to Carlos, it troubled her that his rise to power had been so rapid. Caesar had been imprisoned for less than a year. She knew the Scorpions had probably replaced the SDPD and sheriff's men caught up in the sting with new members and new officers bought and paid for by the gang. Finding those would be a big coup.

Unlike the slimy man she usually saw at the bars, Carlos's house was immaculate, completely modern, and stark white except for his collection of Haitian and Cuban paintings, which hung like violent scars on the sun-drenched walls. He had a wine cellar large enough to serve dinner for twelve, and bragged that at the time of purchase two years ago, the wine had been valued at over a half million all by itself. He also made a point of telling her he never took drugs. "My house is as clean as it looks. "Don't you party?" she asked.

"Nah. Here I relax. I do all my business out of the office or in my car. But when I come home—" he walked around Gina, looking her up and down—"I like to get with my woman, you get what I'm sayin?"

Gina resisted the urge to cringe. Mia was scowling. She held little Ricardo in her arms as the baby grabbed one of her hoop earrings and practically ripped it off her ear.

On the way home, Mia gave her a bit of her own twisted advice. "You know if you get hooked up with Carlos you'll never get out?"

"I know what I'm doing." Gina looked over at the girl she'd actually begun to like. It wasn't her job to reform Mia. Instead, she was supposed to arrest her when the time came.

That would be difficult to do. But if she had to, could she? Knowing what Armando would do?

"I just don't understand why you'd go get in close with Carlos, then. What could you possibly see in him when you got a guy like Sam around? I think you're loco, Gina."

If you only knew.

"Tell you the truth, I'd rather get with your brother. I think he's hot as hell," Gina said and then immediately regretted it. But it had felt good to say something truthful. Mia shook her head. "Girls are all over him all the time. He's a royal pain in the ass to me."

Gina thought a bit before she approached the subject she knew Mia wanted kept secret.

Time to suck it up. "So what happened, Mia?"

"What do you mean what happened? To Armando?"

"What is that thing you don't want to talk about, that thing that happened to you?"

Mia shook her head again. "No way. Just keep your mind on yourself. I don't need any shrinkage."

That was really funny. "Good one. I like that."

"Yeah, well, I've done that too."

"Done what?"

"Screwed my shrink."

They had stopped at the stoplight. Mia turned to her and finally let her have a glimpse of what was going on. "Okay, then. You can't tell anybody this, right?"

"Scout's honor," Gina said.

Mia fixed her with a deadly sneer. "No scouts, either."

Gina was running out of good guys to reference. "I promise, your secret is safe with me."

"My mother's priest molested me when I was thirteen. Confirmation classes and all. My mother has blinders on, just like horses at the races. Wanted me to spend all kinds of time with the creep, and thought I was just being selfish when I didn't want to go anymore. I knew it was wrong to sit on his lap with no panties on."

They continued into the intersection.

"God, that's awful, Mia."

"Found out he'd been doing it for years. The church knew too. Did not one damned thing about it."

"Did you tell your mother?"

"Tried to. She's a brick wall when it comes to the church. She refused to listen."

"How long did this go on?"

"Nearly a year. I got issues about it, you know. I play around and such, but I don't like sex very much. It feels dirty."

"No wonder. You know there are places that can help you with that."

"Oh yeah. I got that too. The priest sent me to a shrink. That man was also a pervert. I think the two of them was comparin' notes. He got arrested last year…you remember that big scandal with the doctor and the young girls?"

"I do. I remember when they—" she was going to say *when they brought him in,* but that would have been incredibly dumb, "they had it all over the news. So you were one of those girls?"

"Police did nothing. I was Carlos's bitch at the time and he was going away. I was pregnant by a gang member. They didn't want me anywhere near that courtroom. Can you blame them?"

So the system had let Mia down. Her mother brought them here for a better life, and Mia had fallen into the clutches of a couple of pedophiles.

"You know, Mia, it isn't your fault. You did nothing wrong."

"Tell that to my mom."

"I think she loves you. Armando does too. I think if you stayed close to them, the life you want for you and the baby, well, you could have that life."

"Says the woman who's going to run money and drugs for Carlos. You should take your own medicine, Gina."

You're so damned right, Mia. Wish I could tell you how it's going to play out.

"I'm just doing it for the money," she decided to say. It was her job, and she did need the money to live on.

"That's prostitution, Gina. You doing those things for money is no different than sucking on a guy's junk for cash. Only a matter of time."

If Mia only knew what she and Armando had done. Her face flushed. A smile crept up to her lips as she remembered he'd be home in two days. She couldn't wait.

"You could!" Mia said. "Shut the fuck up. You could totally do it, couldn't you? You get off on that kind of stuff, Gina?"

"No. I wasn't thinking about that."

"Girl, you are fucked up—"

"No, Mia. You got me wrong." Gina watched the trees and front porches of Mia's now-familiar neighborhood. What would it be like some day to have a little place like this, if she could afford it, with a white picket fence and a garden? A couple of kids running in the yard. Taking the dog to the park. Coming home to a man she loved instead of a sterile apartment pre-staged to look like someone really did live there. It was all a stage. She was walking through the life of a person who didn't exist. Maybe it was time she revealed something about her feelings for Armando. Maybe it would help speed up the process.

"I'm a one-guy lady. I don't do multiple boyfriends or serial dating. I'm pretty much of a loner."

"I know who you like, although you won't let yourself feel it."

Gina looked at Mia's profile as she pulled into the driveway of the Spanish bungalow she called home. The home Armando had bought for her.

"Who?"

"Sam. I see it in your eyes. You do have a thing for him. Don't deny it."

"Not so. Sam and I are over. Never really began. Was just sex, Mia."

"Whoa! We have a winner! Is he that good?"

"No. Definitely not. Not my type."

They got out of the car. Mia unstrapped sleeping Ricardo from the baby carrier. After putting him down to bed she came back to the kitchen.

"So what is his type?" Mia asked.

"You don't want to go there. Honest. You're my friend. He's bad news."

"As in he wears black leathers and rides a Harley. I mean, what does he do for work?"

"Construction." They'd never talked about what Sam's story was going to be. Gina made a mental note to let him know.

"So he works with his tools, then?" Mia's eyes were sparkling. She handed Gina a glass of ice water. "That doesn't sound too bad. I like a guy with calluses on his palms. Rough and scratchy."

"He's into bondage. I don't go there." Gina was surprised she'd finally said it. She watched Mia's expression go from hopeful to concerned.

"How far?"

"I never let him show me. I broke it off before we got there. Something wrong with him, Mia. You should stay away."

"I'm going to quote a really good friend of mine." Mia's stern face didn't reveal an ounce of inner conflict. Without smiling, she said, "I can handle myself."

MIA TOOK IT to the next level when she called Gina up later on and asked her to babysit Ricardo so she could go out on a date the next night. It was an encouraging sign, Gina thought, that it wasn't any of Carlos's crowd.

But her hopes were dashed when she found out it was a date with Sam.

Gina had promised to get the audio download in to her sergeant, so she went in early without her usual slutty disguise.

Several of the detectives were friendly and talkative. It didn't take her long to realize Sam had been telling some tall tales.

"You're a lucky little lady," one of the few female detectives said to her face. "You got a good case, and you get to work with a great cop who knows the ropes." The woman was attractive and athletic and would have been just Sam's type.

"I think the operation is going well. I think I've got enough here to bring in a bunch of the Scorpions' upper leadership." She held up her mini recorder encased in a baggie.

"You and Sam. He just told me the same thing."

Gina looked up and saw Sam seated in front of Kozinski's desk. The sergeant motioned for her to join them.

"Nice work, you two," he said as he closed the glass door behind her. The scene was so totally civil and calm, so far removed from the one a week ago, that Gina was shocked.

"Thanks." She darted a glance at Sam, who had crossed his legs and was leaning back on his chair with a cat-that-ate-the-canary look.

Something was up.

"Sam was just telling me he found Carlos's bookkeeper and the lady has started spilling everything to him."

I'll bet.

"Got a whole notebook full of details," Sam said in a husky voice. The double meaning hit Gina in the gut. Her blood ran cold. His eyes were smiling but he still looked mean and dangerous. Something was unraveling.

"Well, that's good, Sam. I imagine that will help out a lot."

"Enough to put him away for a while, I think," Sam countered.

She turned to Kozinski, clearing her voice, "I've brought in the audio I told you about, Sergeant."

She fished a sealed plastic bag from her purse, containing a mini audio recorder. "In here he talks about his couriers, and he even told me where he keeps some of the drugs."

"Good work." Kozinski grabbed the bag, placing his initials and date on the white square at the top for the chain of custody.

"Hold on a second," Sam spoke up. "I'd like to make a copy of this. By the time they analyze this over at the lab and get a transcription, days could go by. If we're gonna jump on this gang, we gotta act quickly."

Kozinski was still gripping the plastic between his fingers. Gina had a bad feeling in her stomach.

"I can order a copy made and you'll get it tomorrow," Kozinski said.

"Yup, but I can have one in an hour, and then I'll return it to you. Gina and I have worked pretty hard on this case, sir. Let's not put the brakes on now."

Kozinski handed the plastic over to Sam, who tucked it in his parka front pocket. He patted his stomach and gave Gina a smug smile like he was hatching a baby.

More like hatching an evil plan.

"Sam, you make sure and wear gloves. Take precautions."

"Sure thing."

"Just for the record, sir, I'm uncomfortable with this arrangement," Gina said.

"Noted. Now, if you'll excuse me, I have to get ready for a briefing." Kozinski was all business. He picked up his briefcase and motioned to the door, exiting his office behind Gina and Sam. He quickly passed them and sped on his way to the elevator.

Sam caught up to the sergeant and whispered something in his ear. They both laughed. Gina knew her boss was too trusting, and Sam had just told that joke to make Kozinski laugh unwittingly. It was the appearance Sam was after, and Kozinski didn't have a clue what was really going on. But Sam knew exactly what he was doing.

He wanted to be sure Gina knew she was on the outside. Not part of the A-Team. Just in case she thought she could do a better job.

It was intended to put her in her place. She knew the download would never see the light of day.

Good thing I made my own copy first.

WHEN GINA SHOWED up at the house the next evening, Mia looked like the bad girl she truly was. She wore her four-inch stilettos, a scooped neck, form-fitting dress that was sure to get Sam all hot and bothered. She should have just worn a sign, *Fuck Me Now*, on her back.

As if she was Mia's mother and not her girlfriend, Gina greeted Sam at the door while Mia was putting the baby down. Sam's grey-blue eyes were clear and penetrating. He had been a handsome man in his youth, and women would naturally be attracted to the older detective because of his huge frame and arms from heavy workouts. Though he was nearly forty, he'd still be attractive to the twenty-somethings, especially if they liked sex on the kinky side.

She didn't feel an ounce of attraction for him. She knew that face could change, turn dark and menacing in a heartbeat. She didn't trust his motive for taking Mia out. She knew it had something to do with her, as had the conversation in Kozinski's office earlier today.

"Hello, Gina. Nice of you to give Mia and I a little alone time together." He flashed his winning smile, but Gina didn't take the bait.

"All part of the job. Yours, and mine," she whispered.

"With wonderful benefits," he winked and walked past her, lightly grazing fingers against her thigh.

Mia made her entrance. "What benefits?"

Sam stepped back, bringing his palms out to the side. "Holy fuckin' cow, Mia. You're one gorgeous babe."

Mia blushed and returned a smug smile to Gina.

"I was just telling her how beautiful you were, that you had, well, a lot of benefits a guy could get lost in, right Gina?"

Right.

"Enjoy the movie. I'll sleep on the couch if it gets too late." Gina couldn't wait for them to leave the room.

Sam had already fondled Mia's ass by the time they made it out the door. Gina hoped his weaknesses were not as strong as his charge to protect and serve. She still wanted to believe in him. She knew good was stronger than evil.

Eventually.

CHAPTER 17

GINA WOKE UP on the couch. Early morning sunlight shone through the miniblinds in Mia's living room. She checked the street and didn't see a car she recognized. She worried that Mia had never made it home and internally cursed herself for not staying awake.

She tiptoed to the closed door of Mia's bedroom and opened it a crack. Mia was there, tangled in sheets and naked. Next to her was Sam, on his back, sheet draping his naked body low, exposing his enormous chest and shoulders. One of his socks was still on.

Gina sighed and began to close the door, but not before she saw Sam's eyes open, underlined by a wide grin.

So let Sam change the baby when he wakes up. Sam could make her breakfast. What was she anyhow, a maid?

Gina slipped on her canvas shoes and picked up the purse that she'd tucked under the pillows on the couch. She checked her gun and made sure her badge was stowed down low enough not to be easily visible.

She double-checked the room to make sure she wasn't leaving anything. The door opened and Sam stepped out in his shorts.

"You taking off so soon?" he whispered. "It's early." His

hair stuck out in multiple directions.

"I've got paperwork to get caught up on."

Sam leaned against the doorframe and folded his arms on themselves.

"Kozinski said the audio was blank."

"What?"

"I guess you'd never make it in the recording industry. It was blank, even Kozinski tried it. Nothing there."

"Like hell. You erased it."

"Now, why would I erase evidence?"

"You can tell it to the jury when your time comes. Sam, I've had about all of this I can stand."

"You upset about me banging the little nympho?"

Gina knew Mia was anything but that based on their conversation the evening before.

He continued, "If you can do it, I guess I can. She might not be as much fun as that SEAL brother of hers, but I think if we made it a threesome it could get real hot, just like you like it, and you'd forget all about him."

"Not interested." She reached for the door and then stopped herself. "Sam, what about our conversation a few days ago don't you understand? I told you there was to be no 'us' anymore. What's Kozinski going to think when I tell him you screwed Mia to get even with me?"

Sam shrugged. "Don't flatter yourself. Besides, he'll never believe you. And you're wrong, babe. I screwed her because she wanted to be taught how to do it right."

That actually sounded like the first truthful thing Sam had said all morning.

"She wants to try it all. And I'm not kidding about the threesome. I think she'd be open to it." He began to walk slowly toward her. "That way you don't have to feel left out."

Gina was furious. "Never going to happen. You are wasting your time, and mine."

She left through the front door and ran down the red walkway bisecting two green patches of lawn. Everything on the street looked like the Cleavers lived there. The yards were nice; most the places were freshly painted. For some reason, the normal scene brought tears to her eyes.

Get a grip.

She knew she wasn't jealous. What was going on?

GINA WENT HOME and showered, changing into some jeans and a large yellow sweatshirt. She put her canvas slip-ons back on and took off for the office. Kozinski was bent over something at his desk when she knocked on the glass door separating them.

"Come in," he said without looking up.

"Sir. I spoke to Sam about an hour ago, and I understand there was a problem with my audio recording?"

"As in it was completely blank."

"I saved a copy to disc. You can have this one."

"How do I know—"

"Just listen to it first, sir, and then you decide what you want to do with it. I told you I wasn't comfortable with Sam getting access to it. If that recording was blank, then I'm telling you Sam erased it."

"Gina, you understand what you're implying?"

"Yes, I do."

"You're accusing one of our own of obstructing justice, tampering with evidence. That really what you're saying? All because the guy wouldn't go out with you?"

"Excuse me?"

"You heard me. Sam said you wanted to rekindle your relationship and he thought it best not to do so and jeopardize the operation. And now you're angry with him. He warned me you'd be on the warpath when we discovered the blank audio."

"This is ridiculous. It's the other way around. Sam's—"

"Gina, I think you're over your head. You need him. It isn't helpful to put your personal feelings ahead of the operation. You're jeopardizing the very thing we're trying to protect."

"That's just not true."

"I've known Sam for over fifteen years. I've only known you two years. First thing when you get here, you're hot and heavy with one of the guys on the force, someone you're supposed to learn from, breaking up his marriage and putting his job at risk."

Gina knew the truth of what Kozinski was saying. It had been a horrible lack of judgment. She regretted it every day now.

"I'm so sorry about how my time here at the Department started. You are right. It was totally inappropriate and showed my inexperience. But Sam, he knew better. And, sir, he came after me, not the other way around."

"That may have been true before."

"It's the same now. He shows up everywhere Mia and I are."

"He's your backup. These are dangerous guys you're dealing with. He's doing his job. You're taking this all too personally. I told you to bury the hatchet. I don't want to have to tell you again, Gina."

Gina couldn't believe how Sam had worked his magic on the sergeant. He was much better at the office politics than she was. She would have to be very careful.

"So you won't consider pulling him off the case?"

"Not in a million. But I could pull you."

So that was it. Her job was at risk, not Sam's. Good to know. This changed how she was going to go about things.

"Sir. Just listen to this CD, and then you tell me who you believe. I've got evidence here you can use. Not hearsay from a bookkeeper. *Real* evidence of crimes being admitted to."

"Fair enough." He took the CD from Gina's fingers. "I'll listen to it tonight on the ride back home."

"I'd keep it in a safe place, and I wouldn't tell Sam about it, either. Sir, I could be wrong, but I don't trust him."

"Your objection is noted. I think you're wrong, of course, but it's noted. I'll get back to you tomorrow. That agreeable? We'll work on it first thing next week. You go have a good weekend. Then we'll talk."

"Fine."

Two hours later, Armando called Gina. They agreed to meet at her place.

She'd bought some fresh whole wheat bread, smoked chicken, and cherry tomatoes at the Farmer's Market on her way home. She hoped he liked her idea of a healthy, no-frills lunch. She was so distracted with the anticipation of seeing him again she was having trouble concentrating.

In spite of the bright late-morning sun, she lit several candles in her apartment, chilled a bottle of Chablis and jumped into the shower again. She'd just dried her hair and put on lipstick when she heard her doorbell ring. A quick check to the security peephole confirmed it was Armando.

The sight of him standing in front of her with a small bouquet of flowers took her breath away. He seemed anxious to get them out of his hands. She ignored the flowers and pulled him inside by the top of his tee.

"I missed you," she whispered as she began peeling off his shirt.

"Likewise," he said. "Don't you want these in water?" He held the bouquet out between them, where it was in danger of being smashed by their urgency.

"Why, Mr. big tough SEAL. Are you afraid of me?"

"Not a chance." He tossed the flowers on the couch and began pulling at her jeans. Within seconds they were completely naked, heading for the bedroom.

She pushed Armando on the bed, then kneeled in front of the hunky SEAL and held him, rubbing up and down his shaft. She licked the tip and then slowly took the entire length of him in her mouth while she moved her fingers up and down in a ring.

After several minutes, she could feel him trying to slow her down. "My turn," he whispered as he guided her up onto the bed and lay next to her. He nibbled his way down from her breasts to her sex, and then licked her nub until it began to vibrate and swell. His artful tongue made its way into her opening, skirting the outside first and then plunging in deep. He added fingers and pressed her clitoris with his thumb.

She began to feel a slow-rolling orgasm building, as he tasted her.

"You have something?" he asked. The words came out of the erotic fog she'd lost herself in. Of course they had to use protection. What was she thinking?

"Yes," she said as she turned over on her stomach and reached for the bedside table. Inside she'd stashed some purple foil packets with ribbed condoms.

"Nice," he said as she placed one on his tip and spread it down the length of him. "I like your forward planning, Gina."

"I like to be prepared, sir."

"I can see."

In one slow thrust he was inside her to the hilt. She wrapped her legs around his waist and moved up and down as he angled in and out, picking up speed as he did so. Her body opened to him, needing him to fill all the places in her soul that hurt, pushing off all the cares of the day.

He held her wrists together above her head with one huge hand. His fingers massaged her palms. She threaded her fingers through his. His thrusting got more and more urgent until they both started to lose control. She could feel him jerking inside her and that put her over the edge. She arched up and felt her muscles tense around him, squeezing and begging for more.

Afterwards, he collapsed on her chest. His dark, curly hair was wet around his ears and at the back of his neck. She fingered through the silky strands as she felt the glory of his breath on her upper chest.

She faded in and out of a dream state where somewhere in the background she heard the sounds of an ordinary life that was forming in a future very different than the trajectory she'd had just two weeks before. She could see herself in this man's bed, in his arms, at his side, no matter what.

She'd begun to feel as if she'd been created just to love him.

CHAPTER 18

M IA HAD HEARD some of Gina's conversation with Sam, and she was annoyed the two of them had something going on behind her back. And the reference to the three-some? She'd never asked that. But she knew Sam still had a major flame for Gina. In fact, he'd even called her Gina last night during one of the multiple sexual encounters.

The guy *was* exciting, like all men were at first. He was the oldest man she'd ever dated, if that's what this could be called. Somehow she didn't see any future in it, but then there wasn't usually a future with any of the guys she'd dated lately. His body was muscular, not as lean as some of her recent boyfriends, but she kinda liked his size. Size did matter in lots of ways.

But she knew he had secrets, and she suspected they were dark. He'd asked her what she liked and she was forced to tell him about the rape she'd suffered at the hands of the priest. And then he asked the guy's name for some reason, and said he'd met the shrink.

How did that happen? How did he know about their little circle of sickness?

He was clearly on her side, and asked if she ever wanted to exact revenge for the crimes perpetrated against her. That odd question really set her off. Her life wasn't about getting even, but getting away from her past.

Sam also had a thing for her brother. When she complained Armando wouldn't leave her alone, he asked her if she wanted protection.

Protection from Armando? One of the Navy's finest? She'd been angry with him plenty, but to fear her brother? That didn't fit.

She had to clarify that one. She loved her brother, she told him. He was doing what he thought was the right thing, because he didn't have a life of his own outside the Teams.

"So why don't you get yourself one of the Team guys, then? You could all be one happy family." A sneer had crossed his face, as if the idea should be disgusting to her. But when she shook her head and tried to shrug it off, he added the one thing that made her blood run cold.

"I could have him arrested and ruin his career. Say the word and he'll not bother you anymore."

Ricardo was eating baby cereal in his high chair when Sam sauntered into the room barefoot after a long shower she'd begged out of. He smelled of lemons and was bare chested, packed in jeans that hung lower than he had a right to wear, even as a man ten years older than she was used to. She couldn't help but stare. He smiled and walked around to pour himself a cup of brewed coffee. She'd not noticed the obvious scars from two bullet holes above his right hip.

"You have plans for today?" he asked as he looked out the kitchen window. The way his muscles rippled underneath smooth tanned skin was designed to give her just the reaction she was having. So why did she have this terrible feeling she was being played?

"I'm just going to stay home with Ricardo."

"Your boyfriend ever see the kid?" he asked as he turned around to face her.

"No. And I'm going to keep it that way."

"He has a right, you know. When he gets out, he'll come looking for you and your boy there." He glanced down at Ricardo, but his blue eyes were cold and unfeeling. "You have someone who could watch him for you today?"

Mia thought about that. The obvious answer was yes, her mother could do so. But she wasn't sure she wanted to be alone with Sam today. Something was bothering her.

"Can I ask you a question?" she asked.

"Shoot." He took another sip of coffee and leaned against the sink.

"What were you and Gina talking about this morning?"

He frowned and looked down, like he was considering whether or not he was going to answer her. "Suppose you tell me what you heard."

"Is that a way of saying you only want to tell me what you think you have to?"

His eyes sparkled with some kind of dark admiration. She'd hit the mark with that comment. "I'm a pretty much an open book. But I admit I'm an acquired taste, Mia. Not everyone can handle what I'm interested in."

"As in sharing my bed with you and my best friend?"

He nodded very slowly. "I think you'd kinda like it."

Ricardo had started to complain because Mia had been ignoring his efforts to eat. She focused her energy on filling him up and then wiping down his chubby cheeks, his hands, and later his high-chair tray. She set him in a walker in the living room and stood in the doorway watching him. Her back was to Sam.

Sam came up behind her and began nuzzling her neck,

sliding his hands under her shirt and snaking them down the backside of her pants.

"Why did you tell her I wanted to do it?" Mia could not figure that one out.

"Because, baby." He bit her earlobe and reached around to put his fingers down her front until he came to the space between her legs. His knees forced the backs of her thighs apart. He moaned as he inserted his fingers into her quivering sex. "I think you'd dig it. I can show you things about yourself you never knew existed."

"But what about what *I* need, Sam?" She pulled his hand out of her pants and turned to face him. "Where is *my* will in this whole little plan of yours?"

"If you just let me show you, I'll expose your inner demon." He pulled her head to his, devouring her mouth, sucking and pulling her tongue onto his. He placed one hand under her chin and turned her face away so her left ear was exposed to his lips and whispered, "Here, kitty-kitty-kitty."

CHAPTER 19

T HE LITTLE SLUT wouldn't put out for him this morning, saying her motherly duties came first in the mornings. What a bundle of joy this one would be. He'd be tired of her in no time. Not like Gina. Gina was the one he wanted. He'd chase her till the oceans dried up, track her down and have her on his terms once and for all.

He remembered Gina's little surprised expressions when he'd handcuffed her to the bed, when he brought out the riding crop and slapped her perfect pink little derriere. He'd massaged oil into her welts and loved fondling them as he pumped her from behind. She was the perfect shape and size for him, and her channel tightened so deliciously around him. He had to work hard not to spill all over her just looking at her sex before he could get inside. Just thinking about her now made his package uncomfortable.

It was okay with him that she was being a little hard to get. He didn't mind working hard. It was part of the game, after all. Made her submission to his maleness all the sweeter when she finally did realize there was no way out. That's when the magic happened.

That's probably what the SEAL was doing to Gina. He was a well-trained machine. A sex machine on steroids, to be sure. But he couldn't do the things to her Sam had done. He doubted the guy would ever make videos and watch them at home in private as he lay naked on the bed. Jerking off at the sight of her objections, the fear in her eyes, the red marks caused by his mouth, his fingertips and the riding crop. He could be gentle, tickling her with the tip of it. And just when she thought perhaps they'd have slow, beautiful sex, he'd shove his cock up her so fast she'd scream. He loved that on camera.

Yea, she loved it. Every bit of it. She was enjoying the caramel swirl and vanilla ice cream of the Puerto Rican SEAL, but she'd be back for the rich chocolate his twisted dark side could provide. Because he owned her. She just didn't know it yet.

Kozinski was just leaving the office as Sam arrived. The squad room was nearly deserted.

"Didn't expect to see you leaving early, sir."

Kozinski's face looked vacant. The pressures of the job were getting to the man, Sam thought. "Wife's got plans to go shopping for the kids' new home. Only way for me to keep a lid on the spending is to tag along, much as I hate it." He held a briefcase in one hand and his jacket over the other arm. "You should have called, Sam."

"Yes. Sorry. I need to talk to you about Gina."

"Wow, got a lovelorn practice, and here I thought I was a cop."

Sam frowned. "I don't understand what you're talking about."

"You and Gina. Doing a real dance there. Why don't you just sit down and iron out all your differences?"

"We don't have any differences, sir. Other than the terms of our involvement. I choose not to let it interfere with the work."

"Can you tell me why she says she doesn't trust you?"

"I have no idea."

"She thinks you erased her recorder."

Sam plastered on a fake smile. "You really think there was something on it in the first place? She heard I had some evidence, and all of a sudden she has this secret recording."

"Um." Kozinski was studying him carefully. Something made the hairs on the back of Sam's neck stand out. The sergeant continued, "Well, I'll let you know Monday. Have a good rest of the weekend."

"Anything going on I should know about?" Sam asked. He detected a secret he wasn't being made privy to.

"Go home. Stop being so paranoid. That's the same thing I told her."

Sam's stomach fell to his knees. *Damn.* She'd been smart. Something she'd said had resonated with the sergeant.

"She came in today?" he asked.

"Yes she did. Sam, I'm going to ask you the same question you asked me. Anything going on I should know about?"

"No, we're cool. I think she's the one that's paranoid. And she's competitive as hell. Seems to want to go out of her way to show everyone she's better than everyone else, and in particular, me. And you said it so yourself she's way over her head."

"Well, we do have rules and procedures. As long as everyone sticks to them, we'll all be okay. But if I get wind you guys can't work together anymore, I'm more than likely to have you step down than her. Just keep that in mind, Sam. In a way, you have more to lose. You are the more experienced of the two of you. Use it, okay?"

Sam nodded, seething inside.

"Let her cut her teeth on the unglamorous side of police work. Know what I mean?"

"Yessir, I do."

"So run it tight to the vest. Don't inflame the situation, and I'm sure we'll all get along."

Sam gripped a wooden ruler with one hand, folded it over and shattered it, but Kozinski didn't hear. He watched the sergeant walk into the elevator and disappear.

Shit. He'd been asked to keep his emotions between the lines, run it "tight." That's what you told a rookie female cop. Not a guy with his seniority. He wondered what Gina had done. Whatever it was, Kozinski was watching dots on that uncanny radar of his. And Sam's dot was bigger. Something had made him visible. He'd been painted and there was only one person who could have done it.

Sam decided to pay Gina a visit. She'd been a busy girl. He needed to know what else she was up to.

Another car was in Gina's parking spot, and so he figured she wasn't home yet He thought it might be fun to scare her when she arrived, just so she understood he was the one calling the shots, and that he wasn't afraid of any admonitions from upstairs.

After slipping past the security gate when another guest left the complex, Sam donned his Padres cap and maneuvered down the exterior hallway of her complex. He stopped when he came to the first window, hearing sounds of an unmistakable sexual encounter. He inched forward toward the window's edge, but stopped when someone walked past him and turned around afterwards, giving him a glare. He couldn't risk detection.

Sam made it back to his truck and sat with the window open. One hour became two, and it annoyed the piss out of him. The fuckin SEAL was still in there, and Sam knew exactly what the asshole was doing. Gina was turning out to be a real slut. He took out his cell phone and shot a couple of pictures of the Hummer parked beside Gina's apartment.

Maybe she'd flashed her little booty in front of the sergeant, too, because it wasn't right at all she should be in there fucking her brains out when she was supposed to be helping them go after the Scorpions. But that was the flaw with women. They didn't know how to sacrifice like men did. Life was too easy for women. That's why it was a really bad idea to have them work in high-risk drug cases undercover, or on the front lines. They needed to stay home, getting themselves hot and sexy for their man. And they better damned well do what the man said, too.

He tried to get the picture out of his head, but he couldn't. He knew what she looked like all flustered and pinked up. He didn't like that it wasn't him on the other end of that rapture. Her lust belonged to him. The SEAL had no right to any part of her.

He almost drove away, thinking they might make it a whole afternoon and evening combined, like a couple of rabbits. It was just wrong that he'd have to stay and keep guard on their little love nest. Gina had no fuckin' idea what kind of fire she was playing with.

Then he saw the two of them exit her apartment, hand in hand. He wished he could have wiped that little smirky, bitchy trash-mouth look right off her face.

You know I'm the only one that can satisfy you.

He clicked a few more pictures, zooming in on the handholding thing. He caught one shot of her putting her hands down the backside of his pants. Yeah, that would go over really good with the sergeant. She'd be in trouble, all right.

Sam doubted the twenty-something-year-old stud knew half the sexual stuff he did. And Sam certainly did know what Gina liked. This guy was too Boy Scout for the likes of her, Sam told himself. The lady could be a real hellcat in bed, when she was turned on. And, fuckin' A, he knew how to do that in spades.

Fuck it.

He fired up the lowered truck with the blackened windows and slowly drove down the street. They were so preoccupied with each other that neither one of them paid him any attention. Well, she'd pay for that one. She was walking right into a hornet's nest and wouldn't see any of it coming.

He made a hard right and squealed tires down the next street, then gunned it at the next stop sign and took off. He was going to have to make the complaint first. He knew he wouldn't be able to stay away from her. Best to set it up so Armando looked like the bad guy. While they were getting *nekked*, he'd be cooking her goose with the brass. And then she'd either come crawling back to him on her hands and knees, right where he wanted her or she'd be busted off the force. In either case, she'd be all alone, and in need of him like never before.

He couldn't wait to see her beg for it.

CHAPTER 20

ARMANDO OPENED THE door to the Hummer, and Gina slid in. The routine of strapping her down was always an invitation to sex, and he chuckled as she sifted fingers through the hair above his ears and then traced his lips with her thumb.

"So, are we going out to the housewarming, or staying in?" He was fine with either decision.

"Out. In later." She kissed him and he worked not to let it escalate. He needed answers to some of his questions about the big biker dude.

They rode toward Coronado without saying a word. He decided it was time to ask the questions that had been rattling around in his head. And he wondered why she didn't just volunteer something he could latch onto. Things seemed a little out of kilter.

"Something you said last week before we went on our training has bothered me a bit, Gina. I'm just wondering, why is this Sam guy so persistent? I mean, for you to carry a gun, is he following you?"

She nodded her head and looked out the side of her window.

"This is, like, stalking behavior, Gina."

Gina immediately looked to her lap. "I know it is, Armando. But I've got it under control. While you were away, I found someone with connections to the police who can help me."

"Good." But he didn't mean it. He felt she was lying to him again.

The vehicle whined while they sat in silence. Armando was looking for a parking spot along a narrow street several blocks from the water's edge. He pulled in, turned off the engine and sat back, staring in front.

Do I even want to know all about this?

"I'm not getting the feeling you're being one hundred percent honest with me, Gina. It's beginning to bother me."

She exhaled. He hoped he would get the truth this time.

"Can we just table this discussion until later?" she asked.

He was stunned. "You tell me. You're not very careful about your own safety, and that has me more than a little worried. Or is there something about this you like?"

He didn't want to have to ask her, but he knew he would anyway. "Or are you having a difficult time making up your mind?"

Her head shot up. "No." She leaned back and the rear of her head slammed against the headrest. "Fuck it."

Armando waved to a couple who walked past the parked Hummer. He was going to wait as long as she needed. He thought perhaps he would finally get the truth from her.

"He's being investigated by my company for insurance fraud. I'm ordered to stay close to him. Just that he gets the wrong idea sometimes..."

"Sometimes? He gets the wrong idea all the time, Gina. The man is a dangerous person, and I know how to recognize the really bad ones."

"No, he's not. He's just a little high strung."

"You can't be serious. I know what high strung looks like. He's more like a bit off his rocker, if you ask me."

She thought about it for a minute before answering. "Which is why I don't want you anywhere near him, or getting involved, Armando. You've got to stay away. I've got this under control. It's my job. Please, just let me do my job, okay?"

He didn't like it. This wasn't the truth, but it made some sense.

"I trust you, Gina. I just don't trust him."

"If you trust me, then everything will be fine. You'll see. Won't be long now. The investigation is almost complete. I don't want to do anything different to alert him, warn him off."

"What kind of fraud?"

"I'm not allowed to say. I'm sure you understand. In your field, you have secrets, too."

"Yes, we do. But something about all this just doesn't add up properly."

"Can we just put it to bed for a few hours? Let's go to the housewarming and forget about this. We're together. Mia will be there. I'm looking forward to seeing her, and perhaps seeing the two of you more cordial. Promise you'll try?" She smiled at him, and dang, it was hard to say no to her.

"I'm always cordial to Mia. She's the one who has the mouth."

"I even agree. But let's just not stir up anything that doesn't need to be stirred, okay?"

THEY HEARD MUSIC as they approached Cooper and Libby's new little cottage on Sunset Drive. Happy laughter drifted through the air as young couples arrived behind Armando and Gina. Most of the men were members of Armando's SEAL Team 3 since the party was hosted by Kyle's wife, realtor Christy Lansdowne.

Armando was greeted by one of the new guys, redheaded Rory Kennedy, and introduced him to Gina. Rory was scheduled to go on their next deployment. Armando liked him immediately. Single, very shy and uneasy around women, he was the most unlikely SEAL a person could find, Armando thought. That is, until you tried to outswim, outrun or do more reps during PT. The guy was as focused a warrior as Armando had ever seen.

Armando had learned from Rory that the guy had been orphaned as a baby, had lived in a string of foster care homes, and had burned down half of them while living there. He was quick to point out that no one had ever been injured. He and Armando had the fire thing in common between them. So, while Armando was a sharpshooter/sniper, Rory was always the man he liked to consult regarding the equipment, especially the ammo. The guy had invented some metal jackets that sent their projectiles distances the military swore could not be achieved.

After making small talk to a senior guy and being introduced to Gina, Rory quickly escaped.

Gina was watching Cooper and Libby in a very passionate embrace, seemingly oblivious to all the other partygoers.

"How does he afford a million-dollar home on military pay?" Gina asked.

"Libby's dad is loaded," Armando started. "Her parents sort of bought it for them as a wedding present."

"A million dollar house?"

"More like one point six or seven, I hear. But you know how daddies like to keep their girls happy."

Armando saw a frown cross Gina's face. He guessed her own father hadn't cultivated the same sort of relationship.

"Then there's Rory over here." Armando pointed in his direction.

"And?"

"Turns out his dad was a rich, hedge fund trader who had a night of indiscretion with Rory's mom, and was married with kids at the time. She refused everything from the man, and eventually disappeared. The rest of her estranged family put Rory up for adoption."

"So, they found each other after all this time? Recently?"

"In a hospital. Were roommates. What are the odds?"

It was good to hear Gina laugh. Armando introduced her to several Team guys and their wives or girlfriends, but was careful to introduce her as his friend, not girlfriend or significant other. He liked how well she fit in.

He talked to Kyle and Cooper about the deployment coming up, while Christy and Libby fawned over Gina, taking her aside and asking her questions Armando tried to overhear, but couldn't. There was way too much giggling going on. At last he had to break away and go rescue her from the wives of two of his best friends.

"Don't start filling her head with frog-hog stuff," he said to the ladies.

"Armando, she's very pretty, like you are," Christy smiled in Gina's direction. "We think you make a perfect couple."

The air just left the room. It was getting hot.

"Oh, look, he's blushing," Libby pointed out.

Armando scowled and pursed his lips.

"He's got a very sensual side, Gina, but then, I'm sure you've already found that out," Christy said as she fingered his nose. Her tight dress followed every delicious curve of her as she grabbed Libby by the arm and the two vixens joined their men…who hadn't stopped staring in their direction.

"The wives are gorgeous," Gina giggled. "Nice too."

Armando was still following them with his eyes, nodding to their mates when they successfully traversed the floor. "Most women," he began, "seem more preoccupied with the men." He stood close to her, facing her head-on. "But then I wouldn't want that, would I?"

"You not the jealous type?"

"No. I'm confident."

"I seem to remember that. One of the many qualities I enjoy about you."

They smiled in tandem as a small roar started in the background. Fredo had entered the room. It surprised Armando when Mia came in right behind him. She had a scowl on her face until she spied Gina and then shot right over to them.

"Oh, thank God. I thought he told me you were gonna be here just to get me to go out with him," Mia said. Armando winced, holding his hand over his heart.

"Fredo wouldn't do that," he said.

Mia started to give him a glare and then turned back to Gina. "I was glad to have something else to do tonight."

"Surprised Sam let you out of the house." Gina whispered.

"Whoa," Armando interrupted. "Sam, as in the Sam creep who's stalking you, Gina?"

Mia drew her eyebrows together and drilled Gina with a stare. "Stalking? Gina, he's stalking *you*?"

"No he's not. Armando is exaggerating a bit. I'm sorry, I shouldn't have brought it up."

"Where were you this afternoon? I texted you a dozen times." Mia's comment was laced with an undertone of fear.

"Sorry, I was…" Gina stopped, and Armando knew she was unable to go on.

"She was with me," Armando admitted. He hoped the look the two girls shared favored him in some way. What women did with their emotions was a huge mystery to him. Unsecure territory for sure.

He didn't have to wait long for a reaction. He could tell from the look on their faces, he'd managed to piss off both the ladies in his presence.

"What?" he said. "Did I say something wrong?"

"You better behave, my overprotective and testosterone-supercharged SEAL brother. The field is getting a little crowded, or do you like it that way?"

He didn't like any of her comment.

"Not on my watch, Mia," Armando answered, working to keep from getting angry. "I'm a one-girl guy, but then you know that, don't you?"

"Mia," Gina began, "Your brother and I are just good friends. He's helping me with the insurance case I'm working on. Nothing to worry about."

Armando wasn't sure whether he disliked the lie or the easy way Gina was able to deliver it. Flawlessly.

"There you go, Mia. *Just friends*," he repeated.

"Shows you don't know women very well," Mia answered.

She had a point.

"Enough!" Gina interrupted. "Would you both just leave it alone?"

Armando could see Mia wanted to spit out something angry, but was at a complete loss for words. Her legendary Latin temper was sputtering in her chest. He noted her irritation, followed by her self-control. And he liked this change in his sister.

He began to understand what Mia's issue was. She wanted to be in charge, and things were spinning out of control, and she didn't like it.

Could you be sprouting some natural instinct to be decent, Mia? God, he hoped so.

He could see she was weighing her options. She rolled her shoulder, fisted and un-fisted her fingers, shifting her weight from side to side. She was searching for something to say to Gina. In the end, she gave up and addressed him.

"Be careful, Armando. Things aren't what they seem," Mia continued.

"I hardly need protection, Mia."

"That makes two of us, brother," she returned. Staring into Gina's eyes, Mia still addressed him, "You're a son-of-a-bitch sometimes, Armani, but I don't want to see you get hurt. That wouldn't be right. Besides, if I wanted that, all I'd have to do is mention it to Sam. He has a major hard-on for you. Now I can see why."

Mia left, slipping into the crowd that closed behind her.

So if the ex was really the ex, then why was he so over-the-top obsessed with Gina? And what was making his sister jealous of her best friend?

"More secrets, Gina?" he asked.

That was such a dumb question.

CHAPTER 21

G INA WAS WORRIED this would be the last time they could be together. Armando was quiet, pensive. Once they were back in the car, he headed for her home.

It served her right. Things were all messed up. Sam was a loose cannon. She was running out of lies to tell everyone. If she wasn't careful, something would get leaked that would blow the lid off the whole operation.

Maybe it's best we just end this.

It wasn't what she wanted. In a perfect world, he'd be just the right guy for her: handsome, self-assured, attentive to her needs while being private and secretive. She knew she would always be able to count on him if things got really bad. He'd be her safe haven, not that she needed one. He knew about honor, doing the right thing. Maybe she should do the right thing too, and let him go.

But this wasn't a perfect world, either. It was time to make a decision. Would it be a career or her heart? One of them was going to take the hit.

They had driven down her street. Armando slowed the Hummer and carefully studied both sides for parked cars.

"Everything looks okay. No black motorcycles lurking about. I'll walk you to the door," he said. The words felt like a hot spear lodged in her chest.

Her impulsive side was screaming to be heard. She made the mistake of giving it a little too much attention. "Armando," she heard herself say. He'd grabbed the door handle and was ready to get out. "Can we just go somewhere and talk? Someplace where there isn't a bed?"

The leather seats groaned as he swiveled in her direction. She didn't dare take her gaze off the parked car straight ahead of her. She could feel the warmth of his eyes melting her all the way down to her knees. Her breathing became slightly ragged and she encouraged ice-cold thoughts and cold-water nerves to regulate her. She needed calm. But her insides wanted to burst into tears or say something she knew she'd regret.

"So you want ice cream or a drink?" he asked.

She could smell his lime aftershave. His gentle words sent a vibration down her spine.

Damn. Walk away, Gina. You know that's what you're supposed to do.

"I think I'd like one of those strawberry margaritas with tons of whipped cream." She still didn't look at him, but could see from the corner of her eye he broke out in a huge smile.

"Very well. She chooses wisely. Again."

Why did he have to say that? Was she lost already?

You can do this, Gina.

Several swift minutes later they were seated in a booth at Cajun Joe's. The pink flamingo napkins had been placed on the dark tabletop by deft fingers decorated in hot pink nail polish. Gina didn't have to look at the waitress to see if she was pretty. It didn't matter. Nothing mattered except the feel of the warm thigh that pressed slightly against hers in the booth. He didn't force himself on her, but damn, he was so freaking hard to ignore.

"Penny for your thoughts, Gina. You want to tell me what's going on?" he asked.

So she looked at him for the first time since they'd left the party. It was the wrong thing to do.

"I think we both know there is no future in this relationship," she began. "I'm not saying I don't enjoy your company, but you and I both know neither one of us really want a serious relationship."

He was following the movements of her mouth.

Damn.

"I agree. Timing's all wrong. We're deploying in four months, anyway."

Something inside her screamed, and that was ridiculous.

"You might have misunderstood things, Gina. A little harmless sex and some fun evenings don't a long-lasting relationship make. I never said I was out for commitment, or did you misunderstand me?"

Why was it so freaking awful to her that he was saying the exact things she was going to say? Did he possess the ability to read minds?

"Right. I was just thinking the same thing. Wanting to clear the air…"

Their drinks arrived just in time. Hers was ridiculously large, with a huge dollop of whipped cream on the top. Armando's beer was in a long-necked bottle, local artisan brew. He held his up, and she did the same with her drink, spilling some of it on her hand as they clinked.

"To a future that isn't." His smirk was sexy, except it was honest and very, very sad.

The sweet strawberry drink gave her a brain freeze.

"I hate those," he said. He handed her a glass of water. "Here, drink this."

She grabbed it, sliding her fingers across his thumb as she did so. "Thanks."

"So you were telling me about our lack of a future. Why am I here, then, Gina?"

"I just wanted to explain things…"

He reached over, grabbing the back of her head with his powerful right hand and kissed her, demanding she shut up.

Of course she should shut up. What was the point of coming here in the first place? A million scenarios drifted through her mind as she felt herself open to him, as his tongue slipped along her lower lip and found hers. His warm breath on her cheek made her nipples knot in pain. Instantly, she felt vacant, needy, and desperate to find a way to be with him.

When they parted, he studied her carefully, toying with her earlobe between two fingers. He clearly wanted an answer.

"What is this?" she asked.

"I think you know," he said.

"I'm not sure if coming here was a really good or a bad decision," she mumbled.

"Most decisions in life are that way. Hard to tell until the end of the story." He rubbed his thumb across her lips. "There are a lot of things about you and I that don't add up. I'm not sure you're telling me the truth half the time." He grinned that little stupid lopsided grin that brought out the dimple at the side of his mouth. "But for some strange reason, I don't seem to care as much as I think I should."

Her heart was thudding in her chest. Surely he could hear it.

"I don't think I want to hear another story," he whispered.

His fingers slid down her arm, giving her the chills. She closed her eyes as she felt him take hold of her hand and kiss her knuckles.

"Drink up, sweet Gina. Then, I'm going to take you to my place. Unless you say no. But you've got to decide tonight which way it's going to be. I don't like all these indecisions and stories. I'm not interested if Sam is even slightly in the picture. I don't share, honey."

"Thought you didn't want commitment," she whispered. It was dangerous to say, but she had to know.

His dark eyes scanned her face. The lines were getting blurred between who she was as a cop and who she was as a woman.

"All good things start with trust. At some point the stories and the lies have to stop, and we're left alone with the truth. When I'm seeing someone, I expect that she isn't seeing anyone else on the side. I think that's just trust and respect, Gina. Not commitment." He sighed and stared down at his beer glass. "I need to know where you stand on this."

She saw why he was so good at his job. He had the ability to know the difference between what he was feeling and what he needed to do. He'd had the training. She did not. He was able to make those tough choices she was struggling with.

"If you can't decide, then I wait until you do. But I don't sleep around and I won't let you either."

She heard the lyrics and music to an oldies song she'd heard growing up.

He slid away from her, leaving the space between them

cold and empty.

The pink drink with the topknot looked ridiculous. She grabbed it with both hands and gulped away, dipping her nose in the whipped cream.

Before she got to the bottom of the drink she could feel the effects of the alcohol. He was still staring at her.

"What's it going to be, Gina?"

"There isn't any Sam. There really never was."

"So, make a clean break of it. Get your work done, and get away from him. You won't be happy until you confront the way he haunts you, and why."

"Does anything haunt you, Armando?"

"Lots of things, baby. But you have to decide which dog you're going to feed. You let the dog of fear starve. You feed the dog that brings you joy."

"I'm ready to face some of my fears. Can you help me with that? Do you *want* to help me with that?"

He didn't touch her, but she knew he wanted to.

"Absolutely."

"No more lies," she said.

"No more lies. Just the truth," he answered.

She wanted to believe those words, but there were still a few secrets she needed to keep. For now. Just for a few more days. Then she'd explain everything and he'd understand.

"I'm ready, Armando."

"I like to watch how you just throw yourself into things," he said. "It's sexy as hell."

Yup. That's me. I just jump right in where I don't belong. Get myself all tangled up with the men in my life. Can't say yes. Can't stop trying.

Sexy? Did he say sexy?

She exhaled and set the nearly finished drink down on

the table. Her hands were shaking and covered in the syrupy sweetness. He picked up her fingers again and began to suckle each one. Then he concentrated on wiping them down with a napkin he pressed between his warm palms.

"All better." He tipped her chin in his direction. "Shall we go, honey?"

She hoped she didn't have a lapdog look to her face, but his brown curly hair and warm brown eyes made her melt. She felt like she was thirteen with that first crush on the minister's son in junior high.

Her adult voice surprised her. "Yes. Let's go."

She didn't remember the slow ride to his place, over the tall bridge that used to take her breath away when she traveled over it early on. She loved the feeling growing inside her stomach with the knowledge that she would be making love with him tonight, in his bed, in the place he went to for solace, where he repaired himself after missions, where he looked at himself in the mirror in the morning, where he shaved, where he tied his shoes and foraged for granola. She wanted all the regular, ordinary things about this man to be part of her routine, part of what she got to witness. There had never been this kind of connection in her life before.

So satisfying was the thought that they were both circling the wagons, chasing each other, like she used to do as a child. She was trying not to get caught, and desperately wanting to be caught at the same time.

She knew that with the CD she had provided Kozinski, if there was enough there, perhaps this mission would all be over with by Monday. They'd have the evidence they would need on Carlos. Sam would be out of her life forever, just as Armando had requested.

Was this what they talked about when they talked of love? That full feeling at the pit of her stomach, full of promise, sparked with erotic fantasies that came over her all the time now. She wanted to stretch the length of the bed and feel as much of his flesh against hers as was possible. This was the way you felt when you were really, madly, deeply in love.

And to think not more than an hour ago she was considering giving all this up.

Where was my head?

Storm clouds started to rush in, and she bid them leave. Whatever it was, she didn't want to think about anything but what was going to happen tonight in his bedroom.

AN HOUR LATER, Gina woke up in Armando's bed, startled at first. His tanned, sleek, dangerous body was covering hers, his hips pinning her down, just as they had when he'd made love to her. He'd been extra gentle. He let her show him how fast to go and what to do. He asked her what she wanted.

Asked me.

She adjusted her right hip and moved her thigh down the back of his. He awakened with a quick inhale. Those brown bedroom eyes of his immediately honed in on her lying underneath him and he smiled. She traced the creases at the right of his mouth, twisting her head and looking at the growth of stubble already forming on his chin as well as underneath it. Time was suspended in the hush between their two hearts beating, pressed flesh against flesh.

"Thank you," she whispered and kissed him.

"For what?" He winked and gave her a half smile in jest.

"For making me feel safe. Safest I've felt in a long time."

"Oh, really?" His eyes went elsewhere. Then he returned, "I don't hear that very often. Most people are afraid of me."

He wasn't smiling, so she had to ask. "Women are afraid of you?"

"I think so. Self-preservation."

It was her time to frown. "I have a hard time thinking of a SEAL as anything but heroic. Protector of the innocent. Upholding everything good and holy. All that."

Armando smirked.

There was something there Gina wanted to see. "What?"

"We have our dark places too."

"What, making love to women without protection? That's the worst you've done with me." She noticed he'd begun a devilish grin. "Don't you like being thought of as heroic?"

"Yes. I like to be trusted."

"Heroic." Gina didn't understand the distinction.

"You can't trust anyone unless you give them the power to hurt you."

Gina felt this was odd as a ghost shivered up her spine. There had been a threshold crossed into a different room. She wanted to know more. She was desperate to know more.

"I trust you, but far from hurting me, you make me feel…wonderful," she said.

"You don't even know me," he answered, giving her a long, liquid kiss.

"I trusted you to screw me in the back of a pickup truck," Gina began. Armando was biting the side of her neck and her right earlobe. "I trusted you to take me home to your bedroom, your bed. I've thrown a little caution to the wind." She looked at the ceiling to the right of his head.

She was searching for something to say, but couldn't come up with it. Armando found her left nipple and gave her a nip. She did not move away from the pain.

"You regret anything we've done?" he asked.

"It excites me to think about those things." Gina realized this was the missing piece she'd been looking for earlier.

"Screwing in the back of a strange pickup truck."

"With people driving by, maybe guessing what we were doing," she said. The more she thought about it, she remember it had been a totally hot lay. Possibly the best of her life, until today.

"You liked that too, huh?"

"Heightens the pleasure, I think. We couldn't wait to get home."

"And we almost couldn't wait today. But we did." He nuzzled her neck. "Ah Gina, Gina, Gina."

It occurred to her that perhaps he wanted something more for round two. "So what are you saying, Armando?"

"Nothing. We should get up and get dressed." He abruptly stopped kissing her.

He had begun to go somewhere else inside. She could see a faraway look on his face as he stared out the window. She needed his eyes on her. She needed his total focus on her.

"Do *you* want to get dressed?" she asked.

He dazzled her again with a white smile. "Well, this is pretty nice."

"Pretty nice. Gee, just what a girl wants to hear."

"Okay," he said between kisses. "It was wonderful."

She had an idea that began to thrill her. "How can I show you I trust you, then? What can I do?"

A spark registered deep in his brown eyes, some small flame that could flare out of control.

"Everyone has a dangerous side, Gina." He did not smile this time.

"A dangerous side that is in need of someone to trust it."

"Yes." He was looking down at the space between her breasts. His penis was fully erect, and could penetrate her if he moved that way. She decided to resist him a little. Maybe that's what he wanted, after all.

"So, make me trust you," she said.

"No. You already have."

"So do something else." She tried to make eye contact, but he was avoiding her.

"Something dangerous?" he finally asked as he searched her face, and placed his thumbs at her temples.

"If that's what you want," she said. Her heart was thumping. She was heading into dangerous ground. Where was all this leading?

"Is that what you want?"

"I want to give you something I have not given anyone before."

"What are you most afraid of, Gina?"

She wasn't sure. She wondered what fears, demons he had killed off. What kinds of fears had he had to face? Was he asking her to go along that pathway with him?

"Or, who are you most afraid of?" he corrected.

"That's easy. Sam."

"So, why do you let him see you? Is there a place you go, like being in the pickup truck being seen by strangers? Does seeing him make you excited?"

"No. I am actually afraid."

"Because you don't trust him."

"Because I know he wants to hurt me. Deep down, I know he wants to hurt me."

"That's a good instinct. That instinct will keep you alive, Gina."

"Is this what you do when you are over there?"

"Yes."

"You face your fears, you rely on instinct? You starve the dog of fear?"

"Yes." He moved over her, smoothing his callused palms over her breasts. Sifting his fingers through her hair, he bent down and kissed her. "I'm sorry you were hurt, Gina. You've got scars, just like I do."

"Yes. Heal me, Armando."

"Babe, I wish I could. But just being here, close like this, telling each other things like this." He dropped lower and started a slow tongue roll from her nipple to her navel, and then lower. "Letting me taste you," he whispered as he twirled her clitoris with his tongue. "Opening up to me."

She spread her knees further as he inserted two fingers. Gina exploded as a slow vibration began to hum inside her belly.

"Everything that's supposed to happen will happen," he said as he looked up at her from the space between her thighs. "And know this. I would never hurt you, lovely Gina. You'll always be safe with me."

CHAPTER 22

*T*HANK GOD FOR *Saturday mornings,* Gina thought as she stretched. Her hands hit the bedframe and the images of her fingers gripping the cool metal while Armando worked his magic between her legs made her suddenly wet. The bed—*his* bed—was cold and empty beside her. But she could smell fresh coffee and something cooking and she knew he wasn't gone.

The bedroom was sparse, like hers was. But he wasn't undercover, like she was. She'd given up her studio cottage—the one she'd loved down by the beach. She'd toyed with the idea of going back there to visit. She'd have walked down the white sandy spans and turned up the narrow brick pathway to her cottage only a block away. She missed being able to open her windows and smell the salt water and mist first thing in the morning. Until the affair with Sam started, she'd always slept like a baby there.

Like last night. As she moved her legs over his white sheets underneath the green down coverlet, she felt the delicious soreness in her core. That place he had tasted, touched with his fingers, and so royally screwed. Her nipples were still raw from all the kissing and biting. Her wrists were slightly sore where she'd tugged and struggled against the silk.

All good. It's all good.

She saw a picture on his dresser and rose from the bedding naked to take a better look. It was a picture of him in his dress whites. His tanned face was stunning contrast to the bright white jacket with the gold buttons. Above one pocket encrusted with ribbons, she recognized the gold SEAL Trident. Next to him stood a very short woman with salt and pepper braided hair pinned to her head like a crown. The woman was beaming. On the other side of Armando, Mia stood, looking no older than a young girl. She already had a wild and tempestuous look.

There was a picture of five men dressed in fatigues, shirtless, jumping off a bridge together. She recognized Fredo and guessed it was some right of passage their team had gone through.

She separated the blinds and looked outside at the sliver of a view of the ocean. She preferred her old cottage, but the ocean was the same. Rolling quietly, as its namesake: Pacifico.

There wasn't anything else in the room that was personal, and this seemed odd to her. His sliding closet door had been installed with a lock and she guessed he had equipment and probably guns stored there. She placed her elbows on the dresser top and examined her face between her palms. The woman she saw there looked happy. Dizzy in love. She felt safe and taken care of.

Movement out of the corner of her eye caught her attention. Armando was standing in a pair of shorts and white V-necked T-shirt, holding two white mugs of coffee. He had leaned into the doorway and had been watching her. As soon as they made eye contact he smiled that brilliant white smile that made his eyes sparkle.

"How long have you been standing here?" she blurted, embarrassed.

He peeled himself off the doorframe and came toward her, extending one steaming mug. "Not long. I just like to watch you."

"You seem to do that a lot," she said as she accepted the mug. Their fingers touched as she took the coffee. The electric zing she got sent a jolt right to that spot between her legs. Her body ached for him again, just with that little touch.

He must have felt the same, as he set down his mug and came around the backside of her. She took a sip of the wonderfully dark coffee while he nuzzled her neck, bringing his warm palms to her chest. His breathing became deeper. The SEAL smelled of bacon but she still found it sexy. She could barely get another sip in before he brought his face to rest next to hers, cheek to cheek, as they looked at each other in the mirror's reflection.

There were no words to express how wonderful it felt being next to him, waking up in the room that he woke up in every morning—hopefully every morning, that is. To emerge naked from his bed and be here, as he'd told her last night, where no other woman had been before. That felt significant. Could this be the start of something long lasting? Dare she even consider such a hope?

Dark clouds began to gather, but now he was kissing the back of her neck and under one ear. "Gina, I wanted to bring you breakfast in bed, but—" he stopped himself as he turned her around slowly, pulling back her hair and searching her face. "I can't seem to get enough of you."

"I feel the same." She stepped to press herself against his

chest. Her fingers laced over his buttocks as she gently pulled his groin into her belly. She fondled him while he watched the arousal her hands made.

"You up for a shower?" He whispered.

"I am if you'll be joining me."

"I'll be joining you all right," he said as he smiled and took her hand.

The glass enclosure was small, but it didn't matter. She enjoyed the brush of his thighs against hers, the way every movement brought their bodies together. She shampooed her hair while he smoothed shower gel over her backside. He helped rinse out all the bubbles as she rubbed her bottom against his groin. She lathered his back and helped him rinse off.

With water pounding on his head, he knelt and delicately investigated the lips of her sex. Once his fingers found her opening, his tongue soon followed. Gina braced herself on the glass walls, bending to sit on a small ledge, while Armando nibbled her labia. He drew one of her knees up and over his shoulder as he knelt in front of her, taking his fill. Gina's spasms spurred him on deeper. He added two fingers and she began to orgasm out of control.

Abruptly he turned her around and bent her forward. He quickly rammed himself inside her while she was still pulsing. Her swollen lips were sore from the strenuous lovemaking during the long night, but she never wanted the feeling to end, and he started spending deep inside her. He gripped her body by the hips and dug deep until at last he was done.

Afterwards, they helped each other dry off. She felt shy for some strange reason. She wanted to reel in her inner desire to make this a part of her daily routine: great sex in the evening, followed by sex in the shower, the warm kisses and caresses, being held by powerful arms and shoulders of steel.

They ate breakfast in front of the picture window since the kitchen was a small galley. She drank a second cup of coffee. Gina had no idea she'd been so hungry and she ravenously inhaled the cheesy scramble he'd made.

He was watching her eat since he'd finished his breakfast in record speed.

"What?" she asked.

"I just like to watch you."

"Eat? You like to watch me eat?"

"That too." He leaned forward and stopped barely two inches away from her lips. "Gina, anyone ever tell you that you have a lovely mouth?"

She smiled, bridged the distance and kissed him. "I kinda like what yours does too, sailor."

He picked up her hand and kissed her palm tenderly. "You have plans for today, Gina?"

The question thrilled her. "Just what did you have in mind?"

"I'd like to buy you some sexy lingerie today." He studied her face without smiling. He was looking for something.

"Oh, my. No one has ever said that to me before." She could feel her cheeks blushing and his smile in response.

She allowed her eyes to widen. "I think I know what you have planned for this evening. That means I'll need a few things from my apartment."

"Good. I'll drop you off while I run a couple of errands. I'll meet you back there, say in another hour or so? Call me. I've got something I have to check out on base."

"What about the lingerie?"

"I'm glad you didn't forget. That will be the first thing we do after you call me and tell me you're ready."

"I'm ready now, sailor."

He smiled. "But I'm gonna enjoy the kind of ready you'll be after we've done our shopping. And I think you will be too."

She had to agree. "And then what?"

He fingered down the side of her face, tracing over her lips as he whispered, "I'm taking you straight home afterwards for a little show and tell."

Her panties got wet and her stomach lurched. She could have jumped him right there at the breakfast table, but he was right. The kind of ready she wanted to be was going to be enhanced by her struggle to be patient. The sexual play had already begun. Waiting and anticipating what was surely going to happen this afternoon was part of the game.

"Sounds like fun." She leaned forward and kissed him again. "Can I tie *you* up this time?"

"Sweetheart, you can do anything you like as long as it's with me."

CHAPTER 23

THE LONG, LINGERING kiss she gave Armando in the front seat of his Hummer caused a minor traffic jam in Gina's parking lot. The car immediately behind them honked. Neither one of them wanted to separate, but Gina moved first, grabbing the door handle and waving to the handsome SEAL behind the wheel.

"See you in an hour," she said as she blew him a kiss.

Armando drove away as the car behind them slowed and the driver, a young punk, rolled down the window and shouted, "Fuckin' get a room!" He sped off in a cloud of exhaust.

Before getting clothes inside her apartment, Gina decided she'd pick up a couple of things on her own, as a prelude for what she hoped would be a totally wonderful night. She stopped at her favorite food store and placed some cherries and strawberries, as well as a can of whipped cream, in her shopping cart. Didn't have to be a SEAL to know how to improvise. She knew he'd get a chuckle out of it.

She meandered through the aisle with the personal care items. She found some lubricating, warming gel and smiled. She had some pretty good ideas how this could be used.

Returning to her complex, the packages in one arm, she

unlocked her apartment door and was surprised to find Sam sitting in the corner of her living room. She nearly dropped her keys. He wasn't in his leathers, either, so this was a personal visit, not part of the job.

Straddling the doorway, she managed to keep the door ajar with her heel while she struggled to find words. Air was in short supply. Her mind started racing through her options. She could hardly speak, as words got stuck in her throat, but she pushed forward, trying to draw strength from the fact that Armando would be joining her in just a few minutes. She wanted to call him immediately, but didn't want to force Sam to make a move they'd both regret. He wore a dangerous expression. She worked to sound calm.

"Sam, how did you get in here?" she asked as she glanced down the hallway. No one was about. She twisted the deadbolt in the locked position, so when the door closed behind her it hit the extended bolt and remained slightly ajar.

"Showed my badge to your manager." He remained seated. He was not smiling.

Trying to act unaffected, Gina set her packages down in the kitchen, fingering her cell phone to make that 911 call. She pre-dialed the number but left the cell in her pocket as she entered the living room.

Sam was uncharacteristically quiet, and that worried her.

You can do this, Gina. Only call for backup if he comes after you. Her fingers touched the send button, but she did not push it. She'd try some diplomacy first.

"Don't you think that's a little creepy? I asked for your help. I didn't mean you could break into my apartment." She worked to take the urgency out of her voice, but wasn't sure it was working.

"Baby, I can protect you better if I'm around more often."

This was not what she wanted to hear. "No. You broke into my apartment. Let's tell the truth. I said I wanted your assistance but I don't need you doing this. Anything wrong with a phone call? I'll have to report this if you don't get out." She held up her phone and pressed the Send button. The phone began to ring the emergency dispatch.

"Suit yourself." He rose and carefully cracked his back and rolled his neck. He walked like he had a lead weight between his legs as he swaggered for the door. Gina closed her eyes and sighed. She spoke to his back as she heard the dispatcher's voice on the line. Sam could hear it as well.

"Sam, you gotta observe my boundaries or I'm taking you off the case."

Sam slowly turned, an evil grin on his face. "You, little Miss Hot Pants, taking *me* off the case? You don't have that kind of power."

"Nine-one-one. State your name and your emergency, please."

Sam ambled over to her and stood a foot away, showing his lack of concern for her 911 call. Gina chose to stand her ground and didn't flinch. She stuck her chin out, feeling righteous courage. He smiled as if he weren't afraid of any of her threats, or of the dispatcher's voice. "But if you had that kind of power, Gina, Lord knows how good that would feel."

"Please state your emergency."

She slapped his face and was going back a second time when he caught her wrist in midair. His riveting stare was deadly for a second, and then turned soft as he forced a smile. He released her arm and stepped back, giving her a long careful perusal up and down from her ankles to her neck. "You have a nice day, baby. Just wanted you to know I was checking up on you. This is dangerous business, sweetheart. Can't be too careful. Call me if you need anything."

"You'd be the *last* person I would call. Now get out."

Gina was relieved when the big cop turned and left. Her door attempted to close behind him. She undid the deadbolt and sighed as she pushed it securely closed and heard the reassuring click shut. She double latched the lock with shaking hands.

Then she remembered the emergency call. "I'm sorry, my friend's child hit the button by mistake," she said to the cell phone.

The dispatcher started to say something, but Gina quickly disconnected the emergency call. She hoped it wouldn't result in a required response by a patrolman.

Checking her phone, she realized she didn't have more than a couple of minutes left before she was to meet Armando. And she'd not called him yet.

Checking the street outside, she saw no evidence of Sam, but watched as Armando's Hummer pulled into the parking lot. He tweeted the beast locked and gave her a wave that helped ease some of her jitters. She checked the sides of the street, the bushes and around parked cars and still saw no evidence of Sam. She was going to have to tell Armando about Sam's visit.

Later.

She opened the door for him. The first thing she felt was the difference in the energy that wafted into the room. Armando gave her a gentle peck on the cheek and walked past her, into the apartment. He turned.

"Ready?"

"Not quite. I just have to get a couple of things."

Should I tell him about Sam? She watched him scan her apartment, as if making a mental recording of the way she lived.

If he only knew. Shame percolated in her chest. She had to stuff it down, along with her common sense and everything else that fried whenever she was around the SEAL. It was sad, in a way, but he was investigating the Gina that didn't exist. She didn't have any of her houseplants, her watercolors, or her sewing machine. That part of her was a complete stranger to this man.

I can't level with him yet. Soon. But not now.

"Well, I'm ready, Gina. You just going to stand there? Have you changed your mind?" he asked.

Gina stood like her feet were planted in the floor, unable to move. She watched him finger some of her hot sexy novels with the yummy male torso covers and then wiggled his eyebrows.

"These any good?" he asked.

She blushed and grabbed the book away from him. "Of course they're good. Why do you think I have them?"

He flashed her a smile. "Why don't you bring that one, and you can read it to me, tonight, okay?"

"That's silly. You don't want to read this stuff. It's for women."

"If it gets you all hot and bothered, I'm all for that." He handed her one book. "This one stays. I'll bet you could write something hot as hell."

"Why, you wanna give me pointers?" She hoped he heard the flirt in her voice.

"I'm good with that." He smiled. "Go get your stuff or you're leaving without anything."

She turned her back on him and entered her bedroom, stowing her purse with her gun and badge into a duffel bag. Then she added some panties, a new bra and a change of clothes. She tucked in a brush and walked across the hall and added some personal items, including condoms.

"Gina, I see you've been shopping," she heard from the kitchen. She also heard him shake the whipped cream and squirt out a little. Slinging her bag over her shoulder Gina walked to the living room, her excitement heightened. Armando stood in the archway of the kitchen, the tube of jelly in one hand and the can of whipped cream in the other. He had a smudge of whipped cream on his upper lip.

"Which one will it be? Hot or sweet?"

"I'll let you decide this time. I leave it all in your capable hands." She turned to exit. God, it felt great to know that his eyes were all over her ass.

THE *BOUDOIR DE PARIS* was busy this Saturday morning. The parking lot was nearly full to capacity.

The proprietress was Dori Harrelson, who'd retired the year before Gina joined the force. She'd opened the store along with one of her coworkers, a homicide detective who had recently gone through a very tough and publicly messy divorce.

The crusty ex-cop with the baritone voice recognized Gina and greeted her, handing her a wicker shopping basket, but stopped just short of saying her name, after taking a look at Armando. Gina was grateful Dori was so discreet.

Armando held her hand as he led Gina through the

aisles of pink and white lace-covered shelves.

He fingered a skimpy bra and panty set and held them up to her chest.

"You look good in pink."

She relished the spark in his brown eyes. His shoulder muscles rippled under his thin cotton T-shirt when he laid the panties down.

A fanciful display of masks adorned one wall. Below it was a display case filled with creams and lubrication gels. Again, Gina's cheeks began to flame. Armando slipped behind her, wrapping his arms around her waist, pulling her backside into the prominent bump in his pants and whispered in her ear, "I love to watch you blush. I'm going to make you blush all night long, sweetheart."

The kiss he planted on her neck sent a shiver down her spine.

I can hardly wait. "Maybe I should have bought two cans of whipped cream," she whispered in return, reaching behind her to rub her palm up against his erection.

"Maybe I won't let you leave."

She stiffened at first, and then turned to look deep into his eyes. He had no idea what he'd said. She started to tear up.

"What's wrong?"

She shook her head. Bravely, she looked up at him. "Nothing that a night of new things couldn't cure. I have a specific use in mind for that whipped cream, and I won't be stopped.

"Counting on it."

"I get to pick something you'll wear, okay?" she said.

Armando nodded. She found a black satin Zorro mask and held it up to his face. "This. This is you." She stepped close enough to touch her thighs to his, and slipped the elastic band around the back of his head. His brilliant smile offset the traces of curly hair around his temples and at the back of his neck. His face was obscured above the nose.

"Very sexy," she whispered.

He slid the mask up on the top of his head. "And now something for you." He picked a pink sequined fabric mask with jewels around the eye detail. "I think we should try these out to make sure they fit," he said.

He slid his mask down, leaned towards her face and their lips touched. The warmth of his flesh on hers as he slid back and forth over her mouth sent a tingle all the way to her toes. Armando's kisses were expert. She could only imagine how they would feel on her body if all she wore was the dainty pink mask.

They took turns picking up some warming gels, stimulating gels, feathers and flavored lubricants. He brought an expensive box of colored French condoms from behind the counter. Dori's grin as she set them on top made Gina blush. Again.

As Armando paid for their purchases, the door opened behind them and an unlikely couple walked inside.

"Clark, nice to see you two today," Dori said as she extended them a wicker basket. At the sound of the man's name, Armando turned abruptly.

"Detective, Daisy." Armando extended his hand but didn't look at Daisy.

Detective?

Riverton squinted as he searched between Armando and Gina's faces. "Armando, you were perhaps the last person I expected to see in here."

"Watch it," Dori called out. "Don't mess with my customers."

Gina could see Daisy was self-conscious about being ignored. The beautiful blonde woman with the enormous rack extended her hot pink polished fingers and whispered, "I'm Daisy."

Gina was focusing on the tension between Armando and the detective, but she politely shook Daisy's hand and smiled. "Nice to meet you too."

"I need a word with you sometime soon," Clark said.

"Honey, this is Detective Clark Riverton from the San Diego P.D. We worked on something together last year."

Gina shook Riverton's hand. The wizened old cop was no dummy. She wondered what he wanted with Armando. Something about the way he looked at her made her wary.

"Gina here has something perhaps you should know about, Clark." Armando was going to continue, but Gina cut him off.

"Armando?" Her scowl and frown worked.

"I apologize. It seems I stepped out of line for a second."

Gina wanted to get as far away from the detective as she could. Had he seen her before? She couldn't remember his face, so perhaps not. But as one of the few women on the force, she was probably more high profile. Worst of all, he probably knew Sam, and if he did, there was a good chance he'd know about her.

"I think we should be going," she nudged Armando. The pink and black striped plastic bag crinkled in her grip.

"Okay, Armani," Riverton chuckled, eyeing the bag. "Better let you get that stuff refrigerated."

Daisy slapped his arm. "Come on, Clark, leave them alone."

"Nice seeing you, nice meeting you too," Riverton said

as he nodded in Gina's direction. He extended his card to Armando, who examined it. "Give me a call, okay?"

Armando answered, "Sure thing. I'll call you Monday morning." He placed the card in his wallet.

"My cell is on there. Call me tomorrow, tonight if possible. Can you?"

"Not sure about tonight, Detective." He pulled Gina to his side. "But tomorrow works. Have a nice night. 'Night, Daisy," Armando added as he gave her a little wave with his fingers.

Outside, Gina was impatient for information. "Who is she?"

"Daisy? She's, well, she was Cooper's girlfriend for a bit. Before he met Libby."

Gina was noticing the difference between the two women. Daisy was covered in tats, tall, and had work done. The Libby she met yesterday at the housewarming was a classic beauty. Auburn-haired and with one-tenth the makeup Daisy wore. They were from two different worlds.

"I'm having a hard time seeing Cooper with Daisy. Cooper. The tall dude you introduced me to yesterday?"

"The very one. Nebraska born and bred."

She shook her head. Did Armando's tastes vary as much? Did these guys pick up girls depending on their mood swings? It worried her.

"Daisy is the one who does all our tats for Team 3. He showed her his forearm with the frog footprints extending from wrist to the inside of his elbow. "This is one of hers."

"Even the wives?"

Armando stopped. "Ah, no. Not the wives. They use someone else." He gave her a wise-ass smile.

"The wives have lots of tats?"

"Some do. Don't know one who hasn't had a couple, from what I could tell." He winked at her. "They do kid's names, occasionally something more serious."

"Like what?"

"Like the date he didn't come home."

She understood. She'd seen the wives of slain officers, the children who had to face a future without their father. She'd been to too many funerals in her short career.

"That breaks my heart," she said. "Does this happen often?"

"Often enough." Armando went off somewhere else. Gina could tell he wanted to change the subject. She was going to make another comment, but he added. "No, tats are mostly a guy's thing. Especially the newbie SEALs, the young ones. I've seen some crazy stuff. When they're young and first on the Teams, they don't have anything else to spend money on, so they get all painted up like a warrior. Just part of the culture, I guess. We get pretty inked up, but then you've already noticed that, haven't you?"

She gave him a coy smile. Indeed she had.

"It does seem like you wear a lot of ink, but then, I don't have much experience to compare it with."

"And that's a very good thing," he said as he wrapped his arm around her waist.

CHAPTER 24

SERGEANT KOZINSKI KNEW exactly who he wanted picked up based on the detailed account on Gina's CD. He spent most of Saturday filling out paperwork and lining up a grid showing who was responsible for what and whom they reported to. They'd had some undercover information before they'd decided to go after Carlos. What Gina provided were the strong ties that bound everything up in a bow.

He was surprised how clear Gina's recording was, how detailed, as well. That's why he was fairly sure there had been some foul play with Sam and the first audio recording. Gina was a smart cop, and a capable team player. Kozinski didn't think she'd be dumb enough to give him a blank recording.

So now he was acting on that information, not waiting for Monday. Of course, it was possible he wouldn't be able to get the arrests approved, but he knew he'd find someone to sign off on it, and he wouldn't stop trying until he got it. He felt time was of the essence.

The Scorpions had been involved in a skirmish at Babes on Friday night, and they'd arrested two of Carlos's minions who'd had a minor spat over one of the dancers. They were so smart with their operation, Kozinski thought, and yet they'd get themselves into trouble over a dancer. Sometimes the girl was helpful, especially if she had something to lose, like her probation. But most of these were young girls who cruised through town and were gone before his cops could profile them.

So part of his Saturday was finding a judge who would sign off on a search warrant. He had to gather together the manpower so several could be performed simultaneously. Each planned search had to have a backup in case no one was around or got complicated. And it always got complicated. But that's what Kozinski was good at: planning for the unforeseen to get the task done. It was important to catch them with goods of some kind: guns, drugs, illegals, or girls. For the best chance of conviction, he wanted to catch them in the act.

Tito, the youngest courier, who was all of twenty, was the most cooperative. He'd been Sam's snitch for nearly a year, and it had been helpful in building the case against the gang. Tito had been promised extra consideration when the sweep occurred. A very smart sister who was studying criminal law negotiated his situation. God bless her soul, she'd advised her brother to cooperate completely with the police hoping to keep her brother out of jail. He'd had some run-ins with the juvenile authorities, but nothing that would permanently taint his record like this. Even though under age, a stint in lockup would only introduce him to a more seasoned criminal element, she said. Tito had a fake ID that said he was twenty-five. The kid looked fifteen, and Kozinski knew he'd be one of the early casualties of war, if it came to that.

Tito told him that Carlos was doing a cruise up the coast and back with a couple of his lady friends and wouldn't be returning until Sunday late afternoon. That gave them just enough time to start picking up people Saturday and Sunday, and then meeting Carlos at the pier when he returned. The sergeant doubted Carlos would dock a two-million-dollar boat in just any pond. He'd have to come back to his berth in San Diego.

The warrants were issued and shortly afterwards they released Tito to the care of his sister. Kozinski had wanted to release him to Sam, but he hadn't been able to reach the man all afternoon. And with what he was beginning to suspect about Sam, it was probably better—no, safer—for Tito anyway. All Kozinski had to do now was wait for the phone calls to come in telling him how the teams were coming with the arrests.

Which is why it concerned him that Sam was nowhere to be found. Finally he got the call that the warrants had been executed.

Then he got three urgent calls and text messages from Sam and knew something was wrong. He agreed to meet the officer at Ducky's rather than the station, because it was closer. And, based on his suspicions, Kozinski felt he'd better have a few witnesses to this meeting with Sam.

He hoped Sam would get it together fast so Kozinski didn't have to fire the man. That was a bureaucratic nightmare, trying to get rid of someone who had been on the force nearly twenty years. He halfway hoped the man would retire before he learned the truth of Sam's involvement with some of the complaints he'd had from a couple of female staffers lately. And there was that one prostitute that claimed she was one of Sam's regulars, until she broke it off for "personal reasons." Kozinski wondered if Sam's wiring was starting to fry. He hoped he was wrong.

But his intuition was usually spot-on accurate. That intuition had saved his life a couple of times over his career. He wasn't going to abandon his hunches just yet. Certainly not just so he wouldn't have to do something tough like put an officer out to pasture. When it came to right and wrong, the public was to be protected at all costs.

The squealing espresso-maker startled him. He took another sip of his plain coffee and prepared himself for the meeting. He slowed his breathing and settled his nerves.

Sam appeared in the doorway and Kozinski was shocked to see the normally well-groomed officer looking so disheveled. He had a day-old beard, and his hair looked like it had been run through with his fingers instead of a comb. His brown kaki shirt was wrinkled and dotted with several grease stains from a meal.

But his eyes were what worried the sergeant the most. He had a distinctive alcoholic red ring around both eyes, and his lids were puffy, reacting to the allergy that booze definitely was for him. The shit-eating smirk Sam wore tore at Kozinski's heartstrings. Nothing worse than seeing a man going through a breakdown and having the man know you've seen it. No amount of covering up could hide that fact. Both of them had seen enough of it to know what was going on.

But Kozinski decided to pretend anyway. "You look like shit. Whose couch did you sleep on last night, or did you try to make up to the Mrs.?" He decided bringing up something they both acknowledged as painful would be a helpful start to some truth talking.

Sam chuckled. His belly was flabby and his breathing labored "That woman's already got a bedmate. Didn't take her long at all. Another cop, can you believe it?"

"Where?"

"Not here, thank God."

"So then, what is it that you need to talk to me about so urgently?"

"I'm worried about Gina."

You dumb fucker. You honestly believe I'd fall for that?

"Well then, I'm worried about you," Kozinski answered. "I asked that you two bury the hatchet. She's done some really good police work, Sam. I'm kinda proud of her, taking on this job with no real experience."

"So you can make your female quotas?"

"That was originally part of the decision, of course. But she's earning her stripes, Sam. The girl is solid. Gotta give her credit where credit is due."

The sergeant could see it hit Sam right in the chest like it had been a .45 at point-blank range. The surprise in Sam's face was replaced with deep lines showing hatred as he plastered on a crazy-assed smile of pure evil. Now Kozinski was worried for his own welfare and wondered about the safety of the public. He'd have to do something about this. Today. Things had deteriorated too far.

"Mia doesn't trust her anymore. Doesn't consider her a friend, either. Decided to screw the brother instead of doing her job, sir. She's more or less AWOL."

"And you know this how?"

"I've stepped in to help clean this shit up. I've gotten friendly with Mia Guzman and she's been telling me things about Gina...kinky things you wouldn't want to know. Like how she wanted to do a threesome with her and her brother. Can you believe that?"

Kozinski leaned back and took another sip of coffee. Evaluation was always better than leaping to a response. The story didn't add up. And Kozinski knew that meant that part of the story was Sam's and not Gina's.

"And if Mia were here, she'd tell me the same thing?"

"Of course not, sir. But I'm warning you, sir, things aren't what they seem. She's not right in the head."

Someone's not right in the head, Sam. I think it's you.

"Sam, I think this operation is nearly concluded for now. We're taking steps. In the meantime, why don't you just stay away from Gina? Take a couple of days off, and then we'll talk, say, Tuesday or Wednesday. You've been working hard, pushing this thing from the beginning, and I think it's time to sit back and enjoy the fruits of your labor."

"No, sir, I want to see this thing through to the end."

"You got a fishing cabin somewhere you can head to for a couple of days?"

"Nope."

"Take a day or two in Mexico, then. Just get out of town and clear your head."

Sam returned a murderous stare. He got the message. He was being taken off the case. "You can't do this to me, sir."

"Sam, it's already done. You've been part of what I hope will be a very satisfactory operation. You and Gina did the dangerous part, the cooking over the flame. We get to do the cleanup."

"You're making arrests?"

Kozinski decided not to tell him everything, so, he nodded. "Yup. Starting Monday," he lied. "Then you can come back Tuesday or Wednesday, and we'll start helping the DA put together their case against Carlos and all those scumbags."

Sam's face clouded in darkness. "How? The bookkeeper's information helped you that much?"

"Yes. It was very helpful, Sam. That and the things Gina gave us. I think we have enough to put these guys behind bars for a long time. We'll need your help doing that, with your snitches, of course."

Kozinski could see the realization dawn on Sam that Gina had somehow given the sergeant details contained in the recording Sam had erased. And now the erasure was becoming a red flag.

Come on, Sam. Give it up. He hoped the man could. Then maybe all this could just go away.

Not that it was likely.

CHAPTER 25

A RMANDO PARKED IN his garage. She waited while he came around to her side of the Hummer before she emerged, opening the door further, helping her with a firm hand in hers. The pink and black plastic bag containing their sexual goodies made a rustling noise as she transferred it from the floor to his other hand. He laced his fingers through hers while he led her to the rear entrance of his bungalow, her overnight bag tossed over his shoulder. They passed by a bright, azure blue pool and grounds meticulously maintained.

With gentle hands on her shoulders, he dropped her bag, positioned her against the rear door and stood behind, pressing himself and his arousal to the back of her legs, holding her still so he could rub himself against her. He kissed the top of her spine and she began to see stars. Everywhere he touched her she ached for more.

Stepping back, he unlocked the door and showed her inside the kitchen area. She almost forgot her bag on the doorstep, but dumped it just inside. They stood before each other, both of them breathing heavily. She took stock of the man she was about to have sex with, knowing she would miss him with all her heart afterwards if this was the last time.

Am I up for this? She hoped to God her heart would forgive her.

Armando stepped toward her, hands to her face, in a gentle pull until their lips met. She felt savored.

"I'm going to take it real slow, okay?"

"Yes," was all she could manage to say before his mouth fully claimed hers.

He whispered in her ear, "Baby, I'm not going to do anything you don't want to do, okay?"

She nodded as he nuzzled her neck. "You tell me to stop, and I'll stop. Be honest with me. No more secrets, okay? If it doesn't feel good, you just say the word and we end it."

She pulled away, holding his head between her palms. The little crescent-shaped scar under one eye and the pulsing vein in his beautifully tanned forehead reminded her of how fragile life was. How she needed to seize the moment and take what she could. She gently leaned against the solid wall that was his chest, filled the space between her legs with the bulge in his pants, traced his lips with her thumbs and knew, without a shadow of a doubt, that she could give this man everything.

"I trust you," she whispered.

"And I trust you," he repeated.

She had to look away. But damn if he didn't tilt her chin up towards the ceiling, "Hey, like I said, we'll take it slow," he murmured against her neck.

She whimpered inside. He obviously thought it was her fears about the sexual play she was hiding from.

Armando's cell phone rang. "Damn." He examined the screen and swore in Spanish. "It's Mia."

Gina could hear Mia's frantic voice on the other end of the line. Then the unmistakable sounds of Carlos's clipped Spanish.

"You fucking hurt her and you're a dead man," Armando screamed into the phone as he stepped back from Gina. He paced across the kitchen, giving orders in Spanish, swearing and tugging at his hair with his left hand.

"I don't care anything about that. You don't lay a hand on her, hear me?"

The line went dead. Armando looked like he was going to throw the phone at the wall, but thought better of it. Gina could see there was a deadly cat and mouse game going on.

"Tell me," she begged. "I might be able to help."

"No. You don't want me involved in your stuff. You can't get involved in this."

"Armando, I'm—" she almost told him. "I'm so sorry, but you need to call the cops. They need to get involved right away. I have connections who might be willing to help."

Armando looked at her as if she had three green heads. "Cops? Thought you didn't like cops."

The phone rang again before she could answer. He listened and then searched the kitchen for a tablet and pencil. He wrote down an address. Without looking up at her, he added, "I'll be there in a half hour to forty minutes."

He stood up straight and eyed her. "I guess our little party will have to wait." His expression was flat and intent. He was not the same sex machine she had held in her arms just a few minutes before. His focus was on a mission, and she could see there wasn't anything she could do to deflect him.

Gina realized that was what was different about the two

of them. He had a mission in life. Nothing in the world would keep him from achieving it.

And she? She had a vision of a life that could have been. If she'd not been a cop. If she'd never lied to him about the reasons for her involvement with his sister. If she'd only had the strength to just stay away in the first place. Because, unlike him, she lived in a fantasy world, playing a part, acting tougher than she really was, pretending she was whole enough to be loved fully.

And he was the real deal.

"I'm going to take you back to your place, and then I'm going to be gone for a while. I'm not sure when I'll be back." He handed her the bag she had so quickly packed and had expected to use tonight.

"Don't do this, Armando," she said as she slung the bag over her shoulder.

"You think I can just sit back and let them take Mia?"

"It's a trap."

"I know it's a fuckin' trap, Gina. I'm not a kindergartener." His irritation sent a spear through her chest. "I gotta get out of here."

"I can stay here, wait for you."

"No baby," at last he softened. "I can't have you here alone. God knows what's going to go down, and I got stuff here you don't want to know about. Besides, I'm not allowed."

He raced down the hallway to the back bedroom. *His* room. He spoke to someone on the phone, then heard doors opening and knew the unmistakable sounds of equipment being stowed in zipped duty bags. The familiar mechanical clicks and noises she'd heard during her training told her he was loading up ammunition, checking gear created to cause deadly harm. And he was comfortable with it.

She looked down at the little bag of goodies and thought about their precious night of lovemaking now lost. She set them on the kitchen table and waited by the back door. Armando rounded the corner, his shoulders filled with straps from three large black nylon bags. Without saying a word he opened the back door and allowed her to walk through first, then locked it behind them.

The inviting pool and yard looked out of place now. Today someone was in danger. The seedy underbelly of what was a picture-perfect Hollywood scene was creeping in and infecting the day.

He checked the length of the driveway first before crossing it to open up the back of his Hummer. He began stowing the bags and rearranging things while Gina let herself into the passenger side and waited. Soon Armando joined her and abruptly sped backwards out of the driveway onto the street.

This would have been a good time to tell him, she thought. But it might cloud his focus. She doubted he'd do anything stupid, not that having a truck illegally full of God knows what wasn't already stupid. She couldn't have stopped him. But she could make the call and have him arrested. And then he'd hate her even more and just go about doing whatever he had set out to do in the first place. And double that if anything happened to Mia.

She knew that coordinating a rescue would take time, time they did not have. Armando just might have a better chance of pulling it off. She hated to admit it, but she had more faith in his abilities than those of her own department. It wasn't supposed to be that way. But the reality of it was, she did trust him more than she trusted the men and women in the Department.

"You didn't hear or see anything. If stuff happens, you weren't here, Gina."

There he was again, worrying about her, what impact this would have on her.

"So, where are they holding her?" She thought maybe she might get lucky.

"I don't know, some boat."

"That would be Carlos's yacht. Not a very safe place, Armando."

"You know about his boat?"

"I've been on it," Gina said and immediately saw the sadness in his eyes.

"More secrets, Gina? What else aren't you telling me?"

"Don't do this, Armando. I think it's a sting. I think the cops are onto him. I don't want you caught in the crossfire."

"I'm not afraid of crossfire. Hell, I'm prepared for that. I'm gonna have help. And I'll be damned if I'm going to let someone else rescue my sister and botch it up."

"Please slow down for a second or two; I'll tell you something about all of this. Just calm down."

"Baby, later. Then you can explain everything to me. And this time, Gina, I want the full truth. No bullshit. You're somehow involved. Are the cops looking for you too?"

"Yes." She had to lie.

"You know anything about Mia being taken?"

"Absolutely no, Armando. I would never be involved in that." She tried to place a hand on his shoulder, was going to move it up to his cheek. Armando angrily brushed her away.

"You were the decoy," he said bitterly "They sent you to distract me so I'd take my eye off the ball. All this talk about

Sam and an insurance company and shit. You're probably working for Sam."

"No Armando. Please, believe me. I'm a—"

Armando's phone chirped before she could finish. He started swearing in Spanish as he swerved to avoid crashing into traffic and jumped up on the curb taking a right turn. He stayed on the phone, shouting instructions in Spanish, but they made it back to her place in record time anyway. She barely had a chance to say her goodbyes before he streamed out of the parking lot and went barreling down the street. Standing in the late afternoon sun with her bag still slung over her shoulder, loneliness descended all around her. Perhaps this would be the last time she'd see him alive.

And she hadn't even told him the truth. She hoped the God Mrs. Guzman prayed to was listening.

Bring him back safe, sir. He's the real deal.

CHAPTER 26

S AM HAD SPENT the entire afternoon thinking about what it would feel like to have Gina all to himself again. He watched some of his home movies taken from the very bed he was lying on. The CDs, along with this bed and the building were the only things he got from his divorce. He'd lost the house and everything else, not that any of it had any meaning to him.

He fingered the pillow he'd used to prop up her little ass so he could kiss it, ram himself so tight up her little sex that she groaned. He told himself it was pleasure, but this was the last one, the time when she insisted she be let go. He told her he'd be gentle, that this would be a goodbye fuck, and she acquiesced. But then he got rough again. He couldn't help it. And in the end, she just lay there and let him finish. She couldn't stop crying afterwards. She wouldn't let him take her home. He knew he'd lost her that night.

He studied the sheet-rocked walls of the rundown, abandoned duplex he called home. He'd purchased it in foreclosure a year ago when he and Gina were dating. He'd wanted some special renovations, but they broke up before he could take her there.

As far as living arrangements, he didn't need much, just

a bedroom with heat, an efficiency kitchen with a hot plate and microwave, and a decent bathroom. He'd been able to upgrade his unit in one long weekend. He had plans for the other side, too, but everything was on hold now.

After the breakup, he thought maybe if he and Gina worked together, some of the chemistry would come back. He stopped calling her and tried to move on. But no one was like Gina.

He didn't want to share her with anyone, even guys on the force who casually knew her. He didn't want her too close to Kozinski. He didn't want anyone stealing a look, catching one of her smiles, or smelling her perfume. It all belonged to him. It was all he wanted, and he'd pay any price for it.

So when she got sweet on the SEAL, something flipped in Sam's mind. He walked through a doorway of no return, a place of desperation. Suddenly, his obsession with her turned into *he couldn't live without her*.

Tito had let him know about the sweep going on and how successful the task force had been. He knew it was only a matter of time before the operation was called and everyone would go their separate ways. He also knew Gina would make complaints about him and he was facing a dishonorable end to his career.

He tried not to think about it. If he could reason with her, love her in the manner that which he knew she needed, she'd see the folly of her ways. She'd see that he could save her in every way she needed saving. If she felt the power of him inside her, could see how good they were together, then maybe there would be a happy ending.

He didn't want to kill her. He wanted her to surrender to him. Tell him she'd been wrong and he was right. He was the right man for her. He needed to hear that.

Tito had been released and Sam knew right where to find him. Although he wasn't supposed to, he found him at one of their cribs in an abandoned house covered in graffiti. On any other day, Sam would have brought backup, but today he felt like absolute Teflon. He kicked in the front door with his boot and chambered his shotgun.

"Nobody move."

People started scrambling out the doors and windows anyway. Glass broke. Chairs were overturned. Sam scanned the darkened room filled with marijuana smoke and found Tito in the corner, passed out with a needle in his arm.

No one was going to challenge him. He figured with so many of their leadership down at the station, there wasn't anyone in charge. Everyone he'd seen looked to be under-age.

Three quick strides across the room brought him to Tito's feet. Sam grabbed him by the front of his shirt and Tito shook like a rubber chicken, his head lolling back and his mouth drooling something white and foamy.

Sam thought perhaps he was OD'ing. But Tito opened his eyes, at first lazy and glazed over, then full of panic as he recognized the big cop.

He reached down and picked up Tito's kit, tossing the needle. He threw the boy over his shoulder, carrying the shotgun and kit in his right hand. Again, no one challenged him as he made his way back to the pickup truck on the street.

Tito slung against the side of the passenger door in a semi-coma as Sam started the engine.

"You fuckin' piece of shit," Sam spewed.

Tito responded with a warm smile. Sam had an EpiPen

in the first aid kit he carried in the back of his truck, and damn, he was going to use it on the kid. He needed him to play one more part, and then to hell with him.

TITO LOOKED LIKE a zombie in a bad movie, Sam thought. Almost too scary to take him to the pancake house, but the kid was hungry, and Sam needed him to stay awake, while not looking too jittery. So he let Tito order anything he wanted. Sam had lost his appetite.

From the red vinyl booth, syrupy sweet music happily playing in the background, Sam dialed Gina. He wondered if she'd pick up. He had a Plan B if not. But she did.

"Hello?" She sounded groggy.

"You turn in early?"

"It's not early. It's after eight."

"Only time we went to bed that early was to fuck ourselves to death," Sam said. Tito looked up from his pancakes, and smiled as syrup spilled from his mouth onto his shirt.

"Sam, the only reason I picked up this phone was because I hoped you'd seen the light. Everything'll be over in a day or two. You know I'm going to tell Kozinski what went down."

"Well, he's kind of busy right now. Don't know if you've heard, but they've been making sweeps. Got a ton of guys."

"Good. I thought they were going in on Monday."

"That's what he told me too. Seems we've both been left out, for some reason."

She didn't say anything.

"One thing I thought you might want to know, they can't find Mia."

"Well, I'd expect she'd be smart enough to lay low."

"You didn't tip her off, did you?"

"Hell no. I wouldn't do that. You know me, Sam."

He rubbed the front of his pants under the table. Tito looked at him with a scowl. "Yes I do, Gina."

"So that's it? Mia's missing?"

"And we know where she is. She's with Carlos. I got little Tito here, one of Carlos's runners. You remember, the kid who rolled on him?"

Tito frowned and stopped eating. Sam knew he was considering bolting from the booth. Sam put his boot into the kid's crotch and glared at him. He placed his right hand over his weapon.

Tito was going to stay put, for now.

"So, where is she?"

"She told Tito to get you. She's in a building down past Seaside. He's going to take you to her. I think she can convince Carlos to give himself up. You want in on that?"

Gina hesitated. He could tell she knew something. "Sure I do," she said. "But I thought Carlos was on his boat."

"Where did you get that information?"

"I thought that's where Koz and the team were expecting to make the arrest."

Sam knew she was lying.

"Well, we got lucky. We have the better intel. Tito lied to the sergeant."

Tito's didn't look at either of them.

"Kozinski doesn't know about this? Gina asked. "Don't you think we should call him?"

"You want the whole fucking task force there?"

"If it's Carlos, we'll need backup."

"So listen, I'm going to be your backup. Tito will take you to the location and I'll follow behind. Don't want them to see me. But they trust you, so you want this?"

"Why can't you just give me the address, we can call it in?"

"Because Tito won't give it to me, and he's the assurance you're coming."

WITH THE TRAP set, Sam watched as his plan went off without a hitch. He dropped Tito off at Gina's apartment complex, and watched him stand under a streetlight until she came down. The two of them took off. Sam had stashed a thousand dollars on the kid, and told him there would be another after they got to the duplex, so he was fairly sure the kid would cooperate.

He followed Gina's car to the building. From the outside, it still looked abandoned, the lot covered in weeds that stood four feet tall. Next door was a brick warehouse that was also abandoned and had all the windows shot out of it. He was thrilled to be able to bring her home at last.

Tito unlocked the door, just as Sam had instructed him, and they both went inside. That was Sam's cue to go around back to the door bordering the back alleyway. He slipped into the cool cavern and waited for his eyes to adjust to the dark. He heard them talking on the other side of the building.

"I dunno. He said to just wait here," he heard Tito say.

"He? Wasn't it Mia you talked to?"

"Oh, yes, ma'am. Sorry."

"How did Mia know to get hold of you?"

"I guess it was through Carlos. Tell you the truth, I'm just the messenger. As soon as this is over, I'm outta here."

"So I guess Carlos doesn't know you gave him up?"

"Shhh. Careful about that. Don't want him finding out

before it's time. I didn't give him up. I told the cops he was on a cruise, like he told my sister to tell me. I told them he'd be back Monday. He told her that too."

"So he came back early," Gina said.

Tito chuckled. "The fucker never left."

Sam came up behind where Gina stood and with one arm placed a flannel scrap laced with chloroform cocktail across her mouth and nose. At first she stiffened, but then as she inhaled the gas, went slowly limp and stopped struggling.

"Holy shit," Tito's hands were splayed out to the sides, waist-high.

"Shut up and help me," Sam commanded. He could see Tito hesitate. "You do want the other grand, or are you good with just one?"

Tito didn't say anything, but started to pick up Gina's feet.

"No, asshole, come over here and get her shoulders. I'll take her feet." Sam wanted to make sure a generous portion of Gina's skin cells and hair landed on Tito's clothes. Her drool ran down her chin, and over the boy's wrist. The boy didn't notice Sam had work gloves on.

He directed them to the bedroom with the black satin comforter. Tito had to kneel on the bed to get her properly laid out on a pillow. Sam took her shoes off and cuffed her ankles to the lower lip of the bedframe. He pushed Tito aside and cuffed her wrists to the headboard.

"Okay, wow. What are you going to do with her, man?"

Sam stood up and arched his back, cracking it. He gave a wink to the kid and got the reaction he expected. "Nothing she doesn't want done."

"Is Carlos coming over?"

"Fuck Carlos," Sam said.

"But I thought you said he had set all this up for you."

"He did, he did. He just doesn't know it yet." Sam was grateful the kid had been an easy target. "Come on," he said as he tugged on the back of the kid's head, "let's get you your money."

They closed the door, which locked from the outside. Tito didn't notice. He also didn't notice Sam had removed his gloves.

"So what are you going to do with your earnings?" Sam was placing the silencer on the barrel of his .38 while he walked behind Tito. The kid didn't have a clue.

"Shit, I gotta get out of Dodge. Probably Mexico to stay with my cousin."

"That sounds like a plan." Sam reached around as if to give the kid a hug, but slammed the barrel of the silencer against his temple and pulled the trigger. Tito's head exploded all over both of them.

Sam had to wait for all the blood and brains to stop falling around him, and to let the pieces of Tito fall off his clothes. He cleaned his eyes with the back of his forearm, and looked at the detritus that had been the kid.

"You did good, kid. Sorry it turned out this way." He leaned forward and searched Tito's shirt, finding the packet of money still in the bank envelope. It mattered little to Sam if it was all there.

CHAPTER 27

ARMANDO HAD GROUND his teeth so hard his jaw hurt.
Showdown at the harbor.

He stopped by Fredo's apartment picked up Fredo and
Rory. They threw their bags in the back, Fredo taking
shotgun.

"I did tell Kyle," Fredo began, "and man, was he pissed."

"That was dumb, Fredo."

"He reminded me how dumb you are all the time about
Mia. I'm here, my good friend and brother, to watch over
you. I'm your guardian angel."

"Like hell you are. You just complicated things."

"Oh, like Mr. Armani, Super Stud, things aren't complicated enough now?" Rory chimed in "You got a thing about
this gang? This some form of payback?"

The Scorpions had kidnapped Mia over a year ago and
Armando fell into that trap too. Kyle, Cooper, Fredo and
Gunny rescued them.

"You going for a repeat, Armani?" Fredo asked.

"I don't care. Mia's in trouble, and that's just what I do."

Yes there were some similarities, he thought. He'd gotten the call from Caesar the last time. And yes, that one
really did take him by surprise, but then, the gang was after

guns and the guns they mistakenly thought the SEALs would steal for them. They were really stupid to think such a thing. But they'd used Mia as bait, which was a big mistake on their part.

"This time I'm pretty sure Carlos wants a deal."

"What makes you say that?"

"Because he told me Mia was his insurance policy. He promised he wouldn't hurt her."

"Right. And you believed this scumbag? I'm telling you, Armando, you've got your head all twisted. That lady friend of Mia's got you all thinking with your *little* brain." Fredo shook his head in disgust.

"She has nothing to do with it. Besides, it's not little."

"Like hell. It's just too much of a coincidence," Fredo added, ignoring Armando's retort. "I didn't know better I'd think you went all tofu and shit on me, like Cooper did last year. That stuff will rot your brain." Fredo turned to Rory in the back seat. "You know what they make tofu out of? Fermented soy beans, man. They can't even get cattle to eat that shit."

Rory shared Fredo's laughter. Then Armando drilled a glare at him from the rear view mirror. Rory got serious in a hurry. "So, what's the plan, Armani?"

"We go there and I reason with him. I got my Invisio."

"I feel you. So Rory and I sit in the truck and jack off, right?"

"No, if need be, you save the day. But I think the guy is going to be reasonable. Something just isn't adding up right. Piece of the puzzle missing, and I'm going to find out about it. If I fail, you guys will be my seconds. And if you don't want to do it," he pulled over to the curb abruptly, screeched on the brakes, coming to a complete stop, "you get out right here."

Fredo and Rory shared a look.

"Fuckin' nothing better to do on a Saturday night," Fredo mumbled.

"I had a date," Rory said cheerfully. Fredo began to swear.

"So which is it?" Armando asked.

"Well, it's too far to walk back to my truck, so hell, I'm in," Fredo barked. "You gotta be so cryptic all the time? We're halfway there and now you tell us what you have in mind?"

"I'm in, too. But I don't like carrying," Rory said.

"I'm not thinking you'll have to use it."

Rory shrugged and rolled his eyes. "That's the point. We're not supposed to." Armando pulled out into traffic again and sped to the turnoff at the harbor.

"He said it was the Corazon, berth 29." Fredo scanned the nearly abandoned parking lot. One lone light illuminated the asphalt. Ahead lay a sea of twinkle lights decorating the masts of the yachts in spacious rows. A party boat was in full swing out on the bay, but the music carried for miles.

"These guys use sentries, and they probably already know we're here."

Fredo got out the sensitive earphones and the radio kit while Armando inserted his earpiece. "Testing. Testing. Testing," he whispered. Fredo gave him the thumbs up.

"For the record, we're not taping, right?" Fredo asked.

"That's right. The word is Huckleberry."

Fredo gave another thumbs up.

"Rory, you wait a minute, then drop behind me and find some cover on the ledge of that little shop."

Armando closed the driver door quietly, and climbed

into his wetsuit. His night vision goggles were useless around all these lights, so he shoved them up above his forehead for now. Then he softly jogged down the pier without making a sound, counting down to berth 29 and stopping.

At least four guards with semis were alertly pacing back and forth on deck. The cabin was well lit, and when he squinted he could see Mia's form sitting on a white leather couch. Good thing he was lurking in the shadows, out of sight of those sentries.

"We got four and packing heavy," Armando whispered. "She doesn't look in any distress." He noticed Carlos had handed her a drink, and his sister actually smiled.

"I'm up at your two o'clock," Armando heard Rory whisper.

"I'm going for a swim." Armando slipped off his bag and removed his shoes, then slipped without a sound into the murky waters of the inlet behind the taller vessel where Rory was lookout.

He swam to the rear of the ship where no one was posted, grateful for the moonlight guiding him. He mounted the rear stairs and again waited for the roll of the ship to camouflage his movements. "She actually looks good. My little saucy sister is in prime form and dressed to the nines," he whispered, knowing Fredo would appreciate that comment.

He came upon the galley door behind the living room and turned the handle slowly. It was unlocked.

Stepping inside the dark kitchen, he spotted Carlos and Mia sitting on opposing couches. Armando advanced into the room quickly, unhooking his sidearm and aiming it at Carlos's forehead. The red laser pointed right between the gangster's eyes.

"Call them off. I want to hear four splashes, and then I want to see them right here," he pointed to the floor, "on their bellies."

Carlos gave a knowing smirk. "Very good, Armani. The element of surprise."

"Shut the fuck up and tell them."

Carlos began to move toward Mia.

"Don't even think about it...unless you can live with a round between your eyebrows."

"I like your style, Armani." Carlos whistled and told the men to toss their AK-47s overboard.

Before Armando could demand it, Carlos added, "And the pistolas. Then get your asses here on the floor."

One by one the four men entered the cabin and lay prone on the floor. Armando dropped some zip ties at Mia's feet and she quickly secured their wrists. The red bead on Carlos' forehead was beginning to look like a third eye, Armando thought. "My man," Carlos said as he slowly walked forward, "so now we talk."

"I'm not your man, and you know it," Armando answered. "Stop! Right there."

Carlos obeyed.

"Okay I understand. We don't really like each other, but then, I don't like most the people I work with either."

"So where are your other minions?"

"Well, that's partly why I wanted to meet. Are you aware of what's going on around here this evening?"

Armando wasn't sure what he was talking about. "Kids are going to football games, getting laid, taking drugs, people are working."

"That's good. My upbringing was something a little different than that, but that's good. Well, some of those people who are working are interfering with *my* work."

"And that's news?"

"I mean, as we speak, members of my—you'd call them teammates—are being arrested, based on information a certain little lady friend of yours provided them."

"She's a cop, Armando," Mia blurted out.

"Who?"

"Your little bitch. She's an undercover cop."

Armando felt the fire in his belly grow to a roar. He halfway wanted to kill Carlos just because he delivered the message. But he knew that was wrong. Besides, it wasn't Carlos he was angry at.

So that began to explain things. Slowly it began to take shape.

"Gina is a cop?" he repeated in a monotone.

"Yessir, Mr. Armani. And her lover is one, too. That big Sam fella. They been doing the nasty for mostly a year or more now. They're quite the team."

Armando loved his sister, but she was enjoying this way too much. "You knew this?" he asked her.

"Armando, who do you think I am?" Mia's horrified expression wiped away the smirk he hated. "If I knew that, you think I'd have hung around her? You think I'm completely nuts?"

So she'd lied to him. Lied to him all along. Well, he'd deal with that one later. Right now there was the problem of what to do about Carlos.

Carlos continued. "Imagine my surprise when I am out on my little boat, and I get this call, telling me the cops was all over my stuff, and they had a list of some ten names of people they was picking up. You know who else was on that list?"

No.

"That's right, your little bitch was going to have Mia arrested, too, as accessory."

That was the last straw. He'd been a fuckin' idiot, buying her fears and helping her with her stuff. It was all a smokescreen. She'd betrayed him just like interpreters and shopkeepers in Afghanistan had betrayed them. She had a lot of nerve pretending to fall for him and all the while planning his own sister's demise. Nobody got away with harming his family. Rage exploded in his veins.

"So what's the plan?" He knew Fredo would cough at that one. He was grateful he still had the presence of mind to think straight. Fury was way more comfortable to him. Didn't matter that he recognized it as a sign he needed help. It felt good to get angry, because it was some kind of solution he could effect. He was glad he hadn't brought anything but a handgun to this meeting.

"She played you real good, Armando. I told you to be careful. But I didn't know how bad it was."

But then he found a shred of sanity and perspective. Gina had been good at her job. Sucked, but it was what she was *supposed* to do. He knew there was something off, just couldn't pinpoint it, but now it all made sense. And weren't the cops supposed to be the good guys? It still didn't make him feel any better, knowing he'd been used in this manner.

What began to really eat a hole in his gut, though, was her relationship with Sam. Was that all a ruse as well?

"How'd you get this information, Carlos?" he asked.

"I got friends too."

"Like Sam?"

Carlos reacted with a string of Spanish slang. "He's a

crazy man. No way you can trust a crazy man."

"And yet Gina apparently does," he said.

Mia stepped toward him. "Armando, I think she used him too. She doesn't like the dude. Besides, he's a little rough."

Finally something was familiar, some truth was beginning to come out.

"Sam's on Sam's team. He'd never be a player on mine," Carlos said, his eyes forming slits. "Your bitch better be careful. She's playing with some serious shit with that one."

Carlos was right. If half of what they revealed to him was accurate, Gina herself might be in some danger. Danger perhaps she was trying to keep from him. Is that what she meant when she asked him not to get involved?

"So now what do we do?" Armando asked.

"I need safe passage to Mexico. You let me go this evening. I sail away to Mexico until all this blows over. Mia can go home with you. It's like a favor for a favor. You get to deal with the bitch and her master when you get back."

"But that would be breaking the law."

"You're breakin' the law by packing."

"Considering your line of work and where this meeting is taking place, I consider it an act of self-preservation."

"Look, Armando, be reasonable," Carlos took Mia by the shoulders and stood directly behind her. It wasn't lost on Armando that Mia was his shield in every sense of the word. "I'm just looking for the opportunity to lay low for a while, recoup. Lick my wounds. You do me a favor, I do you a favor by giving your sister back. Nobody gets hurt."

Mia wrinkled up her nose and tried to get away from him, but Carlos held her about the waist and put a gun to her temple.

"You starting to feel me?"

"Why you Huckleberry asshole. You'll never make it out alive if you harm one hair on her—"

"Get your fuckin hands off her," came Fredo's voice. Carlos was staring into the barrel of an H&K MP5. The startle effect gave Armando enough time to nudge Mia's knees, forcing her to fall forward and collapse out of the way. He grabbed Carlos's gun. Rory was there in seconds securing Carlos's wrists and ankles in zip ties.

Fredo laid his weapon down carefully as he ran over to Mia, who was rubbing her knees, which were slightly bloody. She glared at her brother.

Sirens and lights flashed. He'd have to stay and give statements. It was too late for him to get Mia away, but she was safe.

As the patrol cars began to descend on the pier, Armando wondered which vehicle Gina was in. Would she take point and come in first? Or wait and show up sheepishly at the end after all the arrests had been made?

As he watched the SDPD officers bathed in the blue and red flashing lights, he couldn't make out Gina's face anywhere in the crowd of uniforms. Nor Sam's. He started getting a worried feeling in his gut. He didn't think of her as a coward and was sure she'd be present for this crowning moment.

He saw the police sergeant in charge coming towards him and Armando decided to make a quick call to Riverton. He needed someone to help cut him loose, and fast.

CHAPTER 28

KOZINSKI SWORE AND threw his cell on the couch in the living room, where he'd spent the night. Again. He was getting updates on their progress. So far, they'd arrested seventeen of Carlos's gang, including some young teenagers who would be delivered to juvenile detention after they got a good look at the jail, where they'd most likely end up if they didn't straighten themselves out. That was always Kozinski's rule, get the younger ones scared so they'd keep to the straight and narrow. Less than 10% ever did, but still.

They'd found a cache of weapons loaded on a semi destined for Mexico. Used to be they would arrest people with vans or station wagons. Now it was semis full of guns and ammo.

Lord help us. He hoped this country lasted long enough that he could see his grandchildren get married and start to have a life of their own. Some days, it seemed as if the bad guys had more firepower and more informants than the S.D.P.D. did.

They'd also found two stashes of drugs and a packaging facility nearby. Was supposed to be a soap plant, making scented bath salts, which was smart, since it partly threw off the dogs, who'd been trained to be so scent sensitive.

He'd just learned that Carlos had slipped away. The man had shown himself at one gun cache, and then slipped into the night like a bat. So much for Tito's intelligence, and Kozinski had a mind to arrest the sister, too, since he was fairly sure she might have been in on the smokescreen.

Nah, you're being too negative, Koz. His therapist wanted him to stop doing the trash self-talk. The tapes weren't working, either. A dumb decision was still a dumb decision, regardless of what you told yourself afterwards.

So there was someone who was feeding information to the gang. He'd been careful not to reveal anything to Sam, and thus he was pretty sure it wasn't him. Sam had been one of his best cops before his steady deterioration into risky behavior. When Gina arrived on the force, it had all come to a head. She was something Sam wanted and could never really earn. He'd seen it happen before, but he thought Sam was stronger than that. Morally, Sam might not be a poster child for a faithful marriage, but Koz doubted he'd ever sell out his brothers in arms for money. The man was weak, but never seemed the type to be greedy, or to be working some angle for extra money.

And maybe that was the problem, he thought. If Sam had some kind of a life off the force, maybe he wouldn't have put all his eggs into that one basket. It was a shame.

The next call was a surprise. He picked it up in one ring, even though it was one o'clock in the morning.

"Kozinski." He sounded like a frog and cleared his throat.

"Clark Riverton S.D.P.D." He'd never met the man, but knew him by reputation as a real bulldog of a detective.

"What can I do for you at this hour?"

"Yes, very impressive. Or are you not sleeping either?"

Riverton asked him.

"Got a big sweep going on, so been getting updates all evening. Don't expect I'll get any rest tonight. What's up? You working too?" If he was calling at this hour of the night, it was important.

"I've heard a little about an undercover operation going on involving the Scorpions."

"You are correct."

"I'm friendly with a SEAL who is personally related, not involved, mind you, but related to the gang."

"You must mean Armando Guzman."

"Exactly. I've met Mia a couple of times. She's a real firecracker. And with Armando, her brother, a SEAL, I imagine he's going to want to interfere."

"That would be understating it."

"*I* don't want to interfere."

"Yes. So, what's your point?"

"I think he's just helped you with your sweep."

"Come again?" Kozinski didn't think he had enough luck left for this.

"Carlos tried to make a deal and the SEALs took him down. You've got men down there at the harbor making the arrests now."

"They killed him?"

"Fuck, no. He's sitting in the back seat of a patrol car with his wrists and ankles tied together like an animal ready for slaughter. I'd prefer that Guzman not get any grief for this."

"He can have a tickertape parade, as far as I'm concerned. He's still at the scene? We let the arresting officers make the determination."

"Surely he's not a target."

"He will be if he doesn't stop inserting himself."

Kozinski took down the address of the boat just as his other phone began to ring. He knew that number to be the officers in charge.

Kozinski wondered where Gina was in all this. And he'd not heard that Sam was a part of any of the arrests, not that he was supposed to be. "Clark, I have a question for you. Is Gina Mancuso with them there?"

"Um, no. I don't think so. I mean, Armando didn't mention her. Why?"

"She's my undercover. Just thought maybe she was there." Kozinski wasn't completely comfortable giving out this information, but with most of the gang rounded up, and Carlos under wraps, he needed to get word to her as soon as possible.

"If she is, I'll have her give you a call," Riverton answered.

"No sir, I'll call her myself. Thanks. And don't tell Armando I'm delighted he got Carlos, or he'll be thinking he can moonlight between deployments."

"Wouldn't be such a bad thing now, would it?" Riverton chuckled.

"I think he does just fine at his current job."

Kozinski called his senior task force officer back and was briefed on the shipboard arrests. He hoped it wouldn't get too messy for the SEALs, who had probably stopped a firefight from the sounds of it. He was actually starting to feel pretty good until he tried several times to get hold of Gina, who was normally very good about answering his calls.

CHAPTER 29

G INA AWOKE IN a tiny, darkened room. She had no idea how long she'd been sleeping, but her internal clock said she'd slept all night. And hard. She mentally checked herself out. She was lying on a bed with…how odd, with silk sheets. Nothing seemed to be hurt or missing. Her clothes were still intact, although she was barefoot. She was unbound, but her wrists and ankles hurt as if she had been tied up. She examined a red ring that was especially tender around her right wrist.

The bed she was sleeping on had dark silk sheets, which seemed very odd. She remembered hearing crying and then realized that's what woke her up.

It's the sounds of my own weeping!

Crossing to the doorway, she found herself in the duplex Tito led her to last night. In the daytime it didn't look nearly as dangerous. She listened for signs of anyone else and heard shuffling. The echoes of her own voice had stopped. When she turned, she recognized Tito's body, even though the head was missing.

Gina's stomach began to lurch. She felt dizzy.

"Come here, baby." Sam's chest appeared from the shadows. It was streaked with sweat and dried, dark burgundy blood. A clump of what looked like brain matter stuck to one of the loops of his belt. His eyes had that vacant and hungry look he used to show her just before he trussed her all up like a chicken at a Chinese market.

She pitched forward and heaved contents of her stomach, nearly covering his boots.

"That's it, baby. Get it all out. Everything's over now. You're safe. I've got you and I'm never letting go."

Then it hit her. He was completely telling the truth. Sam would never let her go. He wasn't the man she thought she knew at all. He was someone who wanted to own her in every sense of the word. She knew she was in mortal danger.

She ran across the dirty living room floor in her bare feet, stepping on sharp pieces of glass and something metallic, but she kept on running. She was looking for a doorway, for a way out. She stopped and vomited all over her toes. When she looked up, she found an opening to what she hoped was an exit.

Where was Sam?

She'd found a bathroom that was surprisingly clean. She fell to her knees and worshiped the white toilet bowl, which smelled almost pleasantly of cleaner. She heaved another round. Then she heard Sam come up behind her. He turned on the faucet and she saw a clear glass of water handed to her.

Before she could take it, she lurched again, but there wasn't anything left in her stomach. The dry heave was painful. Her head was pounding. She should have felt happy her captor had been killed, but why was Sam there?

She looked up and grabbed the water glass anyway. She needed it. The water tasted heavenly. Sam's stubby fingers were caked with a combination of dirt and dark red ooze.

But he didn't hesitate to smooth his callused palms over her shoulders, neck and down her arms as she drank her fill.

After she finished, he took the glass from her and lifted her by the waist, pulling her backside into his groin where she felt his erection as she slid down when he let her feet touch the ground. He didn't remove his hands.

The room was spinning from her quick change of position. She wondered why Sam didn't put a blanket around her and she began to shiver.

"Let's get you cleaned up, and then I'm going to tend to you."

He tried to sound gentle, but the huskiness of his voice was ringing all the bells and alarms in her head. The man had devious intentions, and though she wanted to protest, allowed herself to be led to a sparkling white-tiled shower.

Steam began to fill the small bathroom.

Out of a fog she heard her own words, "I need to get home. I have to make some calls," she said with effort.

"They all know about it. I called it in."

"But Sam, this doesn't make sense. They're going to have to interview me. I can't wash away all the evidence. And where's Carlos?"

"Evidence?" His eyes were tiny slits as he licked his lips. She thought he was going to kiss her he got so close, but he deflected at the last minute and whispered into her ear, "We don't need no evidence to convict that sonofabitch. I blew his head clean off."

She did remember the way Tito's head looked like an exploded ripe melon and she started to feel the sharp pain in her stomach again. Where were Carlos and Mia? Was there anybody else?

She wrinkled her nose; the tips of her fingers began to

feel funny, too. "Why—why am I taking a shower?" she asked as she was led to the steamy opening. Fuzzy cotton balls were bouncing around in her brain. She recalled something about his appearance...oh yes, the brains on his pants. The fact that he had no shirt on. She heard the tinkling of a belt buckle.

And now he has no pants, either. We are both naked. Is he going to hurt me?

Yes. She remembered thinking that just a couple of minutes ago. She held onto the wall behind her, only to find out it was his chest.

"Yes, baby, I'm here."

"Why? Why did you—?"

"Because I had to save you." He pressed himself against her. "Come, let's get clean. Then I'm gonna help you heal."

"What happened to Mia? Where is she?" she whispered.

"I don't know, but it turns out Tito was running his own little scheme."

"Tito? He's just a kid."

"I found a boatload of money on him. I think he was going to sell you, sweetheart. If I hadn't come, you'd be in Mexico already."

It still didn't make sense. "I'm dizzy. Something's wrong. I need a doctor."

"I'm your doctor. I can fix what ails you now."

Her head rolled back and onto his massive shoulder. Smelling of sweat and death, he supported her back and head, lifting her over the lip of the shower pan by her waist.

The water felt wonderful. She leaned into it and lost her balance, but he caught her from behind and turned her around. Putting her under the warm spray, she laid her head against his chest. She was suddenly calm, and very tired. But it felt nice to be sheathed in the warm liquid.

"There you go. I'm gonna take good care of you, Gina. I'm gonna love out all the rough parts until you won't even remember this entire nightmare. You'll see. We will heal each other."

She started to lift her head up but found she didn't have the strength. She smelled shower gel and the touch of his hands rubbing against her back, her bottom and on the backs of her upper thighs. She couldn't help but lay against him as he leaned back, bracing her cheek on his shoulder, holding her with one arm under the spray, rubbing her anus and crevice between her legs from behind. She was losing consciousness, but she thought perhaps he inserted a finger there just before the room went black.

COMING TO, SHE realized she was back in the tiny dark room. Her head hurt like hell, and when she tried to sit up she found she was fully restrained. A collar around her neck held her down. Her arms hurt where they'd been secured with velvet-covered handcuffs to the straight metal bedframe. She tried to struggle, but it was useless. Her ankles were also immobilized with hard steel cuffs. Her sex was wide open for anyone to see. Trying to concentrate on her body and her breathing, she couldn't find anything wrong, and she didn't think she'd been raped.

Yet.

She'd been fixed up for someone's sick pleasure.

And she knew who that someone would be. A camera on a tripod blinked with an eerie red light. She was being recorded.

"Sam?" she cried out. There was no answer. She remembered the shower and it felt like her hair was still wet.

"Sam!" she shouted. She heard running footsteps coming down wooden stairs.

The door cracked open and a golden sliver of light illuminated the hallway behind him. She could see enough of him to make out that he was wearing leather chaps framing his thick hard-on, with a black mask covering his eyes. He also wore long-sleeved plastic gloves that made a crinkling noise. And he was barefoot.

"What's going on here, Sam? Let me go."

He responded by shushing her, then kneeling on the bed. He grabbed his cock and stroked himself as he looked down on her. The fingers of his gloves were peppered with small bumps and ridges she could hear traveling over his flesh. She couldn't see clearly, but thought maybe she could hear evidence he'd covered himself with lube cream. Or he'd come. Either way, she was disgusted. This was sick and twisted. She was in serious danger, because she knew she would have to fight him, and what Sam had in mind might cause pain, even death. But no way was she going to be a willing participant.

"Sam, no. Don't do this," she pleaded. "It's not too late. I'm not into this at all—"

"Hey baby, it takes some getting used to, but you're gonna purr like a kitten."

"Stop it. Stop it now."

Sam abruptly ended his self-fondling and straddled her hips, bending over and placing a large, musk-scented paw over her mouth. "Shut the fuck up or I'll do it to you gagged and fully bound. Or is that how you want it, baby?"

Not. Your. Baby.

She bit his hand and didn't let go until he slapped her across the face so hard she felt like he might have fractured her cheekbone. She saw stars.

"I'm gonna take you, with or without your fuckin' permission, Gina. You're mine. You belong to me."

He got up, adjusting himself, and walked into the bathroom. From what little she could see, he held something in his right hand. Something small.

And then she felt the pinprick of a needle in her arm. A warm glow traveled instantly all over her body and her limbs felt like rubber.

"Yes, baby, let it come to you. You like?"

Seconds later, she was drooling on the pillow, unable to say anything. She worked hard to keep her eyes open. Her headache went away, replaced by a haze that left her powerless to do anything to help herself.

So this is how it ends. Captured, forced to do things. Maybe he's already done them. I must stay alive to see to it he doesn't get away with it. Stay alive to—to see—Armando. Where is Armando?

She began to mumble. He was fondling her sex with the ridged glove, probing and tickling her. She had to say something to make him stop. Or, if there was a chance, maybe, pass out so she wouldn't have to remember what he was going to do to her. That would be better. Nothing else she could do, so she used the only tool she had left.

Her spirit.

Her tongue was thick but she managed to groan, mumbling words in a gurgling whisper.

"What's that, baby? You like my little foreplay? Did he ever do this to you, honey? I think not. I think I got there just in time. Tito coulda fucked you up real good. But I figured it out. He had his own little angle going. So sorry it was almost too late, but I've got you now. I saved you, sweet

Gina. You're a lucky girl, Gina. I'm here now."

She tried to force out the words. She was beginning to lose consciousness. She had to do it now or it would be too late.

"Mmm. Mmm," she groaned.

He leaned over her mouth to listen. She felt the soft hairs of his ear brush against her lips so she opened them just enough to be able to bite down on the velvety cartilage of his right ear.

Sam screamed but she refused to let go. Her chin was covered in blood as the collar dug into her neck. She held on like a pit bull despite his jerking. Finally, he yanked himself free. She was sure she'd bitten all the way through and taken part of his ear. Her stomach heaved, and she had just enough room to turn her face to the side to avoid swallowing her own vomit. She spit the disgusting stuff out onto the pillow still hearing the string of curses coming from the bathroom.

Good. I hope it hurts like a sonofabitch, you asshole. Not a damn thing about this is consensual. The Team will know that.

She passed out.

CHAPTER 30

ARMANDO WAS IMPATIENT after getting the call from Riverton telling him to stand down until released by the task force. The morning light had come while they were waiting. Fredo was attending to Mia. The paramedics asked him several times to step aside, but he ignored them. When he started also ordering them around, Armando had to go over and hook him by the elbow and drag him away.

"She's not hurt, and I'm sure they can tend to a couple of bruised knees, Fredo. She fell onto carpet."

"Carpet burns. You don't want any scarring. They have to clean it properly if it broke the skin, and—"

"Fredo, you're acting like an old woman. Drop it." He leaned into his short buddy, "You're beginning to embarrass us all."

That made Fredo stand up straight.

One thing that warmed Armando's heart was the fact that Mia was giving Fredo a very grateful look. A *very* grateful look. He hadn't seen her look that way for literally years. Fredo hadn't noticed, since he was checking his gear and talking with some of the force who had arrived, no doubt trying to make himself look useful and important.

It was always like this for Fredo. Heart of a warrior. The

guy just wouldn't quit. Like all of them, he guessed.

And then he thought of Gina. Cold fear began to seep into his bones. Riverton had said the operation was nearly over and her boss would be calling her in. He expressly told him not to interfere, but Armando could feel precious time running out.

"You've done enough, Armani. Stay the hell out and let them clean it up," he'd said. "You've done them a favor, now continue to behave and let them finish it. You've got to have faith in what they do. Don't want to make it worse on your sister. She's gonna need you soon."

It was true. He was supposed to let them do their job. But he couldn't shake the feeling that something still wasn't right. He'd asked Riverton if anyone had heard from Sam. Until Armando knew that guy was visible somewhere, he was going to worry about Gina.

The SEALs were allowed to go after being interviewed. Mia had to go downtown with them, which didn't go over very well with Fredo either, but Armando had expected it. After all, she had been involved with Carlos, and that branded her. Hopefully, she could cut a break. Armando thought perhaps Riverton could help in that department. But from now on, it was going to have to be up to her to walk the straight and narrow. Armando figured he'd done enough. He loved her, but he couldn't continue to try to clean up her life. Hell, he needed to clean up his own.

The boys were hungry, so they ate a late breakfast at the Scupper. Kyle and Malcolm Jones joined them. Rory was relating the details, describing the way Fredo had nearly exploded in the Hummer when he heard the "Huckleberry" signal.

"Where the fuck did you come up with that Huckleberry thing, anyhow, Armani?" Fredo wanted to know. "I think it was such a dumb-ass name you stunned Carlos for a second."

Armando shrugged it off and matched Kyle's warm smile. His LPO gave him a high five as they sat across from each other over the table.

"You did good, Armani. But it was a close one."

Rory went off onto a further description of the operation. Kyle took the opportunity to whisper to Armando.

"Where's the girl?"

Armando knew who he was talking about.

"Haven't a clue. She's probably crowing with her buddies right now." Armando hoped this was the case. And hoped she wasn't with Sam.

"Little surprised she didn't call you. I gathered you two were close. Didn't this just help her case?"

"We have issues." That was putting it mildly.

"What, that she didn't let you in on the bust?"

"Hell, no. I don't care about that. She lied to me, Lannie. She never told me who she really was. Plus she used my sister, was planning all along to arrest her along with those scumbags. I just don't see how I could trust her again. I even knew something was off, and I still went in wheels up and hot. I screwed up."

"What did you lose, your pride?"

"I thought I had a read on her. Thought I really knew her, and I didn't. When has that happened, Kyle?"

"You want me to be honest?"

"Shut the fuck up." He smiled but it did needle him in the gut.

Kyle thought before he spoke again. "Who said you did the wrong thing? Anything about this arrest and the roundup of all these bad guys wrong? You *helped* them do it."

"I don't know. I just expected that she would have trusted me with the truth. I don't understand why she didn't."

"Maybe she was protecting you."

Maybe she was. He hadn't thought about that. She did try her best to keep him separated from Sam. He'd never had a woman try to protect *him*. That was always his job.

Holy shit. Kyle's right.

He jumped to his feet and dialed Riverton.

The first ring went to voicemail right away. He left a short message, but while doing so, Riverton dialed him back.

"Sorry Armani. I was in the middle of something," Riverton said. Armando could hear sheets rustling in the background.

"Tell Daisy I'm sorry for that."

"Gotta come up for air some time. What's up?"

"Anybody heard from Gina?"

"Kozinski was going to call her when I spoke to him last night. But, no, like I said, he wondered if she was there with you and Mia."

Armando began to worry again.

"What about the big cop, her ex, Sam? Anyone seen him either?"

"You're asking the wrong person, Armani. You need to talk to Kozinski. Here, I'll text you his number."

"Thanks."

"No problem, son. Look, if you need me, let me know. I'll be there with or without my clothes on."

"Thanks, detective."

Armando waited for the text to come through. He hit

send and waited.

"Kozinski."

"Sir, I'm Armando Guzman."

"Yes, and I want to thank you for what you've done, although I need to caution you never to do it again."

"I understand, sir. There wasn't time."

"Bullshit. Next time you call the proper authorities, hear me?"

"Yes. Well, that's why I'm calling you now."

"Okay? Now what?"

"Where is Gina? And where is her 'friend' Sam?"

Armando was uncomfortable with the silence on the other end of the line.

"Son, you're to stay out of this."

"So where is she?"

"This isn't your concern."

"Then tell me she's okay."

"I can't do that."

"And why?"

"Because we can't find her."

ARMANDO ROUSTED COOPER from bed and asked him to get the location of Gina's cell phone from his friend at the DOJ. He knew he was violating both Riverton and Kozinski's orders, but he couldn't wait. And if it meant his career, so be it.

An hour later Armando, Cooper, Fredo and Rory sat in his Hummer, armed enough for a small invasion. They surveyed the building and Armando saw Gina's rental car around the side, to the rear. Down the street he saw the tail and bumper of an older black pickup he knew to be Sam's.

Gotcha, you son of a bitch.

Fredo agreed to stay in the Hummer while he monitored everyone else. Armando slung his duty bag over his right shoulder, got out, and did a loop around the building using an infrared scope to determine which part was occupied.

The exterior plaster and double sheet-rocked interior made the heat signatures blurry, but there was no question in Armando's mind there was something large present, like a human. But he couldn't be sure if it was one person or two. He also knew that a heat signature would continue to emanate from someone recently killed, but he banished those thoughts as unhelpful right now.

While he was gone, everyone else tested their earpieces. Rory gave a smacking kiss to thin air making Fredo jump with his hands on his ears just as Armando came back to the vehicle.

"Not funny. I'll need a new set of eardrums and that'll cost you," Fredo growled.

Armando interrupted. "Okay, ladies, let's cut the crap. We don't know what's going on inside, but I'm guessing it's personal, just Sam and Gina. And it could turn out to be very personal and very compromising. But we gotta be careful." He realized he was probably saying this mainly for his own benefit.

The team nodded.

Armando would take the front door; Cooper and Rory would take the two at the rear, each entering a different unit. They wore thermal night-vision goggles they could switch on in case of darkness, but the infrared scopes on their H&Ks would give them a body count as soon as they were on the other side of the stucco exterior walls. Cooper had brought along a couple of small IEDs for distraction, and they all carried masks and smoke.

Armando tried the door handle on the front and found it unlocked. "It's open."

"Back door secure," Cooper whispered. "I'm readying it now."

"Copy that next door," whispered Rory.

On Armando's mark, the explosive device blew off the handle on the rear doors while Armando entered the front. All three pulled down their masks and flipped down their goggles as Cooper laid down some smoke, which immediately began to fill the space. Armando switched on his scope and found two green shadows in the rear of the building.

"You see them?" He whispered.

"Roger that," Cooper answered.

"Negative. All clear here." Rory was ordered to stay back and guard both rear doors. Fredo stood guard over the front door, monitoring the listening devices with the computer on his lap.

As soon as the explosive went off, Armando saw the two blurred images merge, and he knew Sam was using Gina as his shield. "I think he's got her by the midsection."

"Agreed. Don't see visitors," added Cooper.

It also appeared that another one of the images was being dragged across the floor.

God, no. Gina, you stay alive. Armando gritted his teeth, hard, and focused his laser on what he hoped was Sam's head.

Armando nearly stumbled on something left in a sticky or oily puddle on the floor. He looked down to see the remains of a body, which he'd missed because the boy had been dead long enough to cool considerably.

"One unknown casualty."

"Understood," answered Cooper. "All clear here, but I hear movement. Going for cover. See you."

Armando quickly scanned for more heat signals and found none. As they'd been trained, Armando was going to deal with Sam head-on and Cooper would try to find a good angle for a kill shot if needed. Armando would have liked to be the sniper, but it was down to Cooper, who was still qualified Expert. He hoped the big SEAL could get his huge 6'4" frame silently into cover as his backup, since Sam was undoubtedly heavily armed.

All of a sudden bright lights came on and the entire room lit up like the 4th of July, blinding Armando temporarily. He dove to the side instinctively, making his footprint small, and almost immediately heard automatic fire sweep the area where he'd been standing. Flipping his goggles up, he breathed through the mask and saw with his own eyes that indeed Sam had Gina, and she was limp and non-responsive.

"Tick tock," he said and Rory lobbed another smoke grenade scuttling through the rear door. Armando knew he had to get to Gina within thirty seconds.

Sam had turned to face the direction of the bomb, spraying the back door with rounds. Armando listened and got the reassuring "ribbit" on the Invisio. Rory wasn't hit.

"I GOT A shot," came from Cooper.

"Aim for the weapon."

The big cop was having trouble wielding his gun with one arm and carrying Gina in the other, since she was out cold and a dead weight.

Armando's heart was racing, and then he saw the green laser light aimed at Sam's shoulder and heard the loud crack of Cooper's H&K. The man went down like a ton of garbage.

Armando ran to Gina and found her completely naked. He swore as tears streamed down his face inside the mask. He placed his palm over her mouth and nose and picked her up, hustling her outside to the front of the building.

Sam was screaming from inside until the smoke overtook him and it was thankfully quiet.

Armando laid Gina gently on the ground, removing his mask and goggles so he could see her with his own eyes.

She was black and blue in patches all over her arms and legs, and had sustained some scrapes on her ankles and knees from being dragged along the concrete floor, but her color was good, and she was alive.

He heard Cooper's squawk, "He's hit, not dead, but won't be getting up anytime soon." Cooper was dragging the big cop outside with Rory's help.

"Let him bleed out," Fredo suggested.

"No. We call it in. Fredo, bring me a jacket or T-shirt from the Hummer. My gal's alive, but she's gonna be pissed if she finds out that four SEALs saw her lying here naked."

Armando held Gina protectively, shielding her private parts while Cooper checked her vitals. Her eyes were dilated and glassy, but she started to moan. Armando was pretty sure she was going to be sick.

"Think she's ingested something, maybe X, or worse, heroin. She's gonna need a hospital, Armani. But her lungs sound good."

Thank God.

"Don't think anything's broken. Of course if you would get your hands off her I could check her out more thoroughly."

"No fuckin' way you're checking anyone out." Armando gripped her, wiping her cheek with his glove. "You okay, baby? Gina, honey, we've got you."

She moaned again and arched up. He turned her head to the side and allowed her to vomit all over Cooper's lap.

"Thanks," the big SEAL grumbled.

"That's for checking out my girl while she's indisposed."

"I'll have to remember that next time I take Libby to the beach with you guys. I've seen how you sneak looks at her when she's sunbathing."

"Fuck you, I do not," Armando lied.

"Don't get your boxers in a twist, ladies, time for a costume change," Fredo said arriving with a pair of running shorts and a T-shirt that smelled of sweat from his last workout. "Pe-*ew*, Armani. You must be back on your high protein diet. Don't you ever wash your workout clothes?"

Armando pulled Gina around and quickly threw on the shorts out of view of his teammates. He threaded her limp arms and head through the T-shirt and admired his handiwork.

"Put her down so I can look at her, Armani. Go call an ambulance, make yourself useful," Cooper said.

Armando didn't take his eyes off Gina's face as Cooper took out his medic pack.

He dialed Kozinski, who answered on the first ring.

"We've got her, and we've wounded Sam."

"Fuck what are you talking about? Did I not make myself perfectly clear earlier?"

"Well, we couldn't wait until you found them. We got intel and went for it. There's a young dead kid we're not responsible for, but Sam's hit in the shoulder. Gina looks drugged but we think she's okay. Get us some medical

ASAP."

He gave Kozinski the address.

"I'm taking her to the hospital," Armando said.

"Is she critical?" asked Kozinski.

"I don't think so, sir."

"She stays, then. She conscious?" Kozinski asked.

"Not yet. Cooper's working on her. She's coming around, though."

"Then you stay right there. I'm on my way and we'll get a crack team."

Armando was rewarded when Gina opened her eyes, at first startled and panic-stricken. Then they settled on his sweaty face, and then he saw that softness he'd lost himself in the first time he looked down on her face in Gunny's old pickup.

Her lips moved. Though she couldn't speak, she mouthed, "Thank you."

CHAPTER 31

B EFORE SHE OPENED her eyes, Gina could smell something familiar. She was riding in a van, listening to voices that faded in and out. She saw tubing, heard a chubby blonde-haired girl with a sunburned nose and freckles speaking to her, but it sounded a million miles away.

What was that?

Her eyes kept rolling up in her head though she tried to keep them front and center. The girl was pointing to her own eyes with the ends of two fingers.

Yes, I'd like to look at you, but I can't—

There was a siren in the background. Her body was bouncing on a bed of some kind. The girl kept talking to her.

Can't you see, I'm trying?

Her arm hurt, and she looked down to find she had an IV running. Her finger was in a clip of some kind. She could hear breathing—wait—it was her own breathing because she was breathing into a mouthpiece.

Her eyes rolled back. She arched up. Sickness overtook her. God she would vomit all over herself again, but no, warm hands held a kidney-shaped yellow plastic bowl. Strong, warm hands with a dusting of black hair on the knuckles. Something familiar about those hands. About the arms she followed. One of them had footprints leading all the way to the elbow. *His* elbow. There was that scent again, and as she raised her shoulder to brush hair from her face, his hands beat her to it. She smelled the fabric of the shirt they'd put on her, and it smelled like, like—

Armando!

Her eyes stopped rolling as she saw his face. Curls of dark brown hair fell over his high forehead. The normally smooth skin above his dark, bushy brows was wrinkled with worry. His warm brown eyes pooled like chocolate, melting chocolate. Something she craved. Something she needed.

And then things began to obscure as water covered her eyes and spilled down her cheeks. He was crying too. He set the bowl down and was holding her hand with both of his. Both his big paws holding hers, rubbing the back of her hand and her knuckles. He bent and his lips traced across her fingers. She extended them to touch the side of his cheek with the back of her palm.

Armando. You came for me. You saved me. You saved me in every way possible.

GINA AWOKE TO a hospital room filled with flowers.

Have I died? She smirked at her own bad sense of humor. In a way, she *had* come back from the dead. She remembered those last frantic moments Sam had her in his grip. She'd felt the terror of his soul, the dark pit he crawled out of just long enough to pull her down into it with him.

How wrong I've been about everything.

She thought she'd lost Armando. As she sat up, she noticed she was all alone.

An IV still trickled into her vein. She knew there'd be a

call button, so she felt along the edge of the pillowcase and found a cylinder with a button on the end of it and pressed it.

Instantly the door swung open. A pretty young redhead leaned over her.

"You're awake. How would you like some breakfast?"

"Breakfast? I can't remember the last time I ate. I'm starved."

"That's awesome. The doctor will be glad to hear it. You want to fill out a menu?"

"I don't think I can hold a pencil. Just some juice, I don't know."

"I'll do it for her."

Armando walked into the room, freshly shaven, light blue shirt immaculately ironed and blue jeans. His hair was still wet from a shower.

A shower!

He laid some roses across her lap and sat on the edge of the bed. "Hello, beautiful. Now what would you like for breakfast?" He leaned over and kissed her tenderly.

Gina felt self-conscious that she wasn't clean. "I'd like a shower for breakfast, and then perhaps some juice, some oatmeal, and a cappuccino."

Armando looked up at the nurse. "Can she?"

"She's not steady on her own. I'll have to assist but I'm still doing rounds."

"Not a problem. I'd love to assist the lovely Gina in her very first hospital shower."

"Are you family?" the nurse asked.

"Yes," he said. He winked at Gina. "I'm her fiancé."

Gina could tell the nurse was affected by Armando's big white smile and handsome face, his buttery voice rolling off his tongue in an almost hypnotic rhythm. She blushed and nodded. "Then of course."

Gina didn't hide her smile. He'd said they were engaged!

"You feel up to a shower?"

"You mean like the last one we took together?"

"Well, if you insist. I guess it would be a shame to get my clothes wrinkled."

"I'm going to need lots of help."

Armando sighed. "I think I'm just the man for the job."

She extended her arms to him. He leaned forward and her fingers found his silky curly hair. "You are exactly the man for the job."

Their kisses gave her the shivers. Her entire body tingled at the touch of the man. He nibbled at her lower lip and then sat back, watching her.

"Armando, I'm so sorry—"

"Shh, baby." He put a finger over her mouth. "We can talk later."

"No, I want to apologize for lying to you, for not telling you who I really was."

He slipped her hair behind her left ear. "I knew who you really were. I knew it all along. And I knew we belonged together; it was something I never doubted."

She let her palm run up his muscled forearm. "It was the hardest thing I've ever had to do, and I won't ever do it again. I'm never going to lie to you, or keep anything from you, if you'll—"

"If I'll what?" His eyes danced with fire. The wide smile on his tanned, clean-shaven face almost made her pass out.

"If you'll forgive me."

"Oh, baby, I've already forgiven you. But I can't wait to

see you prove how sorry you are." He glanced down at her body underneath the sheets. "I think it's time for a shower. And then I'm going to get them to release you to my care, much sooner than they planned."

CHAPTER 32

TWO DAYS LATER they were back at Armando's house. They'd been making jokes in bed after a gentle love-making. Armando had been so careful, Gina began to feel like she was a porcelain doll.

She paused. This was the point in the conversation things could go either way. Would he be able to see her damaged parts? She swallowed and began. "Can you help me face my fears?" She looked for any sign she was losing his interest.

She could see he was confused.

"I can protect you from anyone," he said.

"Can you protect me from a part of myself?"

He rolled to his side and lay down next to her. "What part of yourself do you need to be protected from?" he asked.

How was she going to put this? "When Sam and I…" she looked sideways at Armando but he wasn't reacting. "He used to…"

Armando lay very still.

"There was a part of me that liked it."

There. She'd said it. She closed her eyes and waited for the words she knew would come, telling her he was repulsed, couldn't wait to get rid of her. Hot tears escaped down her cheeks.

Armando was on top of her again. "Gina, look at me."

His face was soft, but alarmed. "Like I said, we all have a dark space within us. All of us do. Not just some of us." He bent down and kissed her, wiping her tears away with his thumbs. "Were you ever really in danger?"

"I'm not sure."

"Think, Gina. Were you really in danger?"

"I think I was. But he unlocked something in me. Like he damaged me."

"You're here. You're safe. You're with me. Nothing bad is going to happen to you as long as you're with me, Gina."

"I'm still afraid." She suddenly wanted to tell him everything about the undercover mission. It would be career ending, but hadn't she already told him her darkest secret?

"Give me your fear. Give me your danger. I can handle it," he whispered.

Their kisses became longer. The rising tide of their arousal was filling the room. She focused on the salty taste of his neck, his shoulders, the way his tongue searched her mouth, how it became all about giving herself to him. She was giving him access again—to all of her.

"*You're* the one who's dangerous," he said between kisses.

"Danger? Me? As in here, in the bedroom?" she asked.

"Always the most dangerous room in the house. Where there is nothing that separates flesh from flesh, where emotions pour out and passions take over." He traced her nipple and then suckled it between his teeth. "Losing control is what lovemaking was made for."

She moaned and he covered her mouth, but gave her

space to breathe. "Don't speak. You must not talk. I want to fill you, Gina. Fill you with pleasure."

"Yes," she whispered. Again he covered her mouth with his palm, and replaced it with his soft lips.

"No talking."

Pressing into her mouth hard, almost causing pain, and then retracting, rubbing lips against lips as he whispered, "We call it release. The French call it the Little Death."

She was feeling that familiar dark blood coursing through her veins. The anticipation and the mystery of what was to follow heightened all her senses.

"Can I show you something about yourself?"

She nodded and was rewarded with a smile.

"Good girl," he said. "Will you do everything I say?"

"Y—" she started and then stopped herself. Looking deep into his eyes, she nodded slowly. It was a commitment to follow along with wherever he was going with all of this. He was asking for her trust. He was asking for a commitment. She scanned his face, centering on his full lips. She licked hers and slowly nodded her assent.

She heard the small moan deep within his chest. He knew what she was giving him.

"Good girl, Gina."

He arched up, lifted both her arms by the wrists and placed them atop her head, pushing them into the pillow. "Let's try something. You don't have to play along if you don't want to. Tell me to stop at any time, and I will. I promise."

She tried to look up to where her hands were crossed above her head, but he held her wrists with one hand while he pulled her head down by the chin with the other.

"No peeking. Trust me?"

She could feel his hungry arousal burning against her. She nodded, and raised her knees to help him find a home deep inside her. Armando's cock stiffly rooted around her opening, but did not penetrate.

"Say it now. I want you to speak now."

"Yes."

"Yes, what?"

"I trust you."

"Good," he whispered as he kissed her. "Hold on to this," he said as he led her hands to a cool metal loop on the headboard frame. She grabbed it. "Good girl," he said.

She heard the sound of silk next to her ears and felt the cool fabric slide over her eyes. Her adrenaline began to kick in when she realized she was being blindfolded. He carefully lifted the silk scarf up so her nose had ample room for breathing. His fingers pressed against her lips and she sucked at them, drawing them into her mouth. The salty remains of her own arousal heightened her senses and her sex began to vibrate. Armando nibbled between her breasts, which felt like they were riding higher since she was holding onto the bedframe above her head.

She felt him leave the bedside and heard water running in the bathroom. When he returned she felt a warm, round bowl tucked between her legs. Armando spread her knees apart fully, which exposed her full sex to him. She wished she could see his face as he looked down on her. It was torture not knowing.

"You are so beautiful, Gina," he said. Now she knew, and the answer made her insides twitch, knowing her sex was bared, fully revealed. Several seconds of silence was followed by the warm feel of his tongue lapping at the lips of her labia. She instinctively raised her knees, presenting her pelvis to him. "Yes. Nice, Gina." He took her further into his mouth.

She released her grip on the headboard to smash his head into her crotch when he stopped her firmly.

"No, no. Bad girl. If you don't leave your hands there, I might have to secure them."

Secure them?

She smiled as she replaced her hands atop her head, twisting her torso carefully from side to side, wanting him to penetrate her, and also wanting to be a good girl and not spill what was in the bowl that rested between her legs. "More," she said.

"Yes. Happy to oblige," he whispered to that private place between her thighs. He blew warm air on her and she moaned, raising her pelvis off the bed again.

"Need you. Need you inside."

"Yes."

She heard water trickling in the bowl. Suddenly a warm washcloth was placed on her swollen peach. He rubbed her carefully, delicately, breathing slowly. Gina's chest was heaving under the aching burden of her engorged breasts. Her nipples hurt, but the rough washcloth between her legs made her come.

He rubbed her nub between his thumb and forefinger. She jerked, uncontrolled, as he played her. His hands left her and she heard the sounds of a brush and lathering cup.

"I'm going to shave you," he said.

Gina's quivering crotch was dripping with her own juices.

"Yes." She said.

The brush tickled as it swirled warm soap over the sides of her crevice and into the depression at the tops of her thighs. Then his fingers delicately spread her folds back and he scraped her flesh with a razor, rinsing it between the long strokes. He was careful not to nick or touch the insides of her lips. He shouldered under her thigh to shave the flesh around her anus. One finger delicately prodded her there and she inhaled.

"Shhh. Careful. I have a sharp tool in my hands," he said.

After he was finished shaving, he applied a fresh washcloth to remove lather and rinse her off.

Far from feeling debased, her heightened arousal made her compliant, needing this strong man to command her to do anything he might desire. When she felt him leave the bed, she surreptitiously stroked the baby-skin-like lips of her labia and then inserted two fingers into her desperately needy vagina. The touch of her own fingers was a welcome pleasure, and something she had never done before. She heard him pour out the contents of the bowl of warm water in the bathroom.

When she heard his footsteps returning to the bedside, he said, "Oh Gina. You have been very, very bad. I asked you not to take your hands off the headboard. I'm afraid that means I will have to restrain you."

CHAPTER 33

A RMANDO KNEW HIS own body, but his goal was to understand hers even better. Each time she would climax, he slowed the pace a little, trying to extend the time they spent in peak arousal. He was so close; he forced himself to focus on little details of her body so he wouldn't go over the edge. Not just yet.

He had tied her beautiful wrists to the headboard. It was a first for him. He'd had fantasies about it, but had never found anyone he trusted enough to explore those regions together. But with Gina he felt like something was building. He suddenly wanted to do everything with her, try things he had never dared before. If she was willing. Only if she was willing.

Looking at those long fingers of hers gripping the bedframe, showing her willingness to be his captive, nearly made him spill. He loved the curves of her hand, the smooth surfaces of the bright pink polish as he sucked on each finger rolling his tongue over every surface, lapping the places between her fingers just like what he was going to do to the place between her thighs later on. She moaned and rose to him, pressing her full breasts into his chest, rubbing them against him as he felt her vibrating sex below his own.

His cock had never wanted something so bad in his life. He licked down the insides of her arms, one at a time. He kissed and nipped at the insides of her elbows. Every shadowy private part of her body was his to devour. *His.*

There was the little hollow under her ears he especially enjoyed, full of the scent from her arousal, mixed with her cologne. He was adapting to her environment, exploring and tasting all her places, learning to tune his body to what she wanted, which happened to be exactly what he wanted. When she moaned, he needed to be there at her mouth to jealously take it all into him. Her breath became his. He would possess every part of her he could.

Something was sliding away as he licked and nibbled over her body. Some heavy shield of steel was being taken from him, dissolved in the scent of her body, in the soft recesses of her flesh. Every place he touched her, she reacted. Nothing was as thrilling as watching her face and feeling her body respond to his.

"Please," she whispered. He loved the baby-fine skin of her now-shaved labia, taking his fill, using his fingers and his tongue. Her nub was red he'd pinched and sucked at it so much. Yet each time he touched her there she jumped. A slow, lazy smile would appear, demanding a moist kiss, delivering her the taste of her own arousal.

"Please," she begged again. He wasn't done teasing her, heightening her pleasure. He had much more in store for her first.

Armando doubted he'd ever be able to go to sleep in this room without thinking about what Gina looked like naked, spread-eagled, tied to his bed and blindfolded. Best thing of all was that she wanted more.

He adjusted his position, straddling her neck. He

rubbed his cock against her lips and she opened to him, taking him inside, and deep.

"Careful, Gina." He was close to exploding. Her tongue rolled over his hardened rod, her lips sucking him, elongating him, making him even more engorged. He moved in and out through her pink lips, increasing the rhythm until he felt his hilt begin to tighten and he withdrew. Her high-pitched whine was a thing of beauty.

"Need you inside me," she complained.

"In time. You trust me?"

"Of course."

"I need a yes or no."

"Yes, Armando. I trust you."

"Good girl, Gina. Now, I'm going to untie you and turn you over."

"Okay."

"What do you say?"

"Yes, please turn me over."

Armando released the silk tie from her wrists but kept her blindfolded. He picked her body up as she wrapped her arms around his neck and snuggled to his chest. He helped her to a kneeling position at the bottom of the bed, keeping her arms stretched above her head, and then retying them together. He tucked a pillow under her belly and spread her knees to the sides, raising her butt high off the bed. He slid two fingers down the crack from her anus to her waiting peach.

She was slick and wet, and so ready for him. At the touch of his fingers, she extended her tailbone higher, presenting herself to him.

"Please," she whined.

His hungry tongue wandered along her cleft, then rooted and planted inside her opening. Her luscious folds were hot, her nub swollen.

He studied the beautiful configuration of her white flesh, and the reddish-pink folds of her sex that glistened as he probed her with several fingers. She bent her elbows and balanced on her forearms, stretching up on tiptoe, legs perfectly straight, in a silent plea for his possession.

Armando decided he couldn't wait any longer. He stood and placed his cock at her opening from behind. He slid the entire length of him in one slow movement, extending him inside slowly, a fraction of an inch at a time, and then back out. Her deep channel accepted him, squeezing him with her internal muscles. The flesh of her cheeks rippled as he rammed in and out of her faster, harder with each thrust. He touched her perfect skin, squeezed the delicious mounds of her bottom that overflowed in his hands as he lifted and separated her for deeper penetration. She responded by pushing against him and grinding herself over his cock.

He picked up the pace even more after several minutes. Kneeling at the edge of the bed, he pulled her knees up under her and continued to stroke. He lost himself deep inside her, and then all of a sudden he began to spill. Her muscles milked him as she gasped, meeting his thrust and opening herself to him fully.

He collapsed on top of her, his left arm covering hers above her head, entangling her bound fingers with his. They breathed in tandem, in the dark, his chest covering her back. His right arm was tucked beneath her while he alternated between stroking her nub and kneading her breasts, bracing his own weight but holding her close. He knew that he would never get enough of this woman. For the first time in his life, all he wanted to do was pleasure her, keep her in his bed.

GINA ALMOST WEPT when Armando untied her wrists and removed her blindfold. They were tears of joy. She was wrung out from the sexual satisfaction she felt for the first time in her life. The glow spread throughout her body, all the way to her fingertips and toes. Every place her body touched his was electric. She felt his rhythmic breathing as his warm chest covered her back. The backs of her thighs felt the muscles in his.

He rocked them to the side and they curled up together on the bed. He reached for the coverlet, slipping it over both of them, and instantly she was in the cocoon of his scent, wrapped in his warm arms, safe and alive with passion unlike ever before.

It was surely a dream. Worries niggled at the edges of her thoughts, but she pushed them aside.

Let me have this. Just this. I'll deal with tomorrow when I have to.

Perhaps unwise, she decided everything she'd ever wanted was resting beside her in the bed.

THE NEXT MORNING, Armando brought her in the breakfast in bed he'd promised the morning before, before their sexual appetites had eliminated their need for food.

He sat on the bed across from her while she looked over everything. He'd made a spinach and cheese omelet, cut up fresh strawberries and added strong black coffee.

"It all looks so yummy. I can't make up my mind where to start. Can you help me?" It felt good to see his smile in the warm sunlight of morning in his bed.

"I can help you with lots of things, as you well know,"

he said as he dipped a strawberry in whipped cream and held it to her lips.

She gobbled it up "Thought we'd exhausted the supply of whipped cream yesterday."

He dipped another strawberry in the bowl of cream, and lobbed it into his mouth. "I always come prepared."

"Yes you do. I like how prepared you are. I like how you demand of me the very best part. Even the damaged parts."

"Together we make quite a team, Gina."

"I agree."

"Which leads us to some decisions we have to make," he said without smiling.

"Decisions?" Doubt began to creep into her otherwise sunny morning.

"Yes. Like how fast you can break your lease, and when you can get some time off from work. I deploy in three months, and I intend to leave a thoroughly married man, if you'll have me."

Gina's heart soared. This unbelievably sunny morning had exploded into a million rays of sunlight, and she realized she was right where she belonged, in his bed, and all was right with the world.

"Nothing would give me more pleasure than to be the woman you come home to, Armando Guzman. I'd consider it an honor to serve the man I love with my whole heart."

*   *   *

Did you enjoy SEAL Under Covers? If so, won't you please recommend it on BookBub or leave a review? Show an author some love?

But wait….did you know there's a Part 2 to this story? Grave Injustice is now out, which chronicles Armando and his family ten years later. You won't want to miss this thrilling chapter of this brave warrior's life. Here's the blurb:

Personal tragedy lands **Navy SEAL Armando Guzman** into the pits of Hell. Were it not for his three-year-old son, this strong warrior would have ended his suffering with a bullet—either as a KIA or by his own hand.

She is his secret enemy; her heart is filled with revenge and hate.

Will their intense and feisty hookup-turned-relationship assure their mutual destruction, or are each of them the key to the other's healing?

Book 3 of the SEAL Brotherhood Legacy Series.

SEAL Brotherhood Legacy Series: A look at some of your

favorite characters from the original **SEAL Brotherhood Series**, 10 years later. Readers can get up to date with what the families in this popular original series are up to now with the passage of time, as their families grow, as the kids mature and life changes force the family to adjust, grow together and in some cases, grow apart.

Continue reading the first chapter of the next book in the SEAL Brotherhood Series…

SEAL The Deal (Book #4) is available here. Check out this excerpt from Chapter 1:

Book 4 in the SEAL Brotherhood Series: SEAL The Deal

Chapter 1

S PECIAL OPERATOR NICHOLAS Dunn shed his shoes and shirt and dove into the waters of San Diego Bay to scrub the left over grit and sand of Afghanistan from his body. It was his first day back ritual. He didn't stop until he'd skinned his knee and taken a serious hit on the chin bodysurfing. The shedding of blood hammered the reality of being home straight to his brain. He'd seen way too much blood this last tour. Friends died. Innocents died too. He couldn't save them all.

And now his sister was dying at home. Not a damned thing he could do about that, either.

He'd stashed his bags at the apartment he shared with Mark "Marky Mark" Beale. Marc had been his best friend ever since they met almost six years ago at the Great Lakes Training Camp, long before they were invited to try out for the Teams. In those days, they were more afraid of marching out of step or getting written up for not having something properly polished, buffed, folded or pressed.

While Nick was swimming, Marc was out scouting for Day One dates. Day One was an automatic Frog Hogs night. Had been their tradition even when they came back from training exercises. Just like having brews at the Scupper and watching the coeds parade by hoping to snag a little Frog interest.

Although he'd agreed, Nick wasn't really sure he was up to it tonight. He looked at his cell phone. No call yet.

Girls on the beach watched him as he dried off, slipped his cargo shorts back over his wet trunks, kicked into his flip-flops and headed for his bright yellow Hummer. The attention was always welcome, and on any other day he'd have reveled in it.

He was interested, all right. Nothing wrong in that department. But the fact was, his sister—his beautiful, outgoing big sister, who loved him like the mother they'd lost to cancer when he was still in high school—his sister was dying. And there was no easy way to deal with it. Death claimed innocents as well as warriors. And all that Sophie would leave behind, thanks to her entrepreneurial streak of independence, was a failing nursery. No grieving husband. No kids. Not even parents to grieve over her. Only Nick.

He knew it would come one of these days soon. *That* call.

He'd worried about her all during his last difficult deployment in the Middle East. Every night he said a prayer for her. He Skyped calls to her as often as he could, and watched the grey rings under her eyes grow as her hoarseness increased.

He'd worried about it today as he boarded the plane to San Diego from Virginia. So he should have been prepared for the call that came as he drove along the Strand. Knew it would come. Hoped it might come a few days or weeks from now, so this one could be a casual, "Hi, welcome home." But it came today, the first day he was back, and that was bad. Very bad.

"Hey, Sis. How's it going?"

"Not well, Baby Brother. I'm in a lot of pain all the time

now."

"You want me to come up?"

"Not right away. Enjoy your homecoming. You deserve it, Nick. Come up when you can. I need to make some final decisions and I would appreciate your help. I'm going to close the nursery down."

Nick was actually glad to hear it.

"But I can't do everything I used to, so need to work on it while I still can."

Nick was *not* glad to hear that.

"I'll be up tomorrow, Sophie. Hang in there. Captain America will save the day."

"Normally, I'd give you hell for that kind of sexist comment, but today I'm just grateful for the help."

Sophie was still pretending to be tough. If she said come in a few days, it meant there weren't more than a few days left. "You can nail me as much as you want on my attitude, Soph—my word choices, and my friends. But I'm coming to help you out, and there's nothing you can do to stop me."

"There's the Nick that charms the pants off all the ladies. By the way, you'll be working with a good friend of mine. Actually, you met her before. Devon. Remember her?"

Nick was scratching his head. He vaguely remembered some noodle-armed high schooler with braces. Knobby knees and ashamed of her tin grin. He was surprised he remembered anything about her.

"And why are we talking about this Devon person?"

"Because you're gonna need someone to spar with when I'm gone."

"Does she wrestle?"

"She'll kick your ass. Little bit of a thing, but I think she knows karate."

"Then she doesn't stand a chance."

If it made Sophie feel better, he'd play along. Last thing he wanted to do was start running around with a female who thought she was Bruce Lee-La, regardless of Sophie's wishes. "I'll be up tomorrow. Can I bring a friend so we can get more shit done for you?"

"You're bringing a girlfriend? Thought I'd never see the day, Nick."

Nick laughed. "Hardly, Soph. I'm going to ask my roommate, Marc. You mind?"

"Sounds good, no problem."

Sophie had never been one to depend on or need anyone, but Nick could tell she was looking forward to his visit and his help.

Yup, it was definitely time.

NICK CRUISED DOWN the Strand in the Hummer, scaring birds, squirrels and tourists with its roar. He was looking for Marky, who'd said he would be at Duckies having an ice cream. When Nick found him, six blonde coeds with legs as long as telephone poles surrounded him. The accumulated glow from their super-white, perfectly straight teeth darkened his convertible sunglasses.

Marky jerked his chin in greeting. "And here he is, the stud of Coronado, ladies," he said to his harem, who obligingly parted like the Red Sea. Marc was wearing an aloha shirt and holding his favorite banana nut crunch ice cream cone dipped in chocolate with sprinkles. Some of the chocolate had migrated to his upper lip.

Nick tried not to make eye contact with any of the love-lies, but damn, it was hard. He was trying to confine his eyes to above the neck, regardless of the signals he was getting from the girls.

"Marky, you up for a road trip north?" he asked.

"North? As in LA, or north as in where you—"

"Sonoma County. Got to go up to Santa Rosa to help my sister."

Nick heard several "ahhs" in the background. He was scoring points he'd only be too happy to collect on any other day. Not today.

He nodded toward the street to give Marc the idea he wanted a private discussion. He didn't want to offend the ladies in case Marc had plans.

"Excuse me. I shall return," Marc said to the crowd.

The two muscled SEALs walked out into the sunlight and stood on the sidewalk facing Oceanside Drive. Marc planted his arm around Nick's shoulder.

"Sorry, man. She that bad?"

Nick inhaled to keep from allowing moisture in his eyes. "I think this is the beginning of the end." He tore his eyes away from the rows of Spanish-style bungalows across the street and peered into Marc's face. "I hate to ask you on our first day back, but would you go with me? She's going to close down the nursery, and I'm thinking she could use another set of arms."

"Gotcha. Well, I didn't make any plans I couldn't break. I'm all yours."

"Thanks, man."

"So we leaving tonight, then?" Marky squinted into the sun as he slurped dripping ice cream from around the base of the cone.

Nick laughed. "Of course."

"That's what I thought. Thank God I washed my underwear, at least."

THE TRIP NORTH was long, but Nick distracted himself with Pashto language tapes. Marc was rocking out to country music on his iPod.

Ten hours later, they turned down a dusty driveway flagged with the Matanzas Creek Nursery sign on the corner fence. They drove past rows of black plastic gallon containers filled with young grape vines and shrubs. Several larger containers held bushy, multicolored flowering clumps. Laid out on black plastic, the ten-acre parcel was stuffed to capacity with neat rows of living plant material. The office was a tin-roofed wooden structure near the back of the parcel. Connected by a breezeway in the rear sat his sister's three-bedroom bungalow.

Nick noticed only one car in the lot in the front parking lot. Sophie's.

"Geez, Nick, it's a Tuesday afternoon and I'd expect things to be slow, but damn, I'd think the nursery would have more than one customer here," whistled Marc.

"That's Sophie's car. I don't ever see any paying customers. I think she's too far out into the country, and she probably doesn't price her things like the big stores."

Nick looked at the greenish gold hills of Bennett Peak and Annadel State Park, where he used to run for athletic training in high school. The valley floor was painted with the beautiful colors and designs of his sister's nursery in a setting that looked pretty much like Heaven itself.

"I'd come for the view," he said to Marc.

"Yeah, but most people only show up for the deals," Marc said as the Hummer stopped. He got out to unkink his long frame, stretching back and then down to touch his toes.

Nick began to do the same. The long ride had been uneventful, even boring. The Hummer was so noisy it made conversation impossible, and so they'd both just zoned out on their electronic devices.

Sophie appeared at the doorway of the nursery office. Her jeans were loose and her sleeveless blouse gaped at the armpits. Nick was shocked to realize she had probably lost another twenty-five pounds. But, characteristic of Sophie, she wore a bright smile accentuated with hot coral lipstick.

She ran up to Nick and threw her arms around him. "Thanks for coming."

Nick squeezed her in his usual bear hug and noticed Sophie hitched a bit in obvious pain. He carefully released her and took a good look at her face, which was turning the hue of grey sand. He knew she wore her lipstick bright, as if trying to convince everyone she was really okay.

Marc was shifting back and forth from one foot to the other. Nick saw him look down at his feet and clear his throat. Sophie looked up at him.

"Welllll… Hello there, sailor," she said in a low, sexy voice, extending her hand. "I'm Sophie. And you must be Marc?"

"Yes, ma'am. Marc Beale."

"Thought he could help out," Nick offered.

"Sweet. *Good of you to come,*" she said in mock British accent. She abruptly turned to Nick and motioned for them to come inside.

Oldies music was playing in the corner, accompanying the numerous water fountains trickling in several sections of the shop. He smelled lemons and realized she was burning lemon candles in the sunny window frames. Under each candle was a mirror. He remembered her little superstition about keeping out evil spirits this way. Even the windows with no candles had mirrors on the ledges. Sophie was taking evil seriously these days, he noted.

"You want some coffee?" Sophie asked as she slipped behind a curtain into the galley kitchen.

"Whatever you got," Nick replied.

"Okay, then. I'll give you a steaming glass of fish oil. How's that?"

"Funny."

She handed him a mug of coffee. From the smell, it must have just been brewed.

"And you?" she looked at Marc.

"Alcohol. Anything with spirits in it."

Marc was served a long-necked microbrew as Sophie brought out reheated minestrone soup with French bread, and the trio sat at a rustic plank and beam table built on metal sawhorses.

"Afraid this is all I've got right now. Tomorrow I go shopping at the farmer's market."

"You make this?" Marc asked.

"I'm not very domestic. Haven't you told him anything about me?" she smacked Nick on the forearm with the back of her soup spoon.

"Sorry, sis."

"No, this started with a can, but added all my own veggies." She lowered her gaze and spoke to the soup. "Supposed to be good for me, and soup is one thing I can keep down after chemo."

The little office suddenly felt cold to Nick.

The three of them ate in silence. Afterward, Sophie gathered their bowls and plates, rinsing them in the sink and setting them on the drain board. "I'll clean the rest of this up later."

"No worries, Sis. We'll do it. You taking off?" Nick asked.

Sophie took off her blue bandana, revealing bald spots on her scalp. She untied the knot, flapped it like a wet towel, and tied it about her head with the bow on top above her forehead. "Time for my beauty treatments. But the good news is, this is the last doctor visit. You know, on the off chance I've had a miracle like the finger of God curing me. This is the last one until they—"

"I'll take you, Soph," Nick interrupted.

"Nope. I want you here in case I don't get back on time. I got that friend coming...you remember, Devon Brandeburg...she's coming over to help me put a price on this place. I want you here when she comes."

"Then I'll drive you," Marc said as he stepped toward her and extended his palm. "Come on, lady, hand over your keys," he said, mimicking a gangster.

Just as Nick expected, Sophie responded with a soft smile, and, if he wasn't totally bonkers, perhaps even a little blush.

Good for you, Sophie. He was also proud of his randy roommate for stepping up and doing the right thing.

After the two of them left, Nick had a chance to look around the place.

Though Sophie's house was behind the little shed office, it looked like she did most of her living, and bleeding, here. With a kitchen sink, a hot plate and microwave, along with a back storage room that had a cot with blankets folded on it, he'd bet that some afternoons, when she had no customers, she'd just slept here.

The space was decorated in eclectic, neo-nursery chic. Recycled timbers made up the underpinnings of an L-shaped countertop covered in hammered aluminum. Various wind chimes and bird houses hung on long fishing lines and tinkled in the breeze.

He imagined the place would be cold in winter, but noted a small pot-bellied stove in the corner with a neat pile of recycled magazines and shredded cardboard boxes, covered with a few pieces of kindling and several round logs.

The oldies continued playing in the main shop, making the picture cozy and complete.

But depressing. Like some of those places overseas. The battle zones.

Looking through the doorway at the nursery beyond, seeing that its dilapidated wooden crisscrossed slats were occasionally missing a piece, and parts of the dark green fabric protecting the plants drooped down in ripped sections here and there, he knew his sister had worked hard to keep this concern going.

And it had killed her. Unlike his team buddies, Nick couldn't save her from herself, rescue her from a life cut short, just like he hadn't been able to save his mom. Maybe it wasn't safe for him to get close to a woman, since all of the most important ones in his life left him. Permanently.

Sophie was one of those women, just like his mother, who refused to go to see the doctor until it was too late. Both women would not be told what to do, or how to do it. Besides being fiercely independent, they were both very strong physically. He remembered wrestling with Sophie until he was in his teens, and his mother always rooted for Sophie. The day he was able to pin Sophie was the last day. She got up and told him never to wrestle with her again.

It didn't surprise him that she hadn't settled down and had a family. She liked men, and dated a few. But mostly she said it just wasn't worth the trouble to have them around. He knew it was because she didn't want to change for anybody, or had never met anybody she wanted to change for. And love? They'd never discussed the topic.

It wasn't on either of their radars.

SEAL The Deal (Book #4) is available now!

ABOUT THE AUTHOR

 NYT and USA/Today Bestselling Author Sharon Hamilton's SEAL Brotherhood series have earned her author rankings of #1 in Romantic Suspense, Military Romance and Contemporary Romance. Her other *Brotherhood* stand-alone series are: Bad Boys of SEAL Team 3, Band of Bachelors, True Blue SEALs, Nashville SEALs, Bone Frog Brotherhood, Sunset SEALs, Bone Frog Bachelor Series and SEAL Brotherhood Legacy Series. She is a contributing author to the very popular Shadow SEALs multi-author series.

Her SEALs and former SEALs have invested in two wineries, a lavender farm and a brewery in Sonoma County, which have become part of the new stories. They also have expanded to include Veteran-benefit projects on the Florida Gulf Coast, as well as projects in Africa and the Maldives. One of the SEAL wives has even launched her own women's fiction series. But old characters, as well as children of these SEAL heroes keep returning to all the newer books.

Sharon also writes sexy paranormals in two series: Golden Vampires of Tuscany and The Guardians.

A lifelong organic vegetable and flower gardener, Sharon and her husband lived for fifty years in the Wine Country of Northern California, where many of her stories take place. Recently, they have moved to the beautiful Gulf Coast of Florida, with stories of shipwrecks, the white sugar-sand beaches of Sunset, Treasure Island and Indian Rocks Beaches.

She loves hearing from fans through her website: authorsharonhamilton.com

Find out more about Sharon, her upcoming releases, appearances and news when you sign up for Sharon's newsletter.

Facebook:
facebook.com/SharonHamiltonAuthor

Twitter:
twitter.com/sharonlhamilton

Pinterest:
pinterest.com/AuthorSharonH

Amazon:
amazon.com/Sharon-Hamilton/e/B004FQQMAC

BookBub:
bookbub.com/authors/sharon-hamilton

Youtube:
youtube.com/channel/UCDInkxXFpXp_4Vnq08ZxMBQ

Soundcloud:
soundcloud.com/sharon-hamilton-1

Sharon Hamilton's Rockin' Romance Readers:
facebook.com/groups/sealteamromance

Sharon Hamilton's Goodreads Group:
goodreads.com/group/show/199125-sharon-hamilton-readers-group

Visit Sharon's Online Store:
sharon-hamilton-author.myshopify.com

Join Sharon's Review Teams:

eBook Reviews:
sharonhamiltonassistant@gmail.com

Audio Reviews:
sharonhamiltonassistant@gmail.com

Life *is one fool thing after another.*
Love *is two fool things after each other.*

REVIEWS

changes to the same old stuff. It made for a more unpredictable read and more adventurous to explore! Vampire lovers, any paranormal readers and even those who love the romance genre will enjoy Honeymoon Bite."

"This is the first non-Seal book of this author's I have read and I loved it. There is a cast-like hierarchy in this vampire community with humans at the very bottom and Golden vampires at the top. Lionel is a dark vampire who are servants of the Goldens. Phoebe is a Golden who has not decided if she will remain human or accept the turning to become a vampire. Either way she and Lionel can never be together since it is forbidden.

I enjoyed this story and I am looking forward to the next installment."

"A hauntingly romantic read. Old love lost and new love found. Family, heart, intrigue and vampires. Grabbed my attention and couldn't put down. Would definitely recommend."

PRAISE FOR THE
SEAL BROTHERHOOD SERIES

"Fans of Navy SEAL romance, I found a new author to feed your addiction. Finely written and loaded delicious with moments, Sharon Hamilton's storytelling satisfies like a thick bar of chocolate." —Marliss Melton, bestselling author of the *Team Twelve* Navy SEALs series

"Sharon Hamilton does an EXCELLENT job of fitting all the characters into a brotherhood of SEALS that may not be real but sure makes you feel that you have entered the circle and security of their world. The stories intertwine with each book before…and each book after and THAT is what makes Sharon Hamilton's SEAL Brotherhood Series so very interesting. You won't want to put down ANY of her books and they will keep you reading into the night when you should be sleeping. Start with this book…and you will not want to stop until you've read the whole series and then…you will be waiting for Sharon to write the next one." (5 Star Review)

"Kyle and Christy explode all over the pages in this first book, *[Accidental SEAL]*, in a whole new series of SEALs. If the twist and turns don't get your heart jumping, then maybe the suspense will. This is a must read for those that are looking for love and adventure with a little sloppy love thrown in for good measure." (5 Star Review)

PRAISE FOR THE
BAD BOYS OF SEAL TEAM 3 SERIES

"I love reading this series! Once you start these books, you can hardly put them down. The mix of romance and suspense keeps you turning the pages one right after another! Can't wait until the next book!" (5 Star Review)

"I love all of Sharon's Seal books, but *[SEAL's Code]* may just be her best to date. Danny and Luci's journey is filled with a wonderful insight into the Native American life. It is a love story that will fill you with warmth and contentment. You will enjoy Danny's journey to become a SEAL and his reasons for it. Good job Sharon!" (5 Star Review)

PRAISE FOR THE
BAND OF BACHELORS SERIES

"*[Lucas]* was the first book in the Band of Bachelors series and it was a phenomenal start. I loved how we got to see the other SEALs we all love and we got a look at Lucas and Marcy. They had an instant attraction, and their love was very intense. This book had it all, suspense, steamy romance, humor, everything you want in a riveting, outstanding read. I can't wait to read the next book in this series." (5 Star Review)

PRAISE FOR THE
TRUE BLUE SEALS SERIES

"Keep the tissues box nearby as you read *True Blue SEALs: Zak* by Sharon Hamilton. I imagine more than I wish to that the circumstances surrounding Zak and Amy are all too real for returning military personnel and their families. Ms. Hamilton has put us right in the middle of struggles and successes that these two high school sweethearts endure. I have read several of Sharon Hamilton's military romances but will say this is the most emotionally intense of the ones that I have read. This is a well-written, realistic story with authentic characters that will have you rooting for them and proud of those who serve to keep us safe. This is an author who writes amazing stories that you love and cry with the characters. Fans of Jessica Scott and Marliss Melton will want to add Sharon Hamilton to their list of realistic military romance writers." (5 Star Review)

Printed in Great Britain
by Amazon